"PASSIONATE, FURIOUS, INTELLIGENT."
— *Cosmopolitan*

"COOL AND ELEGANT." — *The New York Times Book Review*

"Some things which are inexplicable to men will become less so in the light of what Miss Drabble tells us about a woman totally in love." — *Kansas City Star*

"GREAT BEAUTY AND SUBTLETY." — *Newsday*

"Margaret Drabble has perception, wit and great emotional power." — *Boston Globe*

"SHEER MAGNIFICENCE . . . a subtle achievement, a woman's novel that should be read, above all, by every man who's likely to have love for a woman on his mind." — *New Statesman*

MARGARET DRABBLE is the author of many novels, including *The Garrick Year, A Summer Bird-Cage, The Ice Age* and *The Millstone,* all available in Plume editions. She lives in London with her three children.

MARGARET DRABBLE

The Waterfall

A PLUME BOOK

PLUME
Published by the Penguin Group
Penguin Books USA Inc., 375 Hudson Street, New York, New York 10014, U.S.A.
Penguin Books Ltd, 27 Wrights Lane, London W8 5TZ, England
Penguin Books Australia Ltd, Ringwood, Victoria, Australia
Penguin Books Canada Ltd, 2801 John Street, Markham, Ontario, Canada L3R 1B4
Penguin Books (N.Z.) Ltd, 182-190 Wairau Road, Auckland 10, New Zealand

Penguin Books Ltd, Registered Offices: Harmondsworth, Middlesex, England

Published by Plume, an imprint of New American Library,
a division of Penguin Books USA Inc.

BOOKS ARE AVAILABLE AT QUANTITY DISCOUNTS WHEN USED TO PROMOTE PRODUCTS
OR SERVICES. FOR INFORMATION PLEASE WRITE TO PREMIUM MARKETING DIVISION,
PENGUIN BOOKS USA INC. 375 HUDSON STREET, NEW YORK, NEW YORK 10014.

 REG. TRADEMARK—MARCA REGISTRADA

Library of Congress Cataloging-in-Publication Data

Drabble, Margaret, 1939–
  The waterfall.

  Reprint. Originally published : 1st American ed.
New York : Knopf, 1969.
  I. Title.
PR6054.R25W38   1986   823'.914   85-32002
ISBN 0-452-26017-5

First Plume Printing, July, 1986

  6   7   8   9   10   11   12

PRINTED IN THE UNITED STATES OF AMERICA

Drowning is not so pitiful
As the attempt to rise.
Three times, 'tis said, a sinking man
Comes up to face the skies,
And then declines forever
To that abhorred abode,
Where hope and he part company—
For he is grasped of God.
The Maker's cordial visage,
However good to see,
Is shunned, we must admit it,
Like an adversity.

EMILY DICKINSON

The Waterfall

If I were drowning I couldn't reach out a hand to save myself, so unwilling am I to set myself up against my fate.

This is what she said to him one night. He was not interested, and she had not expected him to be so. She had not even thought, as she said it, that it might be the truth. But the image, nevertheless, remained with her, as though she had by accident articulated something of significance, and as she lay in bed at night, swollen and sleepless, she wondered whether it might not have been, after all, as she had said. Because it was not so much the indignity that she feared, not the screams, not the calls for attention, the inconvenience caused, the ugly respiration, the spluttering, the bubbling lungs: it was not so much these, though who could like the thought of them? It was worse than that, some yet greater pride or subjection: for if alone, even if alone, quietly, going under, submerging, she would reject the opportune branch, and fail to make for the friendly bank. Unless cast up there by the water itself, she would drown. There was something sacred in her fate that she dared not countermand by effort. If the current chose to rescue her, it could: providence could deal with her without her own assistance. If she was chosen, she was chosen: if not, then she would quietly refrain from the folly of asserting her belief in her election, in the miraculous intervention of fate on her behalf.

Some weeks later, he left her. She was not surprised. She had been expecting it. She was quite pleased to see him go. Everything seemed a little colder without him—the bed, the house itself, her meals, which she no longer troubled to heat; she ate baked beans and sardines and asparagus straight from the tin. The temperature of her life seemed to be cooling into some ice age of inactivity, lacking the friction of a dying marriage, lacking even the fragile sparrow-like warmth of her child: her child was not with her, he was staying with her parents while she waited to give birth to her second. So she had nothing to do, nothing at all, but to keep herself alive, and to wait for the pangs of birth to begin. She did not ring her parents to tell them that her husband had left her, because she preferred to be alone. She wandered round the cold and empty house, watching the rain fall outside, seeing the windows silt up with London grime, watching the dust thicken on the furniture. She did nothing. She had often, as a girl, imagined such a life: empty, solitary, neglected, cold. It seemed to have happened to her, perhaps as a result of those imaginings. Like a victim, she waited: meek, like a sacrifice. From time to time it occurred to her that she ought to feel desolate, abandoned, frightened perhaps, but she seemed to lack the strength to feel these things. She felt nothing. She walked about, and lay in bed, and made herself cups of coffee, and sometimes waves of familiar dead emotion would softly suggest themselves to her— emotions such as loneliness and physical alarm and social fear. And somewhere else, far away, she heard those mighty abstractions crashing on a distant shore: treachery, love, despair.

Meanwhile, as she waited, the emptiness was almost comfortable. She saw nobody, taking care to shop in shops where she was not known, staring blankly as she handed over a tenshilling note and leaving money in an envelope for the milkman so that she could avoid his irregular, bespectacled, too human face. She held in fact so much to her solitude that when the pains of labor started, she could hardly bring herself to summon the midwife, so reluctant was she to see and to be seen. She lay on her bed, thinking of a True Story she had read once, many years ago, in a woman's magazine: a story of a pregnant woman, stranded by some unmemorable and unimaginable stroke of fate in a hut in the snowy wastes of Alaska. The woman had lived there alone, and had produced her baby, and had survived, and had indeed lived to sell the story of her ordeal. This tale had always haunted her, and as she lay there and felt the ebb and flow of pain she wondered if she had remembered it so well because she was called upon to emulate such brave isolation. Although, of course, she did not: common sense prevailed, as she had always known it would, and after a while she got up and rang the midwife and then her cousin Lucy. So much contact, after so much silence, was exhausting: she lifted the baby's Home Confinement Kit down from the top of the wardrobe, and got out some newspapers and towels, and then lay down once more upon the bed, damp and breathless. By the time the midwife knocked she was too far gone to get up to answer the door, so she called, idly, from where she lay.

It was a cold night, and just after the baby was born snow started to fall. The midwife, distressed by the general in-

adequacy of the arrangements, and afraid lest the baby should
catch cold, had concentrated all available sources of heat in the
bedroom: a gas fire was burning, and there were two small electric fires. The air was heavy and warm and damp. Jane, sitting
there in the bed with the small new child tucked in beside her,
could feel the sweat of effort flowing unchecked into the sweat
of a more natural warmth. They were waiting, she and the
midwife, for the doctor, and for cousin Lucy: the doctor, too
late to assist the delivery, was coming to put in the stitches, and
Lucy was to sit with her for the night. The midwife was sitting
in an armchair by the gas fire: her job ended, and the night
growing late, she was dozing. Jane lay there, propped up
against the pillows, and watched the snow fall beyond the dark
shining pane of the window: there was no noise except the
woman's heavy breathing, and the small feeble movements
of her new daughter, who was trying to suck her emaciated
thumb. Everything was soft and still: the whole night, and
Jane's nature with it, seemed to be subdued in a vast warm lull,
an expectancy, a hesitation, a suspension and remission of trial.
The snow fell outside the uncurtained window, and she could
feel the blood flowing from her onto the white moist sheets.
There was newspaper under the sheets, but it too was warm
now from the heat of her body: warm and sodden, having lost
the dry hard edges and crackling noises that it had made at first,
as she moved and stirred in labor. The bedroom had dark blue
walls, like the night sky itself, and the bars of the fire were red
and glowing. Heaps of white towels and baby clothes lay upon
the chest of drawers, and on a table in front of the fire stood a
large pale yellow pudding bowl, an ordinary mixing bowl, in
which the midwife had bathed the baby. The colors of the
scene affected Jane profoundly: they were the violent colors

of birth, but they were resolved into silence, into a kind of harmony.

She thought that she was happy. It was as though all the waiting and the solitude had resolved themselves into some more hopeful expectation, though of what she did not know. Deliverance seemed at hand. It would be safe to wait, now: it could no longer be missed or avoided. This close heat would surely generate its own salvation.

After a while the doctor came, and stitched her up—drawing the curtains nervously to do so, shutting out the witnessing snow. The shoulders of his coat were covered in flakes and he brushed them off and they fell and melted on the floor and on the sheets. One of them fell on her bare leg as she lay there. His hands were cold. When he had finished, he inquired after her domestic arrangements, seeming ready to be satisfied, producing no refuting evidence when she claimed, deceitfully, to avoid trouble, that her husband would be home the next day. The midwife made them a cup of tea and he drank some, and she drank some too, though it was a drink she did not care for: but in this state, at this time of night, she liked its thin warm wetness. It was liquid and warm, like weeping. It replaced the need for tears. When the baby cried—though she was not crying now, she was silent, asleep, tired by her own birth—when she cried, her eyes were dry and angry, her face red and indignant, protesting against the possibilities of desertion and neglect, unwilling to let such things threaten her: but Jane let her whole body weep and flow, graciously, silently submitting herself to these cruel events, to this pain, to this deliverance.

When the doctor had finished his cup of tea, he looked at his watch and said that he must go: the midwife said that she would stay until Lucy arrived to relieve her vigil; but even as the doctor went down the stairs Jane heard the car draw up out-side and knew that Lucy was there. The doctor let her in: she could hear them exchanging remarks in the hall, and could hear the dry murmur and cough that indicated the presence of James, Lucy's husband.

"That must be my cousin," said Jane to the midwife; it seemed the most personal remark that she had made in weeks.

"I'll be off, then," said the midwife, who had already risen to her feet and was donning the layers of cardigans which the heat of the room had obliged her to cast off. "I'll be back in the morning, nine o'clock."

"Yes," said Jane.

And the woman left. She met James and Lucy on the stairs, and Jane could hear another low-pitched indistinct murmur of greeting and parting, and then the dividing of their foot-steps, the opening and closing of the front door downstairs, and then the tap and push upon her own—and then there, sud-denly, was Lucy, like a visitor from another life, her arms full of parcels, a blank, diffuse and nervous smile upon her face.

"Hello," said Jane, propped up upon her high pillows.

"Hello," said Lucy, dropping the heap of parcels upon the midwife's chair. "We're late, I'm sorry. I couldn't get hold of James, and it would have taken even longer to try to get here without him . . ."

"I hope you didn't mind coming all this way," said Jane.

"Of course not," said Lucy, politely. "Of course not. We'd been waiting to hear."

And the two women smiled at one another, carefully. They were afraid of one another in daily life: tentative, respectful, unsure when they met: but the extremity of the present situa-tion absolved them from their mutual apprehension. They were both so diffident and frail that they were tempted to drift out of contact, out of sight, even when in conversation with each other, both too easily persuaded to abandon hold of any thread or link; but this warm room, and the necessity of their being there, held them together.

"Where's James?" said Jane, as Lucy admired the small sleeping baby.

"He went down again," said Lucy, "to get the cradle from the car."

"Did he mind bringing you?" asked Jane. Lucy smiled, and shook her head, and said, "No, he never minds doing things," as though the fact still after all these years surprised her; and Jane too smiled, because one of the attitudes that they recognized in each other was this shared surprise at James's docility. For he did not look docile, he looked dangerous, he seemed to carry with him the yellow sulfurous clouds of some threatening imminent disaster, but it never happened, it never took place, and James continued to play with his children and to take them to school, and to drive Lucy around in the car, to be polite to her friends, to meet people at stations, to mend electric fuses, to carry heavy furniture, to answer his post. His actions in fact so much contradicted his appearance that Jane, covertly watching him, would sometimes wonder whether she did not see in his place some totally unreal person, some imaginary face and head and voice, and it was only Lucy's air of shared surprise that acquitted her of a conviction of hallucination.

Lucy took off her coat, commenting, inevitably, on the heat of the room, and started to unpack the parcels she had brought—baby parcels, cast-off jackets and socks from her own small son. "Look," she said, "look at this one, I always liked it, how nice to have another baby to put in it—" and she held it up, a small hand-knitted coat of cream wool with small blue buttons and an embroidered ribbon in the neck: and Jane took it, smiling, and laid it on the pillow by her. As she did so, Lucy, profiting from the diversion to speak without the appearance of speech, said, averting her eyes, delicately, staring toward the window, "And what about Malcolm? Ought somebody to ring him?"

"No, no, there's no need to ring," said Jane, stroking the small garment anxiously.

And that disposed of Malcolm, for Lucy would never have asserted herself, would never for a moment have struggled with Jane's faintest expression of wish: and Malcolm, the missing husband, dropped from between them into nothing and nowhere, forgotten, abandoned, disclaimed, cast off.

When James arrived, he was carrying the baby's cradle tucked under one arm, and a bottle of champagne. He stood in the doorway and put the cradle down, and looked at Jane lying there, and said, embarrassed, incapable of the moment and the gesture he had selected, and yet looking at her nevertheless, making the effort to look at her, and not, as usual, averting his eyes as he spoke:

"I brought you a present. To drink your health, if you like."

He did not hand it to her, but stood there holding it, and smiling at her.

"Thank you," she said.

"Shall I open it?" he said, and she nodded, so he opened it while Lucy went downstairs to look for some glasses. The cork came out with a subdued pop, and the baby stirred and moaned in its sleep, and Jane felt herself start to cry, so she bent over the child to hide her tears, which were probably tears of joy, of nothing else: and when she looked up again Lucy had come back with the glasses, and James was sitting on the end of her bed, pouring out.

When she drank, the cold dry taste of the wine frightened her, and she would not accept a second glass. She shook her head limply, and said, "No, you have it, you have it, I've had enough."

So James and Lucy sat there and finished the bottle. They did not talk much—they never talked much to each other, and Jane was too tired to speak, and felt herself freed by recent events from the necessity of effort—so the room was silent, except for the sound of breathing, and the sound of the gas fire, and the faint, small effervescence of the liquid in the glasses. The curtain was half open, and Jane could see that the snow was still falling beyond the glass, whitely, persistently, dimly. She shut her eyes, and rested her head, and listened to the sounds of the room, the quiet sounds, and she thought that perhaps it might have been like that to be with somebody that one loved—to be wanting nothing, to be desiring and suffering nothing, to be without apprehension, loss, or need. The room softly surrounded her; she could tell that there was no dissension in it, for all dissension came always from herself, and having removed it, having removed herself, everything else could but fall gently into its own place, as the snow fell.

Before she fell asleep she tried to open her eyes once more, to see them, but she was too tired.

When she woke in the morning, the baby was crying, hungry, cross, sucking its fist, having abandoned the search for its small elusive thumb: she scooped it out of bed and started to feed it, before she noticed that Lucy was still in the room, curled up asleep in the chair that the midwife had abandoned. The empty champagne bottle was on the floor at her feet, her mouth was slightly open, and she was breathing very heavily. Jane looked away, not liking to look at her in so vulnerable a state, and not quite liking the fact that she looked, unusually, more than her age—twenty-eight, she was, as she herself was twenty-eight—and she had a sudden panic sensation of having observed herself asleep there. There was only two weeks in age between them: their mothers, who were sisters, had had a conspiratorial pregnancy, having coolly resolved to share the troubles and the discussions and the inactivity and the doctor's waiting room. Jane, thinking of this, reflected, and not for the first time, on the amazing apparent control with which her mother's generation had planned their lives and their families—family planning had been a meaningful phrase to them, whereas to her and most of her generation it seemed a fallacious concept quite out of date, a bad joke, like those turban hats that women had worn in war time to conceal their uncherished hair. She herself had never understood contraception, and had disliked what she had understood of it: she had acquired, after her son's birth, a Dutch cap, but she disliked it so

much that when he found it lying in a drawer one day she let
him take it out and sail it in the bath for a few nights, until he
was bored with it, and it perished. She looked down now at
the small child in her arms, evidence of that perishing, and
amazement filled her—amazement that she was a woman, that
knowing so little she was a woman—that babies were so easy to
bear and so cruel to contemplate—and the small child sucked
and sucked, pulling at her nipple, and seeming to pull at her
guts. She remembered the phrase "after-pains," and realized
that she was suffering from them. They weren't bad; like most
things, they weren't as bad as they might have been. The child
sucked with such facility, just as she herself had given it birth
with such facility: it seemed strange to her that so much natural instinctive force could flow through such a medium as
herself, a woman so frail and flawed. She wondered why her
own frailty did not interrupt the process, did not keep the milk
from the child, or the child from the light.

When she took the child off the breast, to move it over to
the other side, it started to cry, and the crying woke Lucy:
Jane pretended that she had done the waking, so that Lucy
should not feel at a loss, and called her name. Lucy yawned,
and stretched, her features snapping back instantly into their
usual even daytime mold; she sat there, stretching, and said,
"How are you? How d'you feel?"

"Oh, I'm all right," said Jane. "I'm fine. The baby's feeding.
It's a clever baby."

"Surely you oughtn't to feed it yet?" said Lucy, staggering
to her feet, straightening her crumpled skirt, running her fingers through her short brown hair.

"I don't suppose it'll hurt," said Jane. "She seemed so hungry."

"I'll make you some tea," said Lucy, standing and gazing at herself crossly and suspiciously in the huge mirror over the mantelpiece. "Christ, it's so hot in here, I feel parched."

"The bed's soaked," said Jane. "I'm sitting in a sea of sweat. The sheets are dripping. She didn't even change them, last night, the midwife. You shouldn't have slept in here, Lucy, you could have slept in Laurie's bed."

"Oh, I just dropped off," said Lucy, swimming closer to her mirrored image, scratching anxiously at a corner of one eye. "I just dropped off. It didn't seem worth moving." Then she turned round and looked at Jane, and said, "It was nice in here, last night."

And Jane nodded, glad of such confirmation.

"When did James go?" she asked.

"About three, I think. He'd have stayed, he didn't want to go, but he had to get the children to school in the morning . . . he'll come back this evening. I'll stay here today."

Jane nearly asked whether that would be all right, but she didn't, because as there was no alternative it seemed pointless to inquire, even for the sake of politeness.

"I'll make you some tea," said Lucy again. "Or would you rather have coffee?"

"I don't mind which," said Jane.

"What about food? Toast? Weetabix?"

"I don't know," said Jane. "I've got pains."

"She'll give you some pills for that," said Lucy, and went off downstairs to put on the kettle.

When the midwife came back, at nine, she produced some pills, and she weighed the baby, which she had forgotten to do the night before. She weighed it in a cloth bag, suspended from a curious gadget that recorded the weight, seven pounds exactly, she said: and the baby, dangling there concealed in the bag, stirring and moaning feebly, looked like a bag of kittens for drowning, or, more happily, like one of those pictures of babies carried by storks on Baby Greetings cards. Jane was glad when she let the child out: it seemed unkind to let it dangle in the air, for however good a reason: unkind, inhuman. She received it back into her arms and tucked it with her into the bed. The midwife said that she had already visited one baby that morning, another newborn, and that the mother, in view of the weather, had resolved to christen the baby Snow White. It was a black baby. The midwife, herself black, thought this was amusing, and roared with laughter, and at the sound of her mirth Jane felt ominously stirring her old anxieties: she wanted to laugh too, politely, but she could not make the right sound, although she tried. What will you call yours, asked the midwife, and Jane said, I don't know, perhaps I'll call her Viola. Violet, said the midwife, nodding, delighted; yes, Violet. No, Viola, said Jane, abandoning the name, which had risen to her from the notion of violation: and then she said, no, I'll call her Bianca. She asked the midwife then if she could get up, to look out of the window at the new snow, and the midwife looked at her shrewdly and said, "Look, Mrs. Gray, it's like this: you're in your own home here. I say you oughtn't to get up for twenty-four hours, but when my back's turned I shan't see much, shall I?"

And she packed her black bag, and went off, and Jane got out of bed and went over to the window and watched her get on her bicycle and ride off through the cold morning to the next baby. The snow lay thin but concealing, all over the road and pavement, all over the front step, all over the roofs of the houses across the way: it lay on the bare branches of the one tree in sight. London was stony, but in the snow its ugliness was concealed. She remembered some snow she had seen once in the Alps, in late spring: it was packed tight by the roadside, thick and dirty, the texture of cement, and it was coated with the dust of the road, yellowish dust from roadworks. She had touched it, by the parked car, and wondered if it ever melted, whether it might perhaps contain in its icy heart layer after layer of dust and grit from that same road, never to be melted, never to be softened: obdurate, each layer of hardening accretion merely concealed by the dazzling white soft beauty of the next winter: and all that melting could do would be to reveal the ugly heart, the brick-like depths. What she saw from her own window had no beauty, had never possessed beauty: a street of London houses, a perspective unalterable, not snow-like brick, but brick itself. In the Alps, there were flowers she had never seen before, trembling on those green slopes below the snowline: perhaps they had been too early in the year, perhaps in June or July even those thick-packed slabs would melt, would submit to the snowdrops, the kingcups, the bells, the fronds, the thin green leaves.

She spent the morning lying in bed, half dozing, listening idly to the radio while Lucy worked: she was editing a book, and Jane quite liked to see the typed bound pages turn. In the afternoon she slept. At tea time, when Lucy brought her her tea, she began to feel a slight distant guilt, and said to Lucy,

"Wouldn't you like to get home? I'll be all right now, until tomorrow."

"I'm going home soon," said Lucy. "I must help put the children to bed—but James is coming, James will stay with you."

"I don't want James to be here," said Jane, suddenly, more

violently than she had meant. "I'll be all right, you let him drive you back."

Lucy looked at her, and said, clearly making some effort—for this was where she drew the line, as Jane had drawn it at delivering her own baby unaided—

"No, you ought to have someone here, you ought not to be alone. It's not twenty-four hours yet, we can't leave you."

"But James won't want to be here," said Jane, feebly, distressed.

"Oh, he won't mind," said Lucy, as though it were indeed surprising, but nevertheless a fact, "he won't mind. He'll bring some work to do. And later, I'll come back. When the little ones are settled."

"It'll annoy him," said Jane, so put out that she was unable to drop the subject, preferring the pain of undignified protest to the pain of acquiescence in a project so unwelcome. "It'll annoy him, and then I'll be annoyed, having him here, and I shan't be able to read my book . . . I'd rather be alone. I'd rather be alone."

"Who wouldn't rather be alone?" said Lucy, rising briskly to her feet and clearing up the tea things, "but alas, in birth, death, old age, and infirmity, it's not possible."

"Oh, all right," said Jane. "I suppose I'm alone enough."

"You're quite spoiled," said Lucy, looking at her oddly. "You're quite spoiled with solitude."

And she took the tea things downstairs. It was the most intimate remark that Jane had heard her make in twenty years or so, and she thought it over for some time.

At five o'clock James arrived, bringing this time not champagne but some salad meal from a delicatessen, in a plastic box.

"This will be our supper," he said, showing it to Jane.

"Lovely," said Jane, peering at the chopped squashed toma-
toes, gherkins, eggs, chicken, and anchovies, feeling quite disagreeable through her gratitude, unable to find any way of expressing simultaneously her gratitude, and her reluctance to
receive gifts, her reluctance to play the role of invalid. He too
seemed equally ill at ease with the role he was cast for: domestic, the brother-in-law, the bringer of food. Panic rose in her,
at their ill conjunction. Such unease had come in the past so
near to killing her: she struggled, lying there helpless, as hot
waves of it, uncontrollable, poured through her, useless pains,
that heralded no birth. When he went downstairs to speak to
Lucy she found herself out of breath, heaving slightly in her
nightdress, amazed as ever that the sight of such terror did not
inflict itself more strongly upon witnesses: that life could continue around it, peaceful, civil, undisturbed.

Lucy left at five, in a taxi, saying she must get back to the
children before the end of children's television. She said that
she would be back again later for the night. Jane, from her bed
upstairs, through the open door, heard her saying to James in
the hallway,

"You'll be all right?" and heard James answering, "Of course
I'll be all right."

And then that was it. He stayed downstairs, and Jane put
her radio on very loud so she wouldn't have to hear him walk
in restless boredom from room to room: she fed the baby, and
talked to it, and looked at her watch, and reflected that there
were five hours to go. Five hours, before she could decently fall
into the oblivion of sleep. She felt the dreadful social strain of
remaining awake up there, while he was downstairs: the contact was too much for her. Even the baby seemed to stare at her
with appraising, prophetic eyes. I'm ill, she whispered to her-

self, I must be ill, this is some kind of illness: but she didn't believe her own diagnosis, she knew it was a normal human state.

After an hour, James came upstairs. He stood there in the bedroom door, looking at her, and said, "I came to see if you were all right."

"Of course I'm all right," she said, in anguish. "What could be wrong with me? It's quite pointless, your being here, I'm so all right I might just as well be on my own . . ."

"It's not good for people to be on their own," he said, still standing there, leaning on the doorpost. "So I'm here to keep you company."

"What a bore for you," she cried, but he did not protest, he merely gently shook his head. And then they heard the knock of the midwife, on her evening round, so he went down and let her in. It was a different midwife, a different woman—Jane was torn between the fear of a new face and the relief of no deepening intimacy with that black Snowdrop woman—and she mistook James for the child's father, addressing him as Mr. Gray. Jane, from the depths of her protest against the visit and the event, was amused, faraway amused, as in another life, by the fact that he did not protest, he did not bother to put her right: he could not be bothered to go through the motions of correction and confusion and clarification. In such a mood, Jane had often thought, one might find oneself marrying the wrong man: too polite to correct or protest, too diffident to say, It wasn't you I was thinking of.

When the midwife had gone, and the baby was asleep, it was quite late—after seven. James was downstairs, nowhere to be seen or heard, and she said to herself that she would force herself to read her book. So she opened the book, and looked at the print, and tried to attach her eyes to its sense. But she was relieved, really, of suspense, when she heard him again on the stair: this time he came in carrying a drink and a glass and a bottle of Scotch. He did not stop in the doorway this time: he came in and sat down in the large chair, and said the words she had been fearing, "Do you mind if I come and sit with you?"

"No," she said, smiling faintly. "No, not at all. But you don't mind if I read, do you?"

She hardly raised her eyes from her dead book.

"No," he said. "I like to see people read. Have a drink?"

"I don't think I should," she said.

"All right," he said.

And she stared down intently at her book once more: trying to make her eyes move convincingly across the lines. After a moment, he said,

"It was cold downstairs. That's why I came up. There didn't seem to be much heat down there."

"Oh, no," said Jane, guilty, confused by this social indictment. "No, there isn't. It's all up here. They made me bring all the heat up here, to keep the baby warm. There *isn't* much heat in this house, we never had much. But if you wanted to take one of the electric ones downstairs . . . it's terribly hot in here . . ."

"It *is* hot in here," he said, "but I like it hot."

"Do stay then," she said, a little more hopefully. "Do stay."

And he stayed. After ten minutes or so she dared to glance up at him, and he was sitting there, doing nothing, sitting in the chair, as though that were in itself a way of spending time. He did it well, with conviction.

Some time later, he said, "I'll go and get our supper," and she looked up at him, and smiled, and said with some grace,

"It's so kind of you." Then she said, presuming on the felicity of the moment, "I think I'll go to the bathroom."

"How do you feel," he said, "about walking?"

"Oh, all right," she said, reaching for her dressing gown from the end of her bed, and starting to pull it round her shoulders. "The stitches aren't too good, but I feel all right."

"I could carry you," he said.

"Would it help, do you think?" she asked.

"I don't suppose so," he said. "But I'll come with you in case you slip. It's my *duty,* to come with you."

And she slid herself out of bed, seeing as she did that she left behind her red blood on the white sheets—pulling the covers quickly over her bleeding—and she started to move, stiffly, to the door.

"I've always thought," she said, standing there feebly, her feet unpracticed on the rough carpet, "that it must be like old age, pregnancy. A premonition of old age. Slowness and help-lessness."

"Do you want your slippers?" he asked her.

"No, I don't suppose so," she said, looking down at her thin white feet on the blue carpet.

He took her arm, and she went with him very slowly down the corridor to the bathroom door, and there he left her; he said, as she went in, "Don't lock the door, because if you fainted I couldn't get to you," and she said, "No, I won't lock it."

But when she was inside she remembered that she had for-gotten her toothbrush, and she called, "James—", the name sounding like a scream in her ears, though she called it as softly as she could: and he came back to the door, and she said, "My toothbrush, could you get me my toothbrush, it's in that pudding bowl by the bed," and he went back and got it for her and handed it to her through the close small crack of the al- most-shut door.

As she washed her face, she thought that it would be good the next day, when she could have a bath. She remembered from the first child the pleasure of that first bath, and the warmth of the water on the damaged flesh, and the flat magic belly, and the curious texture of the salt in the water. She did not know why they told one to put salt in the water: but they did tell one: and religiously she did, and would. It was healing, perhaps: all of her was for healing. Ah never, damaged from birth, beyond repair, damaged before birth, an inheritance of afflictions. She cleaned her teeth and combed out her hair. In the hospital, after the birth of her first child, one of the nurses had said to her, idly, for the sake of killing silence, "I bet you're longing to get off to have your hair done. All the mothers say they *long* to get back into the hairdressers after they've been in here—" and Jane had gazed back, smiling polite acquiescence, but amazed in her heart because she had never been to a hair- dresser in her life, or not above five times since the age of twenty: and she always believed the words of strangers, with their strange authority, and had truly tried to imagine, in that instant, a hospital full of women pining for the ministrations and loving care of their coiffeurs, as she herself pined for she knew not what. Where had she failed, that she lacked such passions? She envied those women, simply desiring what could be simply had. And she pulled a comb through her long tan- gled hair and saw her face in the dusty mirror. A woman's face, despite all. This time, the midwife had not shaved off her other hair, as they had done in the hospital: Jane, unable to be- lieve her good fortune, her release from this indignity, had asked her why not—though at a juncture too late for action, as the child's head burst beautifully out—and the midwife had mumbled that it was a waste of time, doing such things.

"Lovely, lovely," Jane had screamed, and then the child had cried.

When she had combed her hair, and brushed her teeth, and washed herself, she felt better: better able to deal with the evening's massive social problem. After all, she thought to herself, a night out of his life can't kill him: he'll just have to endure me, it won't drive him mad.

Such was her moment of sanity. That is what they were like. She smiled at herself, as though she should wish herself some kind of luck.

When she got back to the bedroom—smelling, even to herself, quite pleasantly of expensive soap—he was waiting there, with the supper on a tray for her, on the end of the bed.

"All right?" he asked her, and she noticed that he was referring to her walking, and she said yes, and took her dressing gown off, as discreetly as she could, and got back into the wide bed. The baby was lying in its cradle by the snowy window, a small pale motionless mound under its white blanket. He handed her the tray, and sat down with his plateful in the chair. She looked at the food, and felt hungry, but just at that instant a dreadful pang of pain, caused no doubt by the effort of movement, went through her, and she stiffened, her face stiffened, and she moaned slightly, before she could stop herself, without forethought.

"What is it?" he said, too quickly, too intimately aware.

"Just a pain," she said, as it released her. "Nothing, it's gone."

"Lucy felt very bad," he said, "after the third."

"It seems a little cruel," she said, pulling the tray toward her once more over the crumpled hot sheet. "After so much, to get pains even afterward. The first baby's a kind of trick, the way one feels so well afterward. A trick of generation."

"There are plenty of tricks of that sort," he said, amused. The thought that he might not dislike the way she talked had never before crossed her mind, but it crossed it then, though merely to disappear in the other hinterland, on the other side of consciousness, the other darkness.

"What a lovely supper," she then said, sincerely, as she embarked on a piece of hard-boiled egg. "Delicious."

"It's all right," he said. "If you like this kind of thing."

And he ate, silently. She wondered whether conversation were called for, over such a meal, in such a place, and ate silently, too. After a while, oppressed, she turned on the radio. It was the Third: they were reading poetry.

"I heard them read one of your poems the other day," he said, when the poem ended.

"You didn't, did you?" she said, almost overcome by this acknowledgment that she existed outside her own head, that he knew what she did, or had done, that he had thought of her in times when she was not there to force such thoughts upon him. Truly, she would not have been surprised to find that (even as he sat there) he could not recollect her name.

"Yes, I did," he said. "A poem about the airport."

"No, no," she said, pedantic even in such a case, "the air terminal."

"Ah," he said. "I don't like either of those places. I keep away from them. Every time I get on an airplane I think I'm going to die."

There was a long silence, while she finished her meal, and

then she said, carefully, "I don't write, now. That was an old poem. I don't write, now."

"Don't you?" he said, equably, uninquiring, accepting the information peacefully: and she, although she had in fact lied, felt better for having said something that was almost, that might have been true.

But there still remained an hour of the evening to kill. After ten minutes or so, covered by a cup of tea, she lost faith in it, and reverted to her book: but he sat there doing nothing, just sitting there, in the chair, staring at the uninteresting flames of the gas fire. She remembered that Lucy had said that he would bring work to do, and wondered whether he had forgotten it, and what work, anyway, he could have done, sitting there in her bedroom—answered letters, perhaps, or written out checks, or done some accounts. She wished he would do it, instead of sitting there with such indictment. As though sitting were all that one could do with one's life. And oh, what else, what else. And then the merciful telephone rang, and he went down and answered it: she strained to hear him speak, and could tell instantly from his tone that it was her mother on the other end. When he came up again he smiled at her, a smile with some edge, and said, "I said all the right things for you," and she said, nervously, "Oh. Oh, thank you"—glad that he had not betrayed her, glad he had admitted the conspiracy of deceit and yet uneasy in her false position. He continued to look at her, surprisingly, after she had spoken, and she shut her eyes against the persecution of inspection, and sank a little farther down in her wrinkled bed as though to remind herself and him that she was ill, delicate, newly delivered, not to be spoken to, not to be judged. The bed beneath her felt so worn, so damp, so warm: she would have liked it to be cold and hard, and he said to her suddenly, to change the subject, but as though, in changing the subject, he were reading her mind:

"Would you like me to make the bed? Straighten it out for you?"

"I wouldn't *mind* having it straightened," she said, still lying there flat, supine, "but I couldn't let you do it."

"Why not?" he asked, looking down at her still, from his considerable height.

"It's too horrid," she said, "too nasty. I couldn't let you see."

"I must have seen worse," he said: but she shook her head, happy somehow to have stated a true emotion: happy to have defined a faint ambivalence. It exorcised, in a sense, the evening's constraints.

"It would embarrass me," she said. And smiled. He smiled down at her, and then they heard Lucy knock at the door downstairs—the bell, like all appliances requiring maintenance, long since defunct—and he went down to open it to her, and, shortly, as she took out the baby, and slipped down the shoulder of her nightdress to feed it, left.

Lucy slept the night not in the chair but in the small bed belonging to the child Laurie. Jane, knowing that a strange person was in the child's bed, wanted him back again, and in the morning made Lucy ring for him: but her mother would not part with him before a week was up, and Jane on her feet again: and moreover threatened to bring him herself. And she could not face the sight of her mother, so she consented to wait.

Most of the next day Lucy spent with her—though leaving her to do the shopping, and take the nappies to the launderette—and she stayed for the evening, too. Jane, watching her sitting there, where James had sat, was aware of relief that it was her own cousin there, not a harnessed stranger: and also of a small treacherous dismay.

The next day, the third day, she felt so much better that she ventured downstairs, with Lucy, to the kitchen, where she ran her finger through the dust on the shelves and gazed at the stains on the kitchen table, as though these things were new, and not part of her, not her own responsibility, although they were always there. She sat on the kitchen stool and watched Lucy make the toast: and after a while Lucy, her back to her, peering at the grill, said, "Did Malcolm ring?"

"No," said Jane, and added, in sudden largesse, "I don't suppose he'll ever ring me again."

"You're better off without," said Lucy, calmly, abstracting the toast, burning her fingers, picking it up from the floor where she had dropped it.

"Yes, of course," said Jane.

"I wonder why people marry?" Lucy continued, in a tone of such academic flatness that the topic seemed robbed of any danger.

"I don't know," said Jane, with equal calm. "Why does one do anything? So much of life seems so unnecessary."

"So arbitrary, really," said Lucy, spreading butter on the toast.

"It would be nice," said Jane, "to think that there were reasons. However bad."

"Do you think so?" said Lucy. "Sometimes I prefer to think we are victims. That we just do things, without knowing why."

"If there were a reason," said Jane, "one would be all the more a victim." She paused, thought, ate a mouthful of the toast. "I am wounded, therefore I bleed. I am human, therefore I suffer."

"Those aren't reasons you're describing," said Lucy, "not strictly reasons."

And from upstairs the baby's cry reached them—thin, wailing, desperate. Hearing it, the two women looked at each other, and for some reason smiled, and then Jane went upstairs to rescue it from its small local need.

That night, she was determined to persuade Lucy that she could sleep in the house alone, and she spent much of the afternoon trying to convince her of the fact: but unsuccessfully, for at five o'clock, James arrived once more for the evening. This time he had brought some work, and as he settled down in his chair with it she was surprised to find that she felt, at such a repetition, not more, but less uneasy. She lay there, patting the baby's back, listening to some music, wondering why she felt such a diminution of anxiety: and decided that it was because his presence there implied some degree of acquiescence. Having gone through such an evening once, he could well have refused to endure another: he could have thought of a dozen reasons for avoiding her. And doing again the things that she had done before—walking alone to the bathroom, feeding the child, eating a meal from a tray—she felt almost a sense of familiarity, of the elusive charm of routine. Actions so difficult the first time seemed easier. And when he said to her, this time, let me straighten the bed, she let him help her, confident that the sheets had been changed that morning and were not too dreadful to behold: she sat in the chair while he pulled the covers straight, and tucked them in for her, and put the pillows back in their high heap. She got back into it, into its warm evasion, and said to him, "That's lovely, thank you, that's lovely," and he smiled at her, as though he knew how much better it felt, and then he looked back at his papers. She watched him, for a while, as he looked at them, and wondered what it was in him that she had always found so threatening: his aquiline features, perhaps, or his pale fanatic eyes. He had a hard face, curiously softened by the soft color of his hair: his hair was blond, a fading, slightly graying blond. Lucy's three children were all blond, inheriting too from him that well-defined face, that cold precision, so unlike the gentle regular tremulous outlines that both she and Lucy, in family likeness, wore. There was distinctly in him some ominous strain: she wondered whether it was merely the reflection of rumors she had heard, stories reaching her feebly over the years through a thousand alterations, or whether it was the man himself that so affected her. A dangerous man, she said to herself: a dangerous man, sitting mildly there, by the fire, reading, smoking, drinking some tea. She had once thought herself a dangerous woman, and it was in fear of such knowledge that she now lay where she was, in the bed she lay in, lost, harmless, weak, her shadow falling nowhere, occupying no space, blotting out no light.

They talked even less than they had talked the night before. And Jane, finally, slipping slowly down into the bed, her eyes drooping over the book, fell asleep, while he was still there. She woke in the middle of the night, as the baby cried for its feed, and she had switched on the small bedside light and was starting to feed the baby before she saw that he was still there, still where he had been: he had not moved. Confused, she looked at her watch: it was two in the morning, and he had been sitting there in the dark. She glanced at him, blinking, trying to clear her eyes, to see if he was awake: he was, he was watching her. So she looked down at the child again, the small child, her ally, and watched her wave her small hands. After a while, as she moved the child to the other breast, she said quietly, into the silent warm room, "I didn't know you were staying, I thought Lucy would be back."

"It's as easy for me to stay," he said.

"You should sleep in Laurie's bed," she said, softly, not to disturb the child.

"I will," he said. "But I thought you might want something."

"Like what?" she asked him.

"Like a cup of tea? A drink? Some things for the baby?"

"No, nothing," she said, shaking her head. "I'm all right, I can manage. There was no need to sit up for that."

"I watched you fall asleep," he said.

She did not know what to reply, so she said nothing. Then, after a while, she said, "Perhaps you could take these wet things out and drop them in the bathroom?"

"There, you see," he said, as he unstretched himself and took them, "it was for that, that I sat up. I sat up to do that for you."

"That was kind of you," she said. "Good night."

"Good night," he said, and she did not see him again until the morning.

The next day Lucy came with two of her children, and did the shopping and the washing, and left a cold supper: and for the first time Jane spent the night alone. I am better off, anyway, she said to herself as the evening wore on, I am better off than that woman in that hut in Alaska, for I have at least a telephone.

She was prepared to spend all the rest of the evenings of her life alone, but the next night, after the midwife and Lucy had left, she was surprised to hear a knock on the door. She had to get up and go down to open it, and she found James standing there on the step. She was weak with relief at the sight of him: she had been afraid, as she descended the stairs, that it might have been her husband. She tried to conceal her relief, but she was so overcome that she could hardly stand.

"I got you out of bed," he said, contrite, as she leaned there breathless against the hall stand.

"I wasn't expecting you, I wasn't expecting anyone," she said, her legs trembling slightly from shock.

"I wasn't going to come," he said, "but I know you shouldn't be alone. We shouldn't have left you alone last night. Come on, let's get you back to bed, you mustn't stand here in the cold."

But she could not walk. She tried to step forward, and could not move. She stood there, feebly, and looked at the stairs, and wondered if she could climb them.

"I'll carry you," he said.

"No," she said, "I'll be better in a moment—" avoiding, with shame, the offered contact, and in a moment she did feel better, and she managed to ascend, clinging to the banister rail, moving with great care. He followed her, and opened the bedroom door for her, and she sank down onto the bed, still trembling.

"I'm sorry," he said. "I frightened you."

"I didn't know who it could be," she said. "I didn't think you were coming. Lucy didn't say you were coming . . ."

"Last night," he said, "we ought not to have left you alone. So I came, I hope you don't mind."

"No, no," she said, softly shaking her head, swinging from side to side her long, moist, sticky unwashed hair. And then she added, with a note of humility, that she had never before heard, never thought to hear in her own voice—and surprised, too, to find that she was speaking, thus gratefully, no more than the truth, "No, I'm glad you came."

"I brought a book this time," he said, as he settled himself into the chair and took off his jacket.

"No more work?" she said, sliding her feet back between the sheets; she was cold, from standing in the cold doorway.

"It was only pretend work," he said. "I never work."

"Why did you pretend to do it then?" she said.

"It was for your sake," he said, looking at her with some kind of knowledge.

"I wasn't truly convinced," she said.

"Well, conviction wasn't necessary, was it?" he said. "It was a reasonable pretext. You needed me to have one, I thought."

"I suppose so," she conceded. "And what about the book? Do you really read it, or do you pretend to read it? What is it, anyway?"

He lifted it up and showed it to her: it was an old Penguin Classic, Zola's *Thérèse Raquin*. She was glad that she had read it, that he was reading a book that she had read.

"A short sad read," he said, and she laughed.

"Mine's the same," she said, and showed him. It was Gide's *La Porte étroite*: he acknowledged, ambiguously, the felicity of the conjunction: she could not tell if he had read it, or if he was merely presuming on her implication.

She read, for an hour or so, and he made her a cup of tea: too strong, the tea was, but she did not complain, and drank it bravely and gratefully, though shuddering slightly at its bitterness. Then, as before, she fell asleep; but because this was not the first time, she fell asleep not carelessly, not as though carelessly detaching herself from him and the room, but gently, accepting his presence, arranging herself upon the bed and the pillows in some way for him and not against him, so that he would know, even as she slept, from the distribution of her arms, that she had been glad of his coming. When she woke later, to feed the baby, he was still there in the dark; he watched her without speaking as she silently fed the child, and when he went out to Laurie's bed, taking with him the wet nappies, he said, "You see, I knew I had a reason for sitting up, this time."

The next night he arrived once more, after Lucy and the midwife had gone. This time she expected him, though neither he nor she nor Lucy had said anything to anticipate his arrival: such reticence amongst people who communicated so little was not in itself unnatural, so his unsolicited appearance was taken by her without surprise, just as she had been unsurprised when Lucy had not mentioned, during the day, the fact that he had spent the preceding night with her. She had repented so much of the indelicacy of her shock the night before, and all its possible implications, that this time she opened the door to him with the calm of weeks of custom: a calm which was not wholly assumed in panic for the occasion.

He made her scrambled eggs, and more tea, and read another two pages of his book, and smoked a packet of cigarettes; the air of the room was dense with smoke and the smell of the gas fire and the faint smell of ammonia and the warm thick smell of milk and wool, and perfume. It was an atmosphere so uniquely constituted that when, months later, years later, she would encounter two or more of its ingredients in conjunction, she grew quite faint with recollection. At one point, looking up from his book, he said to her, with apparent innocence, "I like it here because it's so hot," and she said, "It's unhealthy, the warmth."

"Perhaps that's why I like it," he said.

It was so hot that she sat there in her cotton nightdress, her white winter arms bare, and he in his open shirt. She was becoming addicted to the sight of him, bringing her tea, his shirt cuffs rolled slightly away from his wrists, rolled back from the job of washing up. She looked up covertly from her book from time to time to gaze at his limp hand dangling on the chair arm. She wondered what he had done to the unease that had so wracked her so few nights ago: she acknowledged, her eyes swimming and wavering over dim lines of print, that she liked to have him there. And he, he sat and waited.

She found it hard to fall asleep, having rested too much, having taken no exercise during the day, and suffered no anxiety; but she did not want to break the rhythm of their life together and thus, by doing so, register possible protest or dissatisfaction: and so she lay down, at the accustomed time, and let her book fall to the floor, and tried to breathe with the even quietness of sleep. After a while she heard him get up from his chair and cross the room to stand by the side of her bed: she thought that he must have come to switch off her bedside light, as he had done for her on the other nights. But he did not do so: he stood there looking down at her, as she lay there, hot, damp and limp, feigning sleep. Then he walked away from her to the other side of the room: she opened her eyes discreetly, imperceptibly, and she could see him leaning on the mantelpiece watching her. After a while he said, very quietly, in a voice that would not have woken her had she been truly sleeping, "You're awake."

"Yes," she said, not moving.

There was a long silence, and then he said, across the whole distance of the large room—and with such intention, as though each foot of that space had been measured and ordained, as though the exact pitch of his voice could reach her only across just such a distance, "I want to be in that bed. The only place in the room is in that bed."

She had known it, of course: hearing it, she knew that she had known it.

"You must come, then," she said.

"Could I?" he asked politely, as though unable to trust her generosity: and she, amazed to find herself suddenly no longer bankrupt, amazed to find herself in the possession of gifts, replied, gently, "Yes, of course."

He stayed there, leaning with one elbow on the mantelpiece, in an attitude of such deliberate helpless elegance that she felt the easy tears rise in her eyes at the sight of it—moved as much by its deliberation, by its formal presentation to her, as by its own natural beauty—and then he crossed over to the bedside and sat down on the bed by her. He took her hand, and it lay in his.

"I must, you see," he said to her, as though he were explaining, apologizing; and then he looked up from their hands to her face, and for the first time ever, in their long acquaintance, in seven years of family connection, she met his eyes.

"Yes, of course," she agreed once more, looking away from him, looking down once more at their hands, so oddly joined, upon the sheet. Then, with a sigh, he turned away from her, and switched off the light: she shut her eyes and turned away, moving over for him as he got into the bed, but nevertheless something touched before they parted—a foot, a knee—and then they lay apart, waiting. After a while he said, "I'll have to turn on the light, to look at you," and she sighed, yes; lost, not knowing what to say, no longer knowing where she was. He turned the light on and looked at her face as it lay on the pillows by his, in the circle of light: she shut her eyes, unable to look at him, not daring to look. He reached out his hand, after some time, and touched her cheek, and her neck, softly, as though she might flinch or break. He stroked her hair, not seeming to mind that it was dirty and smelled of humanity, and then he touched her shoulder and her back—she was lying on her side, facing him, in the position in which she always slept—and finally he became still, leaving his heavy hand lying on her, sinking her downward, anchoring her, imprisoning her, releasing her from the useless levity of her solitude. She felt the weight of him, the slope of the bed toward him, the unaccustomed slow declivity. She opened her eyes, to speak to him, but still she did not dare to look, so she looked instead at the familiar cracks and shadows, at the peeling plaster, at the broken molding and all these nightmare images, and then she said, "I think I could sleep, now, like this."

"You sleep, then," he said, and she shut her eyes: and he repeated, very softly, in a voice that was half menace, half solace, "You go to sleep."

So she did. Looking back, she was amazed at the ease with which she had drifted away; there was a sense in which she had taken his words as an order and had, unprotesting, obeyed. There would be no way, she knew, of having again those moments before he had come to her, no way of prolonging the shock of recognition, no way of feeling again for the first time the touch of his hand. She had abandoned these things so readily for sleep that even then, so early, she was signed and pledged away.

When she woke, in the small hours of the night, to the baby's crying, he was asleep, profoundly asleep, and not even the disturbance she made in leaving the bed to collect the baby woke him. As she fed the child, she glanced at him from time to time: he lay there, breathing deeply, so far away that she felt in a sense cruelly abandoned, and yet in another way glad of the distance, because it gave her time to look at him, time to take in this new light on him, this new heap of lovely angles. She had thought that he might look painfully thin on closer inspection, but his back, turned and reared toward her, excluding her, was not the mortal cliff of blades and bone and stretched skin that she had somehow expected: it was smooth and wide. She touched him, through the limp shirt, laying her hand on his averted shoulder: he was hot to touch, his skin burned her through the thin cotton. She was surprised: she would have been less surprised to encounter an icy chill. He looked cold and gray and old: she had not thought he would be consumed right to the surface by such heat. When she had returned the sleeping baby to her cradle, she leaned over him once more, touching his hair, his face, but he started to stir so she turned from him instantly, afraid to wake him: afraid that all his revealed beauty might vanish if he caught her surreptitious vigil, or that he might be taken from her for her too great solicitude, as Cupid was from Psyche when she dropped on him the molten wax.

In the morning, when she woke, he woke at the same instant, or so it seemed: he turned to her, about to clasp her, and then, recollecting instantly and gracefully the circumstances in which he lay, he checked himself, he arrested his movement, and reached out instead for her hand. It was as though she had seen his desire and his hesitation, the one the shadow of the other, both expressed in an instant, both inseparably linked. The unlikely, artificial quality of their proximity, the ways in which they knew and did not know each other, seemed to her to possess a significance that she could hardly bear: such hesitant distance in so small a space, such lengthy knowledge and such ignorance.

When he spoke, all he said was, as though stating a fact that had to be voiced gently before it could be believed:

"I slept all night in your bed."

"Did you like it?" she asked him, rubbing her eyes, heaving herself up a little, propping herself up against the pillows.

"I'd have died," he said, "I'd have died if you'd told me I had to go and sleep in that child's bed, by myself. I wanted to be here so much."

"It can't be true," she said, "it's absurd, it can't be true."

"Of course it's true," he said, lying there on his back, looking up at her: and she noticed that he was shaking slightly, trembling, unable to lie still.

"Touch me," he said. "Go on, touch me."

"I daren't," she said, but she reached out a hand and touched his shoulder, inside the crumpled shirt, the burning smooth flesh of his shoulder, and at her touch he winced and shook, and started to laugh.

"It's no good," she said, amused and yet slightly distraught, as though caught out, "it's no good, there's nothing we can do about it, nothing at all."

He moaned, politely, in assent: she found it hard to look at him, startled by his supine reduction to accessible humanity, startled by nearness of his hitherto so distantly and cautiously acknowledged beauty, alarmed, as ever, by the physical manifestations of otherness, of man: alarmed, most of all, by his appeals to her, herself, as she lay there by him. She had so little expected, ever, to see him in such a strange light: she had so little expected to hear him speak in such a way. Looking at him, now, covertly, carefully, she wondered how she could have known him for so many years, and never have reached out so much as a prophetic hand to touch him, just to touch, in passing.

"You don't mind my being here?" he said, after a moment or two, half opening his shut eyes, as though he too did not dare to risk too much of seeing.

"How could I mind?" she said; and got out of the bed to collect the baby, and started to unfasten her nightdress.

"You might have been horrified by the suggestion," he said, watching her as the baby attached itself, watching her cup its small head in the palm of her hand as it blindly fed. "You might have been appalled. But you're so kind, you're so polite, you'd never have said no."

"How could I have wanted to say no?" she said.

"You're so lovely," he said. "It's so lovely here, it's like heaven in this room, I couldn't keep away from you . . . I kept trying to pretend that I was coming here for your sake, to look after you, in case you noticed that I couldn't help it and sent me away, but I couldn't stay away, all the time I wasn't here I was thinking of you and of how warm it must be in that bed, and of how near I could be if you would let me, of how you might even let me touch you . . . when I sat there in that chair, the first time, and watched you fall asleep, I felt—I don't know, I felt as though you were mine."

"You can't mean it," she said.

"I do, I do," he said. "You're so lovely, I can't bear it. You're beautiful, you know, I've always thought so, I always thought you were beautiful I thought so even before I loved you, when I didn't know you . . ." She flinched and sighed, listening to him, alarmed and yet hopelessly moved by his willing blind suicidal dive into such deep waters: the waters closed over their heads, and they lay there, submerged, the cold dry land of non-loving abandoned, out of sight, so suddenly and so completely out of sight, lost at the sound, at the syllable of the word of love. "I love you, I love you," he said: words she had not thought to hear again.

"How can you, you don't know, how can you," she said softly, smiling, gently, in decorous denial.

"You're beautiful," he said, and she shook her head and smiled incredulously: but at the same time she knew that he was right, she was beautiful, with a true sexual beauty, she had always been so, with a beauty that was a menace and a guilt and a burden: her whole life had been overcast by the knowledge of it, so studiously evaded, so nobly denied, so surreptitiously acknowledged. It had seemed to her a cruel and disastrous blessing, a responsibility, wild like an animal, that could not be let loose, so she had denied it, had sworn that black was white and white was black: but now, for all that, it sat there by her bedside, eloquent, existent, alive, despite the dark years of its captivity.

He watched her as she fed the baby: and when she had finished and returned her to her cradle, he said, with what sounded like a sudden anxiety, "You wouldn't go away from me, would you? You'll wait for me, won't you?"

"How could I go away?" she said. "I've nowhere to go, I'm stuck right here in this bed."

"Yes, of course you are," he said, as though pleased, as though comforted. "You've got to be there, you can't go away, can you?"

"I'll wait for you," she said: long dead through all her bandages, ripped and defeated, she committed herself to waiting.

"You're my prisoner, here, in this bed," he said, "but if you're good, and wait quietly, I'll look after you, I'll bring you meals, and books to read, and cups of tea."

And she smiled at him, slowly, deliberately, capitulating, in complicity, assenting, though to what she did not know, and said, "And in the end, then, will you rescue me?"

"Oh yes," he said, touching her knee under the sheet, very gently and carefully touching her knee with his hand. "Oh yes, when it's time, I'll rescue you."

"I'll be glad of that," she said. "I'll be so grateful for that." And she started to cry, not violently or painfully, but softly and warmly, and through her tears, which flowed down her cheeks quietly, rising unchecked in her eyes and slowly overflowing like a fountain, brimming over like a mild fountain, she said, remembering the first moment of their mutual past, nostalgically recalling it to their transformed present—"I cried," she said, "I cried, when you brought me that champagne."

"I saw that you did," he said. "I saw it, and I loved you for it, I began to love you when I saw you weep."

Weeks later, referring back to that same incident, that same first gift, what he said was, "I saw you, and when I saw your tears I knew that I would have you, I knew that you were mine."

When Lucy came, later in the day, Jane did not look at her much, but then she never looked much at anyone: she had dared to risk more of her vision upon James, over that last night, than she had bestowed upon human features in months. Such reticence as hers, she knew, could hardly be suspected of withdrawal or retreat: she had retreated already so far that there were few further places to go to, and no one with the discernment to follow or measure whatever further acres she might cross. And Lucy herself, so respectful to any reticence, would never attempt to follow her, would never urge or inquire. She would not even, or so Jane thought, permit herself the impertinence of anxiety on another's behalf: and interrogation she would have regarded as a most violent assault on human liberty. She stayed for the afternoon, and talked of her work, and did some of the washing: and then in the early evening she departed to put her own children to bed. Neither of them had mentioned James. And thus they established the silence of months, a silence which took some shattering when the time came.

That evening, James came back, after Lucy had gone, as he had said he would. And he came the next night, and the next. She began to live for his coming, submitting herself helplessly to the current, abandoning herself to it, knowing then at the beginning things that were to be obscured from her later by pain and desire—knowing it could not end well, because how else could it be, what good ends were there to such emotions? And she did not care: she foresaw and surrendered to the whole journey, she did not withhold herself, she kept nothing back. She became possessed by dreadful anxieties: that he would die before she could have him, that he would kill himself in his car, that she herself one morning would bleed to death, that the cracked ceiling would fall upon them both one night. When he left the room to fetch her a drink or to boil her an egg she suffered, acutely, from his absence: she suffered from separation when he sat with her in the same room. During the hours that he was not with her, she lay and gazed at the clock, watching the hands move round the white dial. What amazed her most was that he too seemed to share these anxieties, to fear that she would in some way against every probability elude him: every time, when he came and found her still lying there, he appeared to share her own almost unbearable relief. She was not used to such participation, and had been prepared, heroically, to conceal the desperate intensity of her concern— an artist in concealment and evasion she was, and had always thought that she had to be so, because she had always believed that her passions, if revealed, would in some way scorch and blister and damage their object. She had been prepared to protect him from her own longing, to obscure, by a blank face, her pain and her joy, but he did not seem to want protection. He wanted to hear the worst.

He looked after her with solicitude, as though she were an invalid, as in a sense she was: in his small ministrations they found a pattern, acceptable to both, excusing their situation, that remained with them long after it was needed: an erotic pattern, a chart for their otherwise silent and shapeless love. At night they lay there side by side, hardly touching, hot, in the wide, much-slept-in bed: separated by her condition more safely than by Tristram's sword, or that wooden board that the early Quakers of New England would lay as a partition between their beds, in the first weeks of marriage, to prevent too much surprisal, too much shock, before a more human bond had been established. She lay there, the unachievable *princesse lointaine,* so close that her every breath disturbed him, so close that he was acquainted with all the pains of her still unrecovered body. They talked, and touched hands, and waited for the time to pass. A prolonged initiation, an ordeal more fitting than human ingenuity could have devised.

On the eighth day her mother brought Laurie back. Jane always lied to her mother so much by implication that she found little difficulty in providing yet another excuse for her husband's absence: the truth about the past month being so impossible, what could she do but lie?

"Oh, Malcolm's gone to Birmingham for the day," she said, brightly, putting spoons of tea from the willow-pattern tea caddy into the china pot. "He's so sorry to miss you, he's got a recital there tonight. He's so grateful to you for having Laurie."

"Oh, we *enjoyed* it, didn't we, Laurie?" said her mother, and the boy, clinging passionately to his mother's skirts, obsequiously grinned.

"The baby's lovely, don't you think?" said Jane, watching her mother's gaze as it lit on the thick dust, the round stains, the dirty stove, the tarnished spoons, the rubbish of a careless life.

"A lovely baby," agreed her mother, absently. And Jane, for the thousandth time, wondered whether she ought to comment on the state of her kitchen, to apologize, to show that she suspected the extent of her own failure: whether she ought to say, in extenuation, "I know it's a bit of a mess—" or, "It's a bit untidy at the moment, isn't it?" or whether she might, if she said nothing, get away with it, and leave her mother to go harmlessly home to say to her friends, "Oh, of course, poor Jane's a little disorganized at the moment, but she'll straighten it out no doubt—" nodding, smiling, shaking of heads, understanding looks—"she always was *such* an untidy child, but of course, now she's married, she's so much better now, everything's so much better now . . . " Jane sometimes felt that if she as much as conceded the tiniest mutual moment of recognition, disaster would ensue: screams, abuse, recriminations, madness, collapse. So she said nothing, pretending to herself, uneasily, that all kitchens were like this, all houses in this state. And where indeed could she have started to set it in order? It was quite beyond repair. She knew it, she knew it was too bad to contemplate.

"That's a lovely plant," said her mother suddenly, staring intently at a leafless withered unwatered twig growing in a plantpot on the windowsill, a plant that Jane had for months neglected to throw into the bin because it still possessed, despite its barren decay, small faint green horseshoe scars on its brown stem that proved some hidden life—she did not water it, she did not go so far as to water it, but neither did she throw it out.

"Lovely, isn't it?" said Jane, smiling: laughing, suddenly overjoyed by the grotesque nature of the lie, by the stony obduracy of their denial of the true state of that house, that room, that marriage, that woman, that leafless twig. She wondered, as she laughed, whether she had kept the plant through inertia, or through hope.

"Why did you call the baby Bianca?" pursued her mother, unnerved by the laughter, refusing to be silenced by such tactics.

"Why not?" said Jane. "Because of the snow, I suppose. It was snowing, when she was born. And it's a good pun. Bianca Gray. After all, with *my* name, *I* was fated, wasn't I? So why not make a pun at the child's expense?"

"It's rather an odd name," said her mother. "Your father didn't much care for it. He wanted you to call her Julia."

"Well, truly, to tell you the *truth*," said Jane, pouring out anxiously the watery tea, "to tell you the honest *truth*, Malcolm chose it."

"Oh, I see," said her mother, "oh, yes, I see."

And Jane continued to laugh. This was one of her rare sins of commission: a gratuitous lie.

When her mother had gone safely out of the house and back on to the train to Sussex, she watered the plant, for the first time in months, dripping a little water from a cup onto the dry earth. Laurie watched her, intently, carefully.

"What do you think?" she said to him, when she had done it. "D'you think I might have killed it? It might die of shock."

❧ She often thought that one of the reasons for the total disaster of her sexual life was her own inability to reconcile the practical and the emotional aspects of the matter. The difficulties of both seemed to her to be so great that she wondered how anyone could ever happily overcome them: and the thought of overcoming both at once, so that one might in one instant experience love without pain, without terror, and without danger, seemed beyond the realm of human possibility. Human contact seemed to her so frail a thing that the hope that two people might want each other in the same way, at the same time, and with the possibility of doing something about it, appeared infinitely remote. In her lovely youth she had suffered such torments from problems of underwear, pain, health, and so forth that she had, after the brief despair of marriage, and the ludicrous accolade of pregnancy, given up; and now, as she sat in the doctor's waiting room, after the six weeks of waiting, knowing what she desired him to say, she could hardly believe that she was—as she so clearly, with such forethought, was—about to embark on yet more deception, yet more suffering. Because there was only one end to this visit, and that was the bed, with James in it. She was waiting here in this waiting room, in the chilly unprotected outer world, about to undergo that most intimate and painful of human inspections—and yet prepared to undergo it willingly, miraculously protected from the horror of it by the need to have it done, by that one end in view. What she most dreaded, she was about to endure—the questions, the language, the rubber fingers touching inside her dead flesh, the spectacle of her own terror—and yet for the first time none of it mattered, none of it could destroy her, she knew she would emerge from it as from a dream, the way other, stronger women do. She had never known where they got their strength from, those other women: how could they remember the end, when so trapped by the means? How could one decide on Tuesday to make love on Wednesday, or decide one month to refrain the next? How could one do it? She looked around at the other faces—worn faces, young faces, smiling, busy faces—and she wondered how they all managed it, how they managed to keep alive, when

life was so difficult. For herself, she had almost given up. She
thought of James, waiting for her at home, as she waited for
him here, looking after her two children for her, waiting for
her to come back to him. She suffered, out of his presence, she
suffered and withered and grew dry. He was waiting for her,
in the dusty, run-down, stiffening house.

When she got back, she saw him from the corner of the
street: he was standing in the window, looking for her, holding
the baby in his arms. When she saw him she started to run,
and could hear the sound of her feet on the pavement in the
cold afternoon air. He opened the door to her, and touched her
cheek, and said, "You were gone so long, I missed you, you've
never been out so long," and she said, "Oh, it *was* long, it was
too long, I'm sorry it was so long . . ."

"What did he say?" he asked her, politely, kindly, as he
handed her the restless child.

"He said I was all right," she said, smiling, wondering if
these words could possibly mean what they must mean. "He
said I was all right."

"I knew you would be all right," he said. "Of course you
would be all right."

"I don't know," she said. "I was afraid that because I wanted
it, it might not be so."

He stayed with her for the rest of the day: now that so
many weeks had passed since the child's birth, he stayed with
her less often, finding, she supposed, less pretext, but this night
he had said he would stay. They sat together in the evening,
waiting for the child's last feed, with nothing more to say to
each other. She was sewing, letting down the hem of a baby's
garment that Laurie had worn, converting it into a dress for
Bianca. The children were asleep, and there was nothing hap-

pening in the house at all except for the movement of her hands with the needle, and the small sounds of continuing life—a dripping tap, a passing car, the faint mechanical hum of power. Each time she pierced the wool with the needle she heard the cloth shriek. Finally, when the baby began to cry for her upstairs, she leaned over to him and touched the back of his hand, and said, "Why do you sit with me? Why do you stay with me? Why did you wait for me so long?" and he looked back at her and smiled, acknowledging absurdity, and shrugged his elegant shoulders, and ran his fingers nervously through his hair, and said, "Because you're so lovely, because I love you so, of course, why else?"

She smiled, and sighed, and buried the needle neatly and safely in the dress, and laid it down on the arm of the chair, and said, rising, "I suppose people have loved other people before. It can't be new, can it?"

"It seems new," he said, watching her.

"So pointlessly lovely," she said, shaking her head to herself, unable to understand how she could appear to remain so calm, when a breath of his could have extinguished her. She remembered, as she went up the stairs and slowly undressed herself to feed the child, some story she had once heard or misheard—a story of a ship, drawing in to a beach, cast up there, perhaps shipwrecked, and the passengers straying helplessly along the shore, as the ship put helpless out to sea, reclaimed by the tide. There was more to the story than that—some tale of God, perhaps, or a shell, or death, or a call to salvation—but she could not remember it well. A voyage, anyway, a sandy beach with shells.

He joined her before the child was down; he watched her as she settled her in the cradle by the window. He watched her in such a way as she did these things that what she was doing, in itself a pleasure, became beautiful: she was reconciled in him to weeks of repetition, each act more lovely for its re-enactment. They had constructed between them over the past weeks so delicate a way of being—with subjects neutral, trivial, tender, the quality of the tea, the color of the sky, such innocent things, to avoid the dangerous wastes around them—and now, as she pulled back the sheet and got into the bed, she wondered whether it would be possible for her to join him there in that most dangerous of places without ill words spoken, without destruction or offense. Their warm world was so small, it was little larger than that room and that bed, but that, after all, was where they were, and they had been there before, there was perhaps no need for shock or surprisal.

When he turned to her, she lay still, because despite herself she was frightened: she lay still as he touched her, not daring to move. She was frightened not of him but of herself, of her own coldness, but when he touched her she was unresisting. She wept, later, in amazement: she looked down at him as he lay with his head against her and she knew that there was nothing to be done about such beauty, except to try to keep it. She wanted it, she wanted it for hers. That a desire so primitive could flow through her, unobstructed, like milk, astonished her.

"I want you," she said, looking down at him, reaching down a hand to touch his hair, moving the skin of her leg against his face. "I want you."

"Of course you do," he said, as though it were an obvious thing. "Of course you do, I want you so much that you must want me, it couldn't be any other way."

"You didn't hurt me," she said, bewildered.

"How *could* I have hurt you?" he cried, in the immediate logic of possession, pressing his face into her damp leg. "How could I have hurt you, when I love you so much?"

"It isn't as simple as that," she said, shutting her eyes, able to smile, since it had been simple, in fact.

And so they fell asleep, damp, soaked in a mutual flood of emotion, hardly covered by the stained and wrinkled sheet. One of the things she had always most feared in love had been the wetness. It had dismayed and haunted her, that fatal moisture, and she had surrounded herself with towels and tissues, arid, frightened, fighting like a child for the cold flat dry confines of a narrow bed, superstitiously afraid, like a child, of the body's warmth: and now she lay there, drowned in a willing sea.

It won't, of course, do: as an account, I mean, of what took place. I tried, I tried for so long to reconcile, to find a style that would express it, to find a system that would excuse me, to construct a new meaning, having kicked the old one out, but I couldn't do it, so here I am, resorting to that old broken medium. Don't let me deceive myself, I see no virtue in confusion, I see true virtue in clarity, in consistency, in communication, in honesty. Or is that too no longer true? Do I stand judged by that sentence? I cannot judge myself, I cannot condemn myself, so what can I make that will admit me and encompass me? Nothing, it seems, but a broken and fragmented piece: an event seen from angles, where there used to be one event, and one way only of enduring it.

Because it's obvious that I haven't told the truth, about myself and James. How could I? Why, more significantly, should I? An interesting query, though interesting perhaps to myself alone. And yet I haven't lied. I've merely omitted: merely, professionally, edited. This is dishonest, but not as dishonest as deliberate falsehood. I have often thought—and it's a dull reflection, but then there's no virtue in novelty—that the ways of regarding an event, so different, don't add up to a whole; they are mutually exclusive: the social view, the sexual view, the circumstantial view, the moral view, these visions contradict each other; they do not supplement one another, they cancel one another, they destroy one another. They cannot co-exist. And so, because I so wanted James, because I wanted him so obsessively, I have omitted everything, almost everything except that sequence of discovery and recognition that I would call love. I have lied, but only by omission. Of the truth, I haven't told enough. I flinched at the conclusion, and can even see in my hesitance a virtue: it is dishonest, it is inartistic, but it is a virtue, such discretion, in the moral world of love. And anyway, who could recount, without convicting herself of madness, the true degrees of love? Those endless discussions on that endless theme, the trembling, the waiting, the anguish when he left the room for a moment, the terror—and I did mention this, but abandoned the subject because it seemed too much of an indictment, too gross a conviction of folly—the terror that each time he left my sight he would die? I suffered from his absence, all the time that he was not in my sight, where my eyes could reach him. I had some cause for this—and in a sense I justify myself by recounting it, and in a sense betray by substantiation my feeling for him, I don't know which—I had a cause, because he was in fact slightly more likely than some to die, as he was an appallingly dangerous driver, religiously, consistently dangerous, passionately bad. I have omitted those hours I spent waiting by the snowy bedroom window for his violent car to crash into the curbstone: those hours I spent listening to the radio for news of the spectacular pile-up that would mean his death. He was part owner of a garage, and spent most of his time driving around in a Maserati, at a horrible speed. He was an amateur, in every sense: untrained, inept, he spoke of and drove his cars with rapture. I did not mention this earlier, although it is relevant, because when I first knew him, during those weeks of confinement, my mind could not take it in, so I excluded it, every aspect of it, except for my fear of his death, which seemed a pure and comprehensible emotion. He knew that I could not take this part of him because at this time he never mentioned it, or no more than he had done, for courtesy's sake, throughout those years of family connection.

I omitted, too, my feelings for the baby; I regret that this was necessary, as they were good feelings, pure emotions, but I could not find a place for them in my narrative. I am sorry that they had to go. I would have liked to evoke her, small eggshell head and thin arms and soft nightly murmurs and faint breathings. I am afraid now, looking back, that my failure to include her rested upon some profound and sinister cause that had nothing to do with artistic necessity: I did not want to include one man's child in the story of my passion for another man. I felt compromised, I felt condemned. And yet at the time I told myself—and perhaps rightly, who can say—that it did not matter, that a baby is a baby, no matter whose, and that those who treat it with love and carry it gently are its true parents. But no, it is not so. I admit that it is not so. I acknowledge my guilt, I acknowledge the treachery of my love. Blood is blood, and it is not good enough to say that children are for the motherly, as Brecht said, for there are many ways of unmothering a woman, or unfathering a man. One cannot judge by consequences alone—or I cannot, though I try to teach myself to do so, I tried to say to myself each night, this child knows nothing, she is asleep, she will never know. And yet, how can I deny that it gave me pleasure to see James hold her in his arms for me? The man I loved and the child to whom I had given birth. What could I do? It gave me pleasure, but I omitted that pleasure, and the satisfaction of recording it, because of my own unease, because of my guilt. I would not like it to appear that I did not love her, that I did not notice her. That is all that I am trying to say.

This brings me to another subject, another circumstantial aspect, hitherto tactfully or perhaps crudely neglected: as it was in fact, not only in the telling. What about Lucy? What did she think, what did she know, what did I know of what she knew, what did he tell me of her, what did he think of what he was doing to her? There is no answer to any of these questions, because we never mentioned her name. I am always prepared to believe anything, truly anything, about the lives of others, and I was prepared to exercise my capacity for credit by believing that she didn't know where he was, that he wouldn't have been missed; I never asked him about such things, it wouldn't have been possible to ask. I accepted his presence, I accepted his coming, I accepted him, I opened my door, I gave him a key. I forgot Lucy, I did not think of her—or only occasionally; lying awake at night as the baby cried, I would think of her, with pangs of irrelevant inquiry, pangs endured not by me and in me, but at a distance, pangs as sorrowful and irrelevant as another person's pain. These things were to assert themselves later, these considerations, but then they were weak and powerless, faint shadows of thought, ghosts of considerations, ineffectual, whispering, dry.

So, too, were thoughts of Malcolm, my husband. The discretion of my account may have suggested that he left me, a helpless victim, about to give birth to his child, but this was not so: I neglected him, I abandoned him, I drove him away. When he was gone, I did not think of him. There was no way of thinking of him, just as, with James in my arms, there was no way of thinking of Lucy. So I did not think. Or perhaps I should say—for after all, one's mind is not blank, ever—it is amazing how little I thought of them.

The same is true, too, of my situation. When I look back at the isolation in which I gave birth to Bianca, I terrify myself; I look back to the absurdity of that night, the third night, when I slept alone with the baby in that empty house, and I sweat with retrospective fright. I was frightened then, I admit it, I am no saint, I am not quite mad, I am not unaware of danger. But nevertheless, despite these qualifications, the truth is that I did it. I made that loneliness, I created it alone, it grew out of me and surrounded me: and I chose it, I preferred it to the safety of human company, or a hospital bed. My family would never forgive me if they knew what I went through; it was only Lucy, so like me in so many ways, who could permit it, because to her, as to me, a nature was determinate, pre-eminent. She respected the state I had achieved. It is clear enough, in terms of narrative and consequence, that I would have loved James: what else could I have felt but love for a man who showed love to me when I was so lost, so alone, in such abandon and distress? I loved him inevitably, of necessity. Anyone could have foreseen it, given those facts: a lonely woman, in an empty world. Surely I would have loved anyone who might have shown me kindness, I would have belonged to any man who laid a hand on me? That's what one might think, anyway, and I would find it humiliating but comfortable, were it so, a comfortable explanation: but of course it's not true, it could not have been anyone else. I shall never know what it was that saved me—in him, in me, in both of us—but I know that it was not inevitable: it was a miracle, it was a stroke of amazing fate. So do not let me find myself reasons, do not let me say that the solitude was his cause, that he was born of it, as the phoenix of fire, that what he did for me was easy and expected: if I said that I would be lying. What I deserved was what I had made: solitude, or a repetition of pain. What I received was grace.

Grace and miracles. I don't much care for my terminology. Though at least it lacks that most disastrous concept, the concept of free will. Perhaps I could take a religion that denied free will, that placed God in his true place, arbitrary, carelessly kind, idly malicious, intermittently attentive, and himself subject, as Zeus was, to necessity. Necessity is my God. Necessity lay with me when James did. I looked into its face and recognized it: it made him human, lovely, perishing.

My family had brought me up to believe in a more conventional deity. They believed, or so they said, in the God of the Church of England, and in a whole host of other unlikely irreconcilable propositions: in monogamy, in marrying for love, in free will, in the possibility of moderation of the passions, in the virtues of reason and civilization. And I tried hard to believe in these things, because they made it seem that I would commit some serious offense against them if I did not: and I thought that my distrust was called out by my own wickedness, so I ignored it, I pretended to believe, afraid to distrust my own contradictory hallucinatory lights. But even as a child, I had another notion. I kept it to myself. Through fear—and partly, for why should I deny all virtue, partly through respect and alarm at the thought of denying and destroying them—I lived on the dim outskirts of their world, my life a mockery, a parody of theirs: the shopping, the radio, books, children, a false and equally impoverished friend or two. It seemed, in a sense, better to renounce myself than them, and anyway, I had no clear idea of any other form of life, I had no faith in my fitful dark illuminations.

Respectability is so odd a thing, so strong in its grip, and yet in itself so frail, that when I was at home, in my parents' home, I felt all the time afraid that any word of mine, any movement, my mere existence, might shatter them all into fragments. As a small child, not yet knowing why, I practiced concealment, deviously reconstructing my every thought for them, knowing that if they could see me as I truly was they might never recover from the shock. Sometimes at table I would look down at my plate, afraid that they might see in my eyes the depths of my deceit, afraid that they might see themselves condemned. And it seemed that I was to sweat out this pretense until death, in painful effort: I married a man who would, I thought, help me to share this conspiracy, but there were places where no effort was good enough, and in bed he could see in my cold body the signs of treachery. He was kind at first, he did not accuse me, he tried to share my pretense, but I knew that I had been caught out at last and I could not bear his knowledge of me. So I sent him away, I retreated to a world where nobody could see me but my children: mute witnesses, helpless inheritors. I had thought that I would die there alone, without the comfort of screaming out my failure, claiming till death that my marriage existed, that there were no cockroaches in my kitchen, no gaping holes in the roof, no broken bottles on the steps, no vices in my heart. There was no way out. Divorce, unlike madness, was unknown in our family, structured as it was upon a faintly clerical background. It would have finished my parents, my divorce. But so would one straight look in my face. And it occurred to me even then that by my hesitation, by my delay in declaring myself, I was merely hastening on an assassination, a massacre.

When James looked at me, he saw me, myself. This is no fancy, no conceit. He redeemed me by knowing me, he corrupted me by sharing my knowledge. The names of qualities are interchangeable—vice, virtue; redemption, corruption; courage, weakness—and hence the confusion of abstraction, the proliferation of aphorism and paradox. In the human world, perhaps there are merely likenesses. Recognition, lack of recognition. Faces I know, faces I don't know. The qualities, they depended on the supposed true end of life; they were placed in a scale, steps of an angel-guarded ladder, ascending to, descending from, some possible heaven, some unknown goal—virtue, or innocence, I think I supposed it to be. I sought virtue, but I could not ascend by the steps that others seemed to take: my nature was not large or generous or secure enough to permit me. So what could I do but seek in abnegation, in denial, in renunciation, that elusive quality? The hair shirt, the sack cloth. I thought that if I could deny myself enough I would achieve some kind of innocence, despite those intermittent nightmare promptings of my true nature. I thought I could negate myself and wipe myself out. But when James looked at me it was my true self that he saw: alive, speaking, demanding him, despite all my efforts. So what could I conclude? That all those efforts had been misguided, their goal misplaced? That there were no angels, no ladder? I had lived in denial for so long, had made such virtue of necessity, had built so weighty a case for my own actions, that I could hardly bear to see it all destroyed at a touch of his hand. And yet I could not resist him: I knew that I could not resist recognition. Either way, I stand condemned. Sometimes, in desperation, I think that there are no qualities, and that any human effort is pointless in the extreme: that there are merely the things that I do, the hands that I know, the walls that I look upon. James spoke to me, and I answered. But how then do I account for those other long years, for those cruel efforts, for those entirely unnecessary renunciations? Salvation, damnation. That is what it amounts to, and I do not know which of these two James represented. Hysterical terms, maybe: religious terms, yet again. But then life is a serious matter, and it is not merely hysteria that acknowledges this fact: for men as well as women have been known to acknowledge it.

I must make an effort to comprehend it. I will take it all to pieces, I will resolve it to its parts, and then I will put it together again, I will reconstitute it in a form that I can accept, a fictitious form: adding a little here, abstracting a little there, moving this arm half an inch that way, gently altering the dead angle of the head upon its neck. If I need a morality, I will create one: a new ladder, a new virtue. If I need to understand what I am doing, if I cannot act without my own approbation—and I must act, I have changed, I am no longer capable of inaction—then I will invent a morality that condones me. Though by doing so, I risk condemning all that I have been.

It's odd, really, how completely James represented all that my family was not, so that he was at once an exorcism and an ideal. And all the odder because he was after all a family connection, and not a man picked up in a cinema or a hotel bar, or encountered late at night at a suspect party. Wanting him for myself, and loving him so much, I didn't much care to look back on his past with Lucy, but from time to time the pleasure of thinking of him would overcome the reluctance to dwell on the circumstances, and I would remember his wedding, which I attended, and all the family gossip that surrounded his first introduction. Lucy had met him, after all, through orthodox channels: through his mother, in fact, and what more orthodox than that? James's mother was Norwegian, and she was reputed to be the daughter of famous parents. It was impossible to tell how well founded this reputation was, as naturally enough none of us knew any other Norwegians, so we could not cast any doubts on her claims to distinction. Distinguished or not, she was certainly beautiful, in an arrogant, bony, freckled, voluptuous way; she dressed well, which was something that nobody in our family had ever known how to do. Lucy, who started work for a publisher as soon as she came down from University, met her there: it was evident that she was having an affair with one of Lucy's employers, though I don't think anyone ever said so to me, so perhaps I simply deduced it. She did have some more recognizable connection with the firm—something to do with design, I think. James's father was a businessman—an odd-looking, faintly disreputable-looking small man, much shorter than his lofty wife—who was connected with a firm that dealt in perfume. They were a strange couple: there was something sinister in their very conjunction. They lived in London, in South Kensington. Our family, who had always lived in the country, and expressed, in most circles, deep moral horror at the thought of living in town, were faintly outraged by the idea of their ménage, though I don't suppose they could have put their objections into words. James was the only son, the only child, and would therefore have inherited the money, had there been any, but for some reason there was not, though there was a certain amount of expense—sudden, erratic bursts of expenditure, like prolonged holidays on the Costa Brava, and the purchase of half the garage for James. They lived more lavishly, the Otfords, than our family, and at first my parents were impressed by this, but they gradually became aware that it was being done on a shoe string, that there was not much in the bank, that life was lived in an atmosphere of debt and mortgages and expense accounts and leasehold properties and speculations. There was also some faint explanatory murmur of a distant financial scandal—a weathered bankruptcy, people said, though not loudly or clearly enough for me to understand.

Nothing could have been more different, within albeit narrow limits, from our own family's social ground. Both my father and my mother came from such genteel middle-class descent that Jane Austen herself could have described their affiliations with ease. My mother's family flourished; of her two

brothers, one was a barrister, and one a clergyman. On my father's side, however, some slight disaster had taken place in
the preceding generation, and the three sons had been brought
up in an aura of slight—though naturally genteel—poverty.
My father, the youngest of the three, had ended up as the
headmaster of a prep school in Sussex; a good prep school,
everyone said (though what else would *I* be likely to hear?),
but county rather than smart, worthy rather than fashionable.
Thus, my mother considered herself slightly superior to her
status as headmaster's wife and let everybody know. My father,
too, could not forget that he should have been born to better
things, and was forever reminding everyone of his grandfather
who was a judge, of his cousin who was an admiral, of his uncle who was a well-known advocate. I have never heard such
name-dropping as I heard in our house: I lived with it, it was
what I was reared upon. I remember endless, agonizing conversations between my parents and the parents of boys at the
school: conversations in which my parents would toe, anxiously, the delicate line between flattery and self-aggrandize-
ment. What distressed me most, I think, was to observe how
subtly the line changed, according to the predilections and affiliations of the parents concerned: for one family one set of
relatives would be proudly aired, for another family a different
set altogether. It pained me, it humiliated me, to see my own
flesh and blood so dissemble, so ingratiate itself, so alter with
every word that was spoken, every hint that was dropped. It
confused me utterly. My mother was thought, generally, to be
a charming woman—she was pretty, flattering, gracious—and
yet I know the profound depths of her insincerity, for I would
hear her in private savage, relentlessly, the antecedents of those
very people she took such pains to charm.

And my father was not a clever man; he had the show of intelligence (born of bullying small boys and socially inferior schoolmasters) without its substance. It was difficult for a child to understand that a teacher—and a teacher who was moreover one's own father—should lack intelligence, but so it was: authority doubly betrayed, doubly cast into suspicion. I tried so hard when I was young to reconcile the irreconcilable evidence before me: for how could I say to myself that my own parents were hypocrites, that their social attitudes were dishonest, that the solid virtues to which they paid lip service were as nothing to them compared with the vain honors and titles and glories which, at every speech day, they solemnly denounced? The values that they proclaimed were sound enough, but I found myself forced to repudiate them, I had to cast them out, baffled as I was by the tone in which truths were uttered to me, unable at that tender age (as I am unable now) to distinguish between falsehoods rendered true by passion, and truths made false by duplicity. "What you wear doesn't matter, it's what you *are* that counts," my mother would piously declare, while casting appraising glances at the fabric and cut of her acquaintances' coats, and resting her attitudes and anglings for invitations delicately upon her conclusions: "Marriage and family warmth are *so* important," she would say, "and happy homes like ours so rare"—she, who flinched from any physical approach, whose eyes grew white with alarm and panic when my father touched her shoulder or her hand. "You young people don't know how to enjoy yourselves as we did," she said, as my sister and I dragged restlessly around the house all holidays, afraid to invite our friends home in case my father should crack his sardonic jokes at them and reduce them to tears, as he used to do before we learned to protect ourselves and them. "I can't imagine," she would say, when speaking of other families, "how people can have favorites among their own children," smiling with an appearance of comfort at me as she spoke, knowing—or not knowing?—that she had rejected me at my sister's birth and had disliked me ever since, trying perhaps by her deceitful assertion to right the wrong, to make right in words what had gone wrong in emotion. I never knew how to respond to these lies, lies uttered not with confident ignorance but with a kind of desperate unease that forced me to pretend to believe them, even while I reserved my judgment, because I knew that if I showed my disbelief I would be hitting at something too fragile to sustain even my puny, childish attacks; and I feared even more than her continual evasive misrepresentations those occasional, mercifully rare, days of collapse when some word of my father's or some casual neglect from others would shatter her entirely and reduce her to tears, hysteria, illness.

It cannot have done any of us much good, either, living under the shadow of so many small boys, whose affairs were discussed over the meal table at length with flippant malice; my father affected cynicism as a sign of class distinction, and the way in which he would speak of the major sorrows of a child's life silenced me before I learned to speak. Never would I expose myself, I swore, to provide him with a moment's amusement. Some of the boys would take Sunday lunch with us occasionally; there was one child I shall always remember, a small thin child with protruding ears, whose father, he proudly told us, was standing as Labour candidate for a hopeless seat in an imminent general election. My father teased him unmercifully, asking questions that the poor child could not begin to answer, making elaborate and hideous semantic jokes about the fruits of labor, throwing in familiar references to prominent Tories that were quite wasted on such large and tender ears; and the poor child sat there, staring at his roast beef and Yorkshire pudding, turning redder and redder, and trying, pathetically, sycophantically, to smile. I hated my father at that instant: I could not forgive him for it. I suppose that both he and my mother would have liked a boy of their own, though this did not occur to me until I had a son myself: it would at least have given my mother an outlet for all her flirtatious, coy, and pointless charm, which she never in my knowledge directed toward a legitimate sexual object—certainly she never bestowed any of it upon my father, whom she regarded, as he her, with a thinly disguised contempt. I don't know what had gone wrong between them: perhaps they did not like having to share their mutual knowledge. Some people conspire to deceive the world and find in their conspiracy a bond, but they did it, I think, with a sense of profound mutual dislike. They presented a united front to the world, because their survival demanded that they should, because they could not afford to betray each other in public; but their dissension found other devious forms, secret forms, underhand attacks and reprisals, covered malice, discreet inverted insults, painful praise. Children are lost in such a land, where appearances bear no relationship to reality, a land of hahas and fake one-dimensional uncrossable bridges and artificial unseasonal blooms: a landscape civilized out of its natural shape.

My mother's sister, Lucy's mother, married, rashly, a man in trade, the only one in the family; but she refined him and cultivated him until he was quite at home with his professional relatives, and as capable of verbal malice and sound and useless principles as they were. How I dislike Jane Austen. How deeply I deplore her desperate wit. Her moral tone dismays me: my heart goes out to the vulgarity of those little card parties that Mrs. Philips gave at Meryton, to that squalid rowdy hole at Portsmouth where Fanny Price used to live, to Lydia at fifteen gaily flashing her wedding ring through the carriage window, to Frank Churchill, above all to Frank Churchill, lying and deceiving and proffering embarrassing extravagant gifts. Emma got what she deserved, in marrying Mr. Knightley. What can it have been like, in bed with Mr. Knightley? Sorrow awaited that woman: she would have done better to steal Frank Churchill, if she could.

My parents lived in a large house in a small village, and were treated with respect by the villagers, who were humbly impressed by their claims to rank. James's parents, at the other end of the same small scale, lived in a narrow inconvenient cottage in an expensive street in London, and God knows what circles they moved in, or what battles they fought for their right to them. My parents brought me up well and conscientiously, measuring my feet before they bought me shoes, advising me to get myself measured for a Dutch cap before I got married. James used to sit by his mother's bedside for hours each morning trying on her earrings, covering himself with perfume, listening to her sighing regret and penitence and passion over the phone, as she lay there, tall and lovely, in a beige silk nightdress, her pale hair tied back in a green velvet ribbon, her dark, worn skin freckled with tender marks of sun and age. My mother takes upon herself good works: cycling prettily and cheerily around the village, annoying old ladies, getting them out of bed when they're trying to have a good nap, making them switch off their favorite telly programs to chat to her.

She prevents the village children from amusing themselves by dropping stones on the railway line, and she campaigns against the erection of shiny vulgar new public houses—she, who does not care for alcohol, she who has never set foot in a public bar in her life. She campaigns against these things as the impotent campaign against sex and abortion. Mrs. Otford, James's mother, takes taxis everywhere, and has instilled into her son such a passion for cars that he has forgotten how to walk. Morals and manners: I leave it to Jane Austen to draw those fine distinctions. My mother criticizes Mrs. Otford and her vain amusements and what I once heard her describe, with a pretty, dismissive little laugh, as "her gay social whirl"— though what she knew of Mrs. Otford's life I cannot imagine, and I fear that its pleasures, had she known them, would have caused her more outrage (though perhaps less envy) than any supposed social gaiety. But the truth is that it is my parents themselves who are so obsessed by the notions of class and rank that my heart bleeds for them in shame. In moral, as in social shame: or for my own sake I need to believe it to be so. They live where they do in order to appear the better as large fish in a small pond, gasping in the muddy shallow water. With them, awareness of rank is a disease: it seems to be the core of their existence, it has displaced any of the significant centers of life, it eats them up, it devours them. It is not with them a peripheral weakness; it is central. It is the gestures of charity, of public spirit, that are peripheral, covers for their true malady. They live in that small, self-justifying prep-school world, marooned in it: petrified, ossified, worse than that, mad—mad, dryly shaking their dry branches against the high gales of newspaper truths. I repudiate them, with pain I do so, dangerously I do so: I repudiate in them the human condition, my birth, my sustenance. Inequality is our lot. I bleed, I resign, I reject.

My mother, once, put the wrong middle initial on a letter to a titled parent, and posted the letter before she found out what she had done. I saw her grow pale, I saw the hours lengthen, I saw her bite her nails, I saw her panic, I saw her weep. For her error, for her crime. I saw her hair turn gray, for a G where there should have been an H. A whole obsessive nature attached to such an offense. There is no end to suffering for such a nature: and it transmits itself, it multiplies, it gives birth. The object may change, but not that passionate destructive attachment. If only she could have cared less. If only I could have attached myself to some more harmless object.

Ah, love. We lay in bed, with the two children, as the night grew beyond the blue curtains into the pale late light of morning, and he would talk of his childhood, and I of mine, and I would listen with such tender voracious rapture, as though I could have devoured in him his whole past and made it mine. He told me of a sailor suit he had worn as a child, and of a children's party on Hampstead Heath, and I lay there stroking his arm, resting my teeth against his shoulder, faint with love. He told me of a master at his prep school who had loved him and who had said that he looked like Shelley. I buried my fingers in his hair and tightened them, and his head fell obediently backward on the pillow, his mouth gently parting for me. I loved him, I was ill with love for him.

At first we were careful and modest in our recollections, remembering only the safe and distant past, confessing our infancies, making no mention of more entwined and recent years, but to myself I remembered him, I remembered him and Lucy at those family gatherings—weddings, Christmases, christenings—to which, with Lucy, he would meekly come. I loved him so much that it seemed I must always have loved him, and I searched my memory for faint forecasting shadows of the future falling across that cold past where I had never touched or known him. I found them; they are always there. Hints, signs, moments. I thought of one evening, one Christmas Eve, at Lucy's mother's house: we were all there, her parents, mine, James and Lucy with their first baby, and Malcolm and myself, engaged but not yet married, and Lucy's two brothers, and my younger sister. It was after dinner; we were drinking coffee. I was wearing a brown woolen dress that irritated, though slightly, my skin; it was a pretty dress and I endured its discomfort for the sake of appearances, knowing that none could divine my irritation, smiling bravely in it at the world's ignorance like the mermaid in the fairy story who walked on swords. A rough and knobbed texture, it was. A secret sorrow. We were talking about my sister's A Level syllabus, and she was complaining about something called Ancient History, and about lacrosse. It was one of those dull, oft-repeated conversations that acquire their only interest from familiarity. Lucy and James were sitting together in a corner: he was sitting on a small buttoned Victorian chair upholstered in a nasty shiny pale-green color, and she was sitting on the carpet at his feet. He was smoking. She was wearing a thick green jersey, and trousers, and her knees were bent, and she had her arms around them, and her head was leaning against his knees. He was listening to what my sister was saying, and to my father's remarks about a classical education and the follies of the state's approach to such matters, and he had an air of such calm masculine politeness, and he nodded from time to time, and made noises of assent. He appeared to be listening; he sat there on that chair as though simply sitting in his body, idly smoking, was enough to do. I am always so ill at ease in my body, so estranged from it, always nervously approaching it and withdrawing from it, unable to take it calmly: destructive, I am, yet helpless, confined, an everlasting destroyer of my own nails, of bus tickets, of the fringes of tablecloths, of the wicker seats of chairs.

Nobody seemed to notice what a threat the presence of James was, what nonsense it made of the whole scene. I truly felt that if he were to rise violently to his feet the whole room would collapse like paper; that if he were to speak, decades of careful pretense would shatter at the sound of his voice like old dead flesh exposed to alien air. But he did not rise, he did not speak. Carefully he sat there, gently, delicately silent. How did I know then that there was treachery in his heart, and that it matched my own? In Malcolm, whom I was to marry, there was no such treachery; he was subdued to that room, to its pastel shades and flocked wallpaper and magazine racks and light fittings, to its good taste and its observances. He did not belong in it, but he had not the means to destroy it. The way that James held his cigarette was in itself a menace. I watched him, covertly, not yet aware what I was watching; he was the only stranger in the room, the only person there to whom my father's familiar references to the headmaster of Winchester and other dignitaries could betray me, and I thought that I was waiting, as I had waited as a child, for those sickening signs of boredom and distaste, those judgments from equal ground, those perishings by the same sword. But James did not judge; he nodded, politely, and knocked his ash mildly into the gray glass ash tray. "Last time I saw Hugh," my father was saying, "he told me that this new system for admitting local children was simply an agreement for the sake of peace and quiet—" and James shifted slightly the angle of his arm as it rested upon the chair. I felt my own arm, my elbow grating on the harsh weave. I should have known then: it was all foreordained in that slight transference.

After a while, the discussion of the wickedness of the very notion of compulsory state education died a merciful death, and the conversation turned to domestic help, as it always did upon Christmas Eve, when the prospect of stacks of unwashed dishes loomed. My mother and Lucy's managed to maintain, in the face of every probability, a deep amazement at the fact that their charladies—treacherous, fickle women, all of them— would not work on Christmas Day, and this amazement spread, as usual, into reminiscences about past betrayals, about charwomen falling sick on the eve of dinner parties, about butchers neglecting to deliver vital joints of meat, about gardeners deserting for more lucrative pastures and more tasteless rockeries. After a while James and Lucy, claiming virtuously to take their cue, got up and took the coffee things out to the kitchen to wash them up. I could hear them laughing as they did so: I missed them, they were my allies, they were of my generation, like me they were corrupt. When my uncle said something about fetching glasses for a drink I sprang obediently to my feet, casting off my habitual leaden apathy and, glad of the pretext, I said that I would go and get them. I went into the kitchen, and there was Lucy sitting on the table defiantly eating a banana. James was drying his hands. His shirt-cuffs were turned back from his wrists. I noticed them: his wrists, his hands. And he, he noticed my attention, he received it, because I can see in recollection that his hands became slow and heavy in the towel, and he turned and hung it on the silvery rail with a special kind of care.

"I came for some glasses," I said. "They were going to have a drink."

"Were they really?" said Lucy. "How marvelous. What an event. Will we be allowed one too?"

"I can't see why not," I said, as I opened the cupboard and started to lift the glasses out onto the tray. "If we're good. And so far we've been very good. Don't you think?"

James smiled. I was so sure that he did not like me, that his smile appeared to me the effect of intention, of deliberation, of a sudden polite desire to communicate, from one who had hitherto thought such an effort too pointless and exhausting to undertake. And I think I was all the more affected by it, by the sudden somber lightening of his face, than I would have been had I believed him to be amused or in any simple sense friendly. I was sure he could not like me, that house, those people, because I did not like us myself, and as he was alien and silent I endowed him with judgment, and with the credit for maintaining a discreet silence in his judgment. I could not see why he did not condemn, why he did not walk out. I thought his abstention a virtue: I did not suspect that it might be a weakness, that he might be subject to the same foolish social pressures as myself. I endowed him, in my mind, with freedom, and saw his patience as a voluntary martyrdom. I think that this attitude was not as unfounded and subjective as it might seem, for I was abetted in it by certain anxious glances from Lucy, who appeared, from time to time, to fear from him some revelation too awful to ignore, some word too shocking to be unspoken. But it never happened; her anxiety was never fulfilled.

James smiled, and then he said, "I think we've all behaved *very* well," and he took the tray of whisky and brandy and cut glass from me, and we went back into the drawing room, leaving the kitchen and its moments of sedition, its brief defiance. When we got there I declined a drink, to my own surprise; I could not resist trying to outwit my mother at her own abstemious game, as though only by such deceitful gestures could I protect and color my true desires. If I declined even the permitted measure, how could they know how much and what I really wanted?

James drank Scotch. When he was asked if he wanted some more, he said yes, and got up and helped himself. Angel-like simplicity. I saw in such simple acts of selfishness the lovely flower of moral courage, so long sought.

The next day, as was customary, Lucy's family drove over and joined mine for Christmas dinner. Lucy's child sat in a highchair at the corner of the table, and James fed it off his plate, tenderly and accurately selecting for it the bits that it would eat. We drank champagne, and my father even suggested that the baby should be given some in a teaspoon, but James shook his head and disapproved and mashed up a little more sprout and potato with the back of his fork. He protected it, too, from the Christmas pudding. As I had no children of my own I did not pay the baby much attention, but I noticed his solicitude, and I thought of it, more often than was reasonable, while I was anxiously expecting my first child. I even think that when feeding Laurie I would try to imitate the successful texture of the mash which James made for Charlotte, and perhaps this is not so ludicrous, for all information must come from some source and from whom should one learn but from one's friends and relations? I remember to this day the first potato I ever boiled, the first sausage I ever fried, and the blueprint for each act is as clear in my memory as the act itself.

After the meal, all the adults—and by that I mean the middle-aged, I mean my parents' generation—went into the drawing room and cracked a few worldly witticisms about the Queen's speech, and fell asleep. We were left, the children, in the kitchen, with the debris of the meal, slightly drunk but not drunk enough, slightly gay but not gay enough, overcast by the occasion, unable to leave those sleeping parents, unable to abandon them and their somnolent weight. We did the washing up, and Lucy's brothers, to evade it, went out on their bikes to call on some neighbors. Then, as we stood around in the kitchen wondering whether we ought, through boredom, to embark on drying the wooden spoons and potato peelers and egg whisks and casseroles that we usually left to drain or rust or rot, James said, "We could go for a drive." And I remember how wonderful a suggestion it seemed, how appropriate, how liberating, how inspired, and how I concealed my enthusiasm beneath blank features, turning away to wipe down the draining board, leaving the others to agree and to put the project in motion. My heart lifted, the air thinned.

"Supposing they wake up and find us gone?" said my sister, nervously, as we put on our coats and gloves, and looked for our boots. It seemed treachery, to her, to leave them sleeping, to leave the house without their knowledge and consent.

It seemed so to me, too, but I was not prepared to share with her my uneasiness, so I said, briskly, as though her doubts were nothing but unfounded shadowy effects of her own immaturity, "Oh," I said, "we'll leave them a note." As though it were as simple as that. And I wrote a note and left it on the hall dresser. It said: "Gone out for a drive."

James, at that time, had an old Citroën. It was a big car and he drove it too fast. Lucy and the baby sat in the front, and Malcolm, my sister, and I sat in the back. The occasion seemed to me full of a great charm: a family occasion, yet purged of the elements which made such occasions so generally intolerable. We drove to the sea, along the dry withered lanes, and Malcolm and James talked about cars, like real men. He drove very fast, too fast, and I was frightened, I thought I was about to die; the car moaned around the corners, brushing against the dried grasses, the shaking heads of old seeded flowers, the embrowned brambles; and on the long stretches it gathered speed. Past James's shoulder I could see the speedometer, recording his folly on that minor road. And all the time he talked evenly to Malcolm about engines and cylinders and acceleration. I wonder if I knew then that he was frightened, that he scared himself. I think I knew. I think it was there, in the even tone of his voice, mildly and elegantly counterpointing the notion of voluntary danger. We were all afraid, but nobody told him to go more slowly.

At the sea, we stopped and got out. It was a penance that had to be endured, the getting out into the cold, and even James, untrained as we were, submitted to it as we had submitted collectively to his seventy miles an hour. It was a small bay, with a beach of pebbles and no houses near; the sky was gray, the sea was gray and flat. It was cold: I walked on to the pebbles, my

ankles weak and ready to snap, cold inside their Wellingtons,
my fingers turning to sticks in my pockets. I could never wear
gloves; my hands are ill in gloves. My feet, in their nylon stockings, were comfortable inside the large rough gritty linings of
the boots. Cold, worn. I was glad to have dismissed the thick
woolen socks of childhood, the compulsory disgusting thick
protecting wads.

There was a post in the water, standing some way out. James
threw a stone at it and missed it. Malcolm threw one and hit it,
which pleased me. (I protected him in my thoughts.) We all
threw stones. By some mistaken distribution of providence, I
have a good eye: I hit the post each time. They clapped, they
applauded, they marveled. The stones fell from the sodden post
into the gray salt water, deflecting dully from it, falling with
a splash.

"I could have played tennis well, I suppose," I said, amazed
as I was always amazed by my heavenly gift. "But I never cared
for it."

"What do you care for?" said James, picking up one last
smooth black round stone, circled with a pale eternal streak of
whiteness. I could hear the water, sucking the pebbles from under my feet.

"Nothing much," I said, smiling, turning away, gazing at
the dead horizon. "No, nothing much."

Then Lucy, who had returned to the car, called us: the baby
was cold and crying, she said. So we got back into the car and
drove home and had tea and cake with icing on it; the parents were quite civil about our defection, restraining their comment to some veiled allusion to the misplacement of a sugar
bowl which they had had to look for before they could get their

tea. That night, as I fell asleep, I thought of the speed of the car, and of the pebbles, crunching, damp, beneath my boots: pebbles worn round and smooth, all of them, by the endless knocking. Strange, I thought, that so much ceaseless soft and endless violence should create such tender shades, so fine a grain, such cool and delicate surfaces. I would have liked to write a poem as round and hard as a stone. But words, but thoughts obtrude. A poem so round and smooth would say nothing. And being human, one must speak.

The narrative tale. The narrative explanation. That was it, or some of it. I loved James because he was what I had never had: because he drove too fast; because he belonged to my cousin; because he was kind to his own child; because he looked unkind; because I saw his naked wrists against a striped tea towel once, seven years ago. Because he addressed me an intimate question upon a beach on Christmas Day. Because he helped himself to a drink when I did not dare to accept the offer of one. Because he was not serious, because his parents lived in South Kensington and were mysteriously depraved. Ah, perfect love. For these reasons, was it, that I lay there, drowned was it, drowned or stranded, waiting for him, waiting to die and drown there, in the oceans of our flowing bodies, in the white sea of that strange familiar bed.

And so, if you would check, if I would check, it ends in the same place. There is no other conclusion, at this point. And since there is no other way, I will go back to that other story, to that other woman, who lived a life too pure, too lovely to be mine.

✦ Two months after the baby was born, when it was already spring, he said that he would take her out. For those two months she had hardly left the house, being afraid to expose herself to the multiplicity of objects in the outside world and afraid to expose her baby to the cold. She lived indoors, making brief excursions to the shops or to the playground, and for the first time she felt that the house did not threaten her in its own decay. Once, one afternoon, he took her to the square, with the two children; there were swings there growing from the concrete, and a roundabout. They sat on the roundabout, all four of them, and revolved slowly, entranced, transfixed, in the dull darkening February air. He looked at her across the center of it, as the trees and houses moved around them in their stately way, and he said: "Next week, I'll take you out. Next week, we'll go to the country. Next week it will be spring."

"We'll do what you say," she said.

"I love you, I love you," he said to her, across the turning wheel. And she believed him: she believed, through faith, each word that he said to her, even when she thought that she knew that he was lying. I lie to you because I lie with you—the loveliest of ambiguities, though sadly restricted to one language: untranslatable, and lacking therefore the absolute truth that seemed to inform it.

They went out in the car, the next week. She could tell, as he held the door open for her and helped her to sit down, handing her the baby to hold upon her knee, that this event was important to him: that it was important to him to put his woman in his car. It was a fairly new car, a Maserati sedan. She had known that men took such things seriously, but she had never thought to be able to submit herself to so strange, so unfamiliar an addiction. She had thought that she would judge and condemn, but there was no judgment left in her. She wanted to be what he wanted, to do what he said. She watched him as he got in beside her: he sat there, then turned and smiled at her.

"I have to call at the garage, first," he said. "And then we'll go. We'll go to the country, perhaps. Or to Hampton Court. Would you like to go there?"

"I don't mind where we go," she said. "I don't mind where."

"We'll go there," he said. "We mustn't go too far, yet. We'll go farther later, when you're well."

"Yes," she said. "Yes." She was not ill at all, she had never felt better in her life, but she found it easy to respond to such solicitude: it took away all effort from her, all responsibility. She wondered what instinct could have taught him such a way of speaking to her.

He switched on the engine: Bianca moved inside her flowery shawl. Laurie jumped in excitement on the back seat. The car moved forward. She sat there, watching him, happy in the knowledge that neither he nor she could get away. She faded away into stillness by his side. She hardly watched the passing houses as they drove south toward the Bayswater Road, across the park, along Knightsbridge, seeing instead the movements of his hands. Knightsbridge distracted her a little, with the shops she had not seen for so long, the crowds of people, but façades and features that had once closed in upon her now fell flatly backward into their true place, they reeled backward to the vertical, they no longer closed overhead or thrust at her their sorrowful deformities.

In Hammersmith, they stopped at his garage. It belonged to him, the garage, he was part owner of it: it was the source of his insubstantial, mysterious, fluctuating income. She had never been to it before, but she had heard Lucy speak of it often, with a mocking indifference, not wedded to this passion, able to dissociate herself from it, indifferent, superior. (Though even Lucy, she remembered, in the days before she married, had been unable to disguise her profound delight at being driven around by James in a sports car: and who could have resisted such a joy?) The garage was in a mews; they drove into it, and as the car stopped she saw men emerging from the doorways, men in blue overalls, their first witnesses. James opened his door and got out, and one of them said, "How's it going, Mr. Otford?" and she knew that he had foreseen that she would take pleasure in the mere sound of his name in a stranger's voice: substantiation it gave him, substance and a shadow.

"All right," said James, "all right," standing there with one hand on the open door, looking for something with the other in his jacket pocket, with such elegance of gesture that her heart stood still, for the vanity of her love.

"I wondered if anything had happened about that chap from Brussels," he said, finding the letter in his pocket, and handing it over to one of the men in blue. "He seemed quite a serious bloke. It'd be a pity not to do something about it."

"The car was in a shocking state," said the man, glancing over the letter. "Shocking."

"I know," said James, "I know. But he was a nice man. Didn't you think?"

"He was all right," said the man, assenting.

Jane listened to this interchange, entranced. She wondered what men could find in a man from Brussels, to make them speak of him in such terms. It touched her, such approval. Music was surrounding them, two different tunes, one from a transistor, one from a first-story window. She gazed at the car bodies, at the rusty corpses, at the rescued ones awaiting collection. There were some racing cars, small flat tiny things too near the ground, like children's toys: they frightened her, they were a menace of death.

"Come and have a look at it," said the man in blue, wiping back his hair from his forehead with a greasy hand.

"All right," said James. And he turned to her, as she sat there, and said, "You don't mind, darling, do you?" and she shook her head, repenting of years of impatience and wasting grief, and said, "No, no, not at all, not at all." She would have waited for him, unprotesting, for two hours or more, listening to that conflicting, harmonizing, disembodied music, which surrounded her like music in a Shakespearean masque, like the music from under the earth that heralded Cleopatra's death; inappropriate, heavenly: listening to the enchanting absence of those past mute screams and screeches from her past life, from those other waits and absences. Wait for me, Malcolm would say to her, and she would wait silently, her whole self weeping with bitter vexation, for a night, for a week of solitude, it was all the same: and when her own body cried out to him wait,

wait, he would not wait, he left her there each time, abandoned, forsaken, desolate, until mutely, in silent pride, she
died, and pushed him from her, into a cold and stony death.
Cruel, they had been to each other.

The mews was full of budding foliage; there were plants in
window boxes, and creepers climbed past the blue doors, putting out their small new leaves. They decorated the mechanical
paradise, they made it live and grow. When James came back,
he was still with the man in blue, and they stood by the car
door, talking of cars; she listened to their voices, which were
dull with an authentic rapture. When James talked of such
things his tone took on a hypnotic, even chant such as she had
rarely heard, such as people use of their obsessions: she had
heard it once, its apotheosis, in the voice of an elderly poet she
had met who had described to her, late at night at a party, the
new decorations he planned for his new house. "The ceiling a
dark blue," he had been saying, "a dark greeny blue, not black
blue, green blue, and the molding in green, and the curtains
gold with blue, and on the table a white—a white flower? a
white vase? and the walls that texture, that silk texture . . ."
and so on, meandering, beautiful, mad, dull, obsessed, the
rapture of another passion, a passion of colors and textures,
where James spoke of cylinders and performances and speeds.
She listened to his voice, not understanding a word he said, its
emotion quite unobscured by meaning, as though, in a foreign
language, he had been declaring to her through a third party
an unmistakable love.

Finally, he took his leave. "I'd better be off," he said to the
man in blue. "I'm taking my cousin out." And he smiled at
Jane, proprietorial, unambiguous: she was amazed that he
should claim her, though she knew that he had brought her

there for precisely such a reason, and she smiled back, and acknowledged the glance and nod of the other man, his registering of her existence there. She wondered how many other women James had taken there, he had the event so smoothly in the command of his movements and his looks. As they drove off, she said to him, "I liked it there, you knew I would like it there," and he smiled to himself, gazing blindly through the front window, and reached over and touched her waiting hand. "I thought you might," he said. "How do you know what I like?" she asked him, as they drove through Fulham to the river, and he shook his head, still smiling, and said, "I daren't say." Then, a little later, as they crossed the bridge, he said, "Do you want me to know?" "Of course I do," she said, "it's what I love in you, that knowledge." And it was so: she loved him for these carefully chosen encounters, for his delicate widening explorations of their islanded world, for the gradually increased speeds on the speedometer, for a mile more here, a word more there, all staggered, all arranged, all chosen, not wildly or blindly undertaken, but done with such care, such art, such dedicated frivolous love, each word sinking gently into its rightful place in her heart, each touch received so gently into her body.

At Hampton Court, they got out and walked. The sun was shining with a pale early watery light, the grass was a yellow green, and under the trees grew the long blades of flowers to come. The snowdrops and crocuses were already in bloom. Jane pushed the small folding pram and the baby, James held Laurie's hand. They looked like a happy family, idly entranced by its own idle afternoon, and passing ladies smiled at them comfortably and with approval as they walked under the bare budding trees. And she thought, this peace, then, is the peace of treachery: this calm, the lovely calm of infidelity. She wondered if it would kill her, the thin clear air of so much happiness.

"It's nearly spring," he said to her as they stared together into the ancient depths of the round pond.

"Yes," she said.

"When it's summer," he said, "will you still love me?"

"Of course," she said.

"In the summer," he said, "we'll go away. You and me and the children. We'll go abroad. Will you come?"

"Of course," she said.

Though she did not think that they would go. Or that love could last so long.

The next week he took her to one of the race tracks near London. He had a car and a man there, he said, and he had said he would go. Would she like to come? What about the children, she said, but he said that the place was always crowded with children, that they were to come too. So they went. On the way there they listened to the car radio: it was on the Third, and they heard her husband, Malcolm. He was singing, accompanying himself, singing that Elizabethan song, "Weep you no more, sad fountains, what need you flow so fast, look how the snowy mountains heaven's sun doth gently waste." His voice, with its plangent profundity, filled the car, and filled the space between them, but they did not switch it off. They had never spoken of him to each other, they had hardly mentioned his name, and there his voice was, between them, as they drove. Hearing it, she remembered the days when the sound of that voice had meant something quite different to her, and when the song was over she said suddenly, rashly, in panic:

"It's so easy, to love a person that one doesn't know."

He did not answer, so she was wisely silent. But as she sat there waves of panic, so familiar to her, evoked by that disembodied voice, began to possess her—guilt, senselessness, terror, failure, betrayal. She could not make sense of where she was, of what she was, of what she was doing: she wanted to write poetry and she could not, she wanted this man and she could not have him. It seemed so simple, she said to herself that she ought to be able to take it, but she could not take it: she started to cry, for the first time for weeks, like a child, confronted by impossibility. He noticed that she was crying, and reached across and took her hand, and she said, "There's something wrong with me, I'm going to die, I'm going to die," though that was not at all the reason for her tears.

"Then let me kill you," he said, holding her hand in his.

"I want you and I can't have you," she said, the tears drying on her cheeks.

"Of course you can have me," he said.

"I'm mad," she said, "I'm wicked, and I'm mad."

"I'm not interested in that," he said, "that doesn't affect me at all."

"Doesn't it really?" she said, hope beginning to reassert its grip.

"Not at all," he repeated. "It doesn't inconvenience me in any way, your madness. I can't see it, I can't touch it, I can't hear it, why should I worry about it?"

"You're lovely," she said, feeling better. "It's so lovely, when I'm with you."

And she forgot, deliberately, for the sake of survival, that warning voice and its unfelt, undirected perfect technical lament.

The race track was exciting. She had heard about race tracks from Lucy, who spoke about them with that mixture of envy and contempt with which clever women talk about beautiful women and expensive clothes: one could never tell, from the way she spoke, whether boredom or enthusiasm on each occasion had finally conquered the battleground of her heart. Jane found no such problem: subdued as she was, enthusiasm filled her, she offered it no resistance. When they arrived some motorcyclists were going around the track with a violent deafening irregularly rhythmic roar: she liked the noise, she liked it with sincere affection. She could hear Lucy's mother's voice complaining away somewhere in the back of her head about jet aircraft and sonic booms, her favorite antipathy, but the voice for once meant nothing, nothing at all: it was so much fainter than that grinding ear-piercing wail, it had no hope of prevailing. The noise seemed to her to satisfy something very noisy in herself: it drowned and deafened the shrieking of her heart, the unmodulated, unlovely shrieking, just as Malcolm's singing had once seemed to drown the more plaintive notes of her adolescence and her youth. Ah, she had grown too loud for him, in her deathly stillness and her silence, she had lain there too loud and still and violent.

On each motorbike there seemed to be two people: as she got nearer she saw that each bike had a passenger, and that at the corners the one who was not driving leaned over, balancing the bike, scraping the cinders, an inch or two from the earth. It seemed dangerous, but she could see why they did it: a thing that she had never seen when watching such events idly on the television news. James took her up onto the rickety, shoddy, empty grandstand, and she watched them go around and around, and Laurie jumped from bench to bench. Then James said, "Come and see my car," and she followed him to the car park; there were more people there, standing about, mechanics, engineers, addicts, wives, children, goggled drivers. James's car was a small Mercedes sports car: he introduced her to the man who was driving it, a man called Mike, and once more he introduced her as his cousin. He himself had no cousins, and she was beginning to see that he liked the word, the connection, the relationship. "My cousin, Jane," he said, and Jane held out her hand to the man called Mike, and he shook it. He was a tall man, an Irishman with hair much more blond than James's own, and he was brown and weathered from much exposure. On the back of his hand he had a tattoo, which said:

B

B O B

B

and she very much approved of the poetic symmetry of this declaration.

"You going around yourself?" said Mike to James, grinning, baring his golden teeth.

"I thought I might," said James.

And they smiled at each other, as though taking part in some unmentionable conspiracy, like the subversive conspiracy of sex.

"You take her around first, then," said Mike. "When the solos have finished."

"Right," said James.

"Seen Ciciiarelli's latest?" said Mike, and when James said that he had not, they all had to troop off to see it: it was a curious ochre-colored car, surrounded by a group of amazed, admiring spectators, all of whom were peering into its exposed parts with expressions of well-informed concern. Jane, who had too little knowledge for amazement or admiration, stood there and watched them, and wondered why she was not bored: she could not have said that she was interested, but on the other hand she was a hundred miles away from boredom. Perhaps, she thought, what I like is the feeling that nothing, nothing at all is expected of me: I am merely a woman, merely an attendant woman, I don't have to do anything but stand here. She thought that perhaps she was learning to be a proper woman, at last. Though, formulated in that way, the idea did not in itself seem safe. It could not, surely, end well, if she became something that she had so much resisted. Surely the other twenty-eight years of her life would take their revenge? She thought that they would, but she did not much care.

After some time, when the solo motorbikes had been around, James said that he was going too. She was treacherously afraid that he would look a fool, in his goggles and helmet, and she could not bear him to look anything less than perfect, but luckily, when he had them on, he looked all right. She realized that he knew he looked all right in them or he would not have risked putting them on. Then, as he got into the car, she was afraid that he would die: sudden, acute terror possessed her, so pure that it was almost a delight, and she could see that he saw it in her face, and was equally delighted to see it there. They looked at each other, and she could not tell if it was a moment of true corruption that united them or a moment of true love.

"Don't kill yourself," she said, smiling at him tenderly.

"You needn't watch," he said, "if you don't want to." And he disappeared amid the ghastly roar of acceleration. As he went she knew what he had brought her there for; he had brought her there to frighten her, to torment her, to make her suffer for him: and she was doing it, she was doing what he wanted. She couldn't believe it, that she, so selfish, so recalcitrant, so cold, so obdurate, was doing what he wanted.

She watched him go around the track twice, around the dreadful bends and inclinations, envisaging his death, the not-having of him: it had always before, when she had bothered to think about it, seemed childish to her, this courting of danger, this titillation of fate, but now it appeared to her as something quite different, and she thought that she perhaps had never in her heart thought it childish, she had merely been afraid, or possibly even envious, desiring this danger for her own. When she had seen him go around twice she could not stand it any more, and she asked Laurie if he would like to go to the children's playground, which she had noticed as they drove in. Laurie was pleased, he skipped and ran. She never made such suggestions usually, she hated the cold muddy park, the grimy squares, the dead ends of her freedom, the walled, railed plots and enclosures where she walked her guilt. This place looked different: it was high and open, with grass, and no attendants, and she could see James from it, furiously cir-cling in the dark green car. There were no other adults there, and only a few children. She could smell the curious dangerous

sulfurous burning smell from the track, and wondered what
it was, what name it had: she thought she would ask James,
and find if the name corresponded to the hot cinders and petrol
and rubber. Perhaps it would be a word she would never again
be able to dispense with, an important word, a necessary word,
that she now still at that instant lacked. Learning was so dangerous: for how could one tell in advance, while still ignorant,
whether a thing could ever be unlearned or forgotten, or if,
once known and named, it would invalidate by its significance
the whole of one's former life, all of those years wiped out,
convicted at one blow, retrospectively darkened by one sudden light? It seemed at times too dangerous to find out those
most important things, in case, having found them, one should
also find that nothing else would do, no other word, no
other act. Yet how could one not know? Like a nun, she had
held on, in wise alarm, to her virginity: through marriage,
through children, she had held on to it, motionless, passive, as
pure as a nun, because she had always known it would destroy
her, such knowledge.

When they reached the playground, she helped Laurie up
the steps of the slide a few times, and then he gathered confidence and started to climb up and descend by himself, so she
parked the sleeping baby and went off to sit on one of the
swings. There was nobody to turn her off so she started to swing
herself, a luxury she had not attempted for years, not since a
fat, sour, blue-overalled threatening woman had asked her, in
a playground, if she was over sixteen. She remembered that she
had jumped down, saying to herself, trying to be reasonable,
trying humbly to convict herself of paranoia: *after all, the
woman's only doing her job.* But she knew, at the same time,
that the sane view was not right: she knew that she herself was

not paranoid, that the woman had enjoyed turning her off, that she enjoyed stopping people doing things, that she enjoyed shouting at small children, corrupted like a prison wardress or a matron into sadistic practices by her trade. She knew that the malice was in the outside world, that she was right to fear it. She thought of that fat woman, as she swung herself higher and higher, into the cloudy, fast blue sky, and she thought of all those other mothers who had found themselves, amazingly, over sixteen, not children any more but mothers, real women, proper women, forbidden to swing. Where were the adult joys? Dressing and undressing those tiny babies, saying to each other, in that dreadful whine, oh, isn't she a proper little doll, what a good thing it's a girl, you can dress them up real nice, can't you; and Jane, listening, sick with effort to understand, sick with effort to trace in their features the true lineaments of maternal passion, and ill with relief, weak with relief, when occasionally, in a tender smile or an anxious cry, she caught it. Oh, redeem yourselves for me, she would cry to herself: let me redeem myself, in you.

The swing was marvelous: on iron chains, rooted in concrete, it was strong, and she could swing herself very high. She had always liked movement; as a child, she had been intoxicated almost unbearably by fairground roundabouts and rocking chairs and rocking horses, and until recently she had liked all forms of transport, boats, trains, cars, even buses. There was even something in her that wouldn't have minded going around that fatal track with James. She wondered how many people had died on those steep corners. Once James had left lying on her bed a copy of one of his racing magazines, and she had opened it, clutching passionately to this remnant of him, and she found that it was full of elegies of early death: "We regret to report the death of Mike Stanning of Bromley, who was fatally injured when his Syracuse B-type Connaught went off the road at the meeting at Hadbury Park, and hit a tree. Mike, a greengrocer by trade, was in his early twenties." And so on, familiar, condoling, inevitable, sad. Why, she thought, as the air sucked past her, I'm older now than Keats was when he died. She had always measured achievement by the death of Keats.

She could see Laurie on the slide. He had been joined by another group of children, the only other children in the playground, and she could see that he was playing with them, joining their games—going down the slide backward, trying to run up the wrong way, going down in twos and threes. She liked to see him with other children, like that, because she felt that he was better when he was away from her, when he was free from her, when his dreadful inheritance was diluted by foreign influences. She felt so strongly about the child: she loved him, and yet she knew that because he was hers he was doomed. She had felt this before he was born, and had said so, had wept and moaned and suffered real torments of apprehension for the unborn child, torments which had been slightly assuaged by the sight of a real live baby, for it did seem to have, somehow, more of itself and less of her in it than she had expected. But recently, while expecting Bianca, she had known that those moments of comfort had been biological merely, a trick of procreation, and that the child would inherit her disastrous nature as surely as he had inherited the color of her eyes. It was all predestined: a fate handed down by necessity through the generations. This was why she kept herself from him, why she withheld herself from him. And that withholding was in itself a part of the child's fate. She was grateful, for such moments as this, when his happiness was independent of her, separate, part of others: and grateful too for her own happiness, because it would make his life less heavy to bear. She could say to him, in years to come, I was happy then, and perhaps he would believe her. It would be true, it would be true. What doom could be worse for a child than its parents' grief? What guilt worse than the giving of such an unwanted, unsolicited painful gift? I didn't ask to be born, she had screamed in childhood at her own parents, observing at the same time their wry adult smile; and now she waited daily for Laurie to learn enough of the language to scream those same words at her. What wryness could she summon up to meet them? Or what love?

After a while the children abandoned the slide and came over to her, and gazed at her, until she slowed the swing and sat there looking at them.

"That your mum?" said one of the other children to Laurie, and he nodded.

"What's your name?" said the child to Jane, and she answered, "Jane." She could see that the children were all one family: she asked them their ages, and the eldest answered, saying that they were aged 11, 9, 8, 6 and 3, and that their ages, added together, came to 37. Jane laughed, and the child laughed. They all had appalling teeth: even the smallest had teeth that were black and of a startling irregularity. They were clad in a strange mixture of garments, some of which looked as though they had been hastily apportioned by a busy mother to the wrong child. They all wore plimsolls, and one of them had a jacket that was scorched all the way down the back: she could see the bars on it where it had been hung too near the fire to dry.

"That your baby?" asked the eldest child, pointing to the pram.

Jane nodded. She liked talking to children like this, and knew that it was because they could not judge her.

"Can I take him a walk?" said the child.

"Her," said Jane. "It's a her."

"Can I give her a push?" said the child.

"All right," said Jane, "but don't take her too far."

And the large child set off, in her red woolen knee socks, and old gaberdine raincoat, pushing the small pram with an air of serious pride. Jane never ceased to be astonished by the delight which some children take in babies: she herself had always thought babies too boring even to look at, and when, as a young wife, people had handed her theirs to hold she had been filled with trembling apprehension lest their heads should roll off their necks, lest all their limbs should snap.

The child woke Bianca, unintentionally: the pram stuck on an uneven bit of long grass, and her efforts to disengage it roused the baby.

"Never mind," said Jane. "I'll go and feed her; it's time to feed her anyway."

And she pushed the pram back along the cinder path to the car, and got in, and undid her coat and her dress, and unwound Bianca, and started to give her her feed. All the children, who had accompanied her, gazed at this event in surprise, and after a while the spokeswoman of them said, "What's that you're doing?"

"I'm feeding the baby," said Jane.

"She don't have a bottle then?" said the child.

"No, not often," said Jane.

"Why not?" said the child. "We all of us had bottles. I used to give the bottle to Karen, and Mark, he had to have one too, he was that jealous."

"Children are like that," said Jane, amused by her audience, by all the faces pressed against James's car window. "They always want to have what the little ones have got, don't they?"

"They certainly do," said the large child, fervently, her wide face expressing adult depths of knowledge. "They certainly do. You should just hear them. Squabble, squabble, squabble. They drive me mum and dad mad."

"Do you help look after them?" said Jane.

The child heaved an exaggerated sigh, and nodded her responsible head.

"I have to," she said, smiling, and yet at the same time trying to imitate that authentic adult look of proud exasperation. "I have to, because there's so many of them. I have to keep an eye on 'em, see?"

"Your mum must be glad she's got you to help her," said Jane.

"Ah, well," said the child, with a rare philosophic distance from the situation, "I suppose I was a nuisance, too, when I was small."

"I suppose you were," said Jane, whose heart was quite melted by the child's concern: it seemed so important to her to see family relationships from time to time absolved in this way, absolved and beatified. Tenderness between brothers and sisters always touched her, she did not know why; she remembered a small boy she knew, a five-year-old, who was afraid of the noise that the lavatory cistern made when he pulled the chain, and whose smaller sister, only three, would bravely pull it for him, explaining to questioning adults that she did it so he wouldn't get told off. She thought too of a brother and sister she had seen on a bus, a largish eight-year-old boy, in charge of a two-year-old girl, whom he had held firmly clasped on his inadequate lap, grappling with her as the bus swayed around the corners, talking to her all the time, telling her not to be afraid, they were nearly there, not to cry. Finally, at one particularly violent corner, he dropped her, and he picked her up, pulling her back onto his slippery knees, wiping her face, as she wept, with a dirty handkerchief, offering her his own gobstopper out of his own mouth, and all the while smiling proudly around the bus, meeting the soft indulgent admiring glances of mothers and housewives, proud of her, loving her, with her huge wide streaky cheeks, her baby face, his own, his own sister. Hansel and Gretel, the Babes in the Wood.

She was holding the milky baby upright on her knee when James came back. He stood there, looking down at her, and the children gaped up at him.

"I couldn't watch," she said, "it was too frightening. I thought you might die."

"Nonsense," he said. "You got bored."

"I was bored too," she admitted. "Frightened first, then bored. I took the children to the playground; Laurie went on the slide."

"You collected some more children," he said. "You've got an audience."

"It's nice, to have an audience," she said, but the children nevertheless melted away, knowing that her attention had gone from them.

On the way home, on the way back to London, they went down a hill labeled Death Hill, and laughed. "Poets and people who fool around with racing cars die young," she said, thinking of Keats, and that greengrocer from Bromley. They talked constantly of death, it seemed a way of preventing it. If sufficiently evoked, it would surely elude them. They wanted to live forever, there in that car.

Laurie got bored in the car, so to amuse him Jane made him show her his collection. Whenever they went out he always collected things—tin lids, toffee papers, match boxes, fag packets, stones. He turned out his pockets for her: he had acquired eleven wooden lolly sticks, relics of the past summer joys of others, and three stones from the dirt track. One of them was round and smooth, and she held it in her hand and thought of the day when James had asked her what she cared for: Christmas Day it had been, and before she was married. Thinking that he would surely have forgotten, she said to him, "Do you remember that day by the sea, that Christmas Day years ago, when we all threw stones at that post?"

He turned and half looked at her, and said, "Of course I remember. I asked you what you cared for."

"What did I say?" she said, breathless.

"You said, nothing much," he answered, luxurious, triumphant, giving her a whole recollection, a whole piece of their past.

"Darling," she said. "Darling. I didn't mean that. I only said that because I hadn't known what you'd meant. I didn't want to say the wrong thing."

"What I meant was that *I* wanted *you*," he said.

"Ah, rubbish, rubbish, darling, you make it all up, you know I like to hear it," she said, enchanted, not even caring whether he was lying or telling the truth, quite sufficiently enchanted by the elegance, the tactful charm of the lie, and knowing at the same time that he must be telling the truth, because he must have wanted her or he would not have found the words to lie with; she felt that she had known then that he had wanted her, that his attention to her had colored that flat gray sea, that whole winter afternoon. And then, just as they were about to embark on more discursive reawakening of the past, Laurie fell off the back seat and she had to turn around, and comfort him, and rearrange him in a new cross, tired heap. After a few moments they entered the Blackwall Tunnel, under the Thames, and thinking to distract him by this lucky change of environment, she said, "Look, Laurie, look, we're in the tunnel, look at all the pretty lights," and James laughed, and said, "Why, it's just like fairyland, down here," and they both stared out at the high white tiled curved walls, at the deadly pallid fluorescent glare, and they both laughed, helplessly, she laughed until she choked, and the innocent child sat there listening to their laughter, wide-eyed, silenced, until they emerged into the open air.

Lies, lies, it's all lies. A pack of lies. I've even told lies of fact, which I had meant not to do. Oh, I meant to deceive, I meant to draw analogies, but I've done worse than that, I've misrepresented. What have I tried to describe? A passion, a love, an unreal life, a life in limbo, without anxiety, guilt, corpses; no albatross, no sin, no weariness, no aching swollen untouchable breasts, no bleeding womb, but the pure flower of love itself, blossoming out of God knows what rottenness, out of decay, from dead men's lives, growing out of my dead belly like a tulip. Reader, I loved him: as Charlotte Brontë said. Which was Charlotte Brontë's man, the one she created and wept for and longed for, or the poor curate that had her and killed her, her sexual measure, her sexual match? I had James, oh God, I had him, but I can't describe the conditions of that possession; the world that I lived in with him—the dusty Victorian house, the fast car, the race tracks, the garages, the wide bed—it was some foreign country to me, some Brussels of the mind, where I trembled and sighed for my desires, I, a married woman, mother of two children, with as much desperation as that lonely virgin in her parsonage. Reader, I loved him. And more than that, I had him. He was real, I swear it, and I had made myself a true loneliness, and in it, I had him.

Perhaps it is merely dull, this claustrophobic dialogue. The two of us shut together, locked together, touching, not touching, naked, clothed, remembering, foreseeing. I can't even describe him, for description is treachery: I feel for him as those Africans feel who defend their loved ones from photography, regarding it as a wicked theft of virtue. It's not much of a narrative. It's a dialogue: the only other parts are nonspeaking parts—my two small children, a midwife, a doctor, some garage mechanics, a policeman who shouted at James at some crossroads. Perhaps love can't survive a contest; perhaps it dies if it admits the outside world, or crumbles to dust at the breath of coarser air. But that air is the real air, I know it. I can't make the connections; I can't join it up. And yet love has a reality, a quotidian reality, it must have, everything has, and it's merely my own inadequacy that can't face it, my own guilt that winces from knowing it.

I must make some effort to comprehend. I am tired of exclusion. First of all, I must tell some of the truth about Malcolm. If I told it, and found that love could still rottenly, beautifully blossom, I would feel better, I would forgive him. And then I will turn my attention to Lucy, that other ghost, that other torturer.

I married Malcolm because I thought he was safe. I thought I was safe with him. I thought that he would be safe with me. In view of the mutual damage that we finally inflicted, this seems a curious basis for choice, but so it was. I thought that our weaknesses and virtues were well matched: and so in a sense they were, alas, on all levels but that most profound one that might have saved us. Malcolm is a guitar player, of the most elevated, classical nature; he also sings. He does not descend toward the popular; he is a purist, a musician, and just good enough to be able to afford to be so, even in so competitive a world. Guitarists and garage owners: God knows what defects in me this lunatic selection represents. Where are the proper people, the politicians, the academics, the lawyers, the company directors? Cast out on the family rubbish heap: gone forever.

I first met Malcolm at a party, a small dull awkward party after a recital at which he and one or two others had been performing. I was twenty at the time. The recital had not much interested me, as I do not care for music, and had gone through a sense of duty to my hostess, who was teaching me Elizabethan literature and who had asked me during a tutorial if I would like tickets: and unable to say no, I had naturally said yes. The program consisted of music played on various ancient instruments such as viols and lutes and harpsichords, and I kept hoping that it was instructive, as it was certainly not enjoyable: or so I thought until Malcolm sang. The first song he sang did not impress me particularly—it was one of those Fa la la, Hey Nonny Nonny lyrics, and he sang it with rather a feeble plaintive charm as though he did not quite trust its fabric, as though he knew it balanced on the edge of foolishness. He had an interesting face, though not a noticeable one: I wouldn't have picked him out from a group of people to stare at, but singled out as he was by a solo performance and the small eminence of a platform and the surrounding dullness of the proceedings, he repaid attention. He had a thin, sensitive girl's face; fair, rather wavy hair, with a parting and a forelock; he was small and slight and had a kind of pleasing intensity about him, a nervous energy, a performer's energy. Although he looked very young, it was indefinably clear that he was not as young as he looked and that he would continue to look the same for the next fifteen years; his features would not thin out or harden into masculinity, he would remain slight, he would preserve that vulnerable boyish air. His voice, unlike his face, had the firmness of certainty; it was thin and clear and high, a tenor, with a choirboy's innocent assertion.

I waited for his next song—preferring always words to sounds, addicted in fact to words, at that age, my only passion— and as he started to sing it I felt my hair rise, my scalp stiffen, my heart thud, my blood drain in one violent flow from me, as his voice threw itself into the dusty thrumming silence. He was singing that lyric of Campion's, the one that starts:

> *When thou shalt home to shades of underground*
> *And there arrive a new admired guest,*
> *The beauteous spirits do ingirt thee round,*
> *White Iope, blithe Helen, and the rest—*

and he sang it with a note of impersonal purity that brought tears to my eyes. How can I describe such an emotion without even more lamentably convicting myself? But I was young at the time and I confused myself: I thought that that stillness in my head was something of significance and that it might in some way attach itself to the man that was singing. Love at first sight: I have heard of it, and like a doomed romantic I looked for it and found it, released into the air by the words of a long-dead poet—words which should have been long rendered harmless to me by familiarity but which unjustly received such new power from this new medium that they went straight to my heart. How well I concealed, subsequently, that first moment's power, how well I dissembled, covering my shallow heart from the more serious world, seeking nonexistent virtues and sympathies between that singer and myself; it was for that moment that I married him, without it I would never have listened. I blame Campion, I blame the poets, I blame Shakespeare for that farcical moment in *Romeo and Juliet* where he sees her at the dance, from far off, and says, I'll have her, because she is the one that will kill me. And I, watching Malcolm up there in that little brown varnished room, said to myself, I will have that note of suffering, that cry of unrequitable pain. I forgot that the words were not his, that singing was his profession, that words and inevitable rhymes move me inhumanly: as a man may forget that a woman's limbs and face may be expressive of a profound movement while she lies in them, inert, immobile, hardly touching them at all. Oh God, if I had met Malcolm elsewhere, amid a confusion of other, more significant faces, or if he had confined himself to foolish little ditties, it would all have been so different (just as it would have been so different had James never, by such unforeseeable circumstances, seen me asleep and uniquely vulnerable in that bed in that hot blue room): but that was the song he sang, and as it moved on to its conclusion, I thought, in listening to him, that I was about to faint:

> *Then wilt thou speak of banqueting delights*
> *Of masks and revels which sweet youth did make,*
> *Of tourneys and great challenges of knights*
> *And all these triumphs for thy beauty's sake:*
> *When thou hast told these honors done to thee*
> *Then tell, O tell how thou didst murder me.*

And so it was: the song was prophetic, it made its own conclusion of our lives; for I did in a sense murder him, and I murdered him in the true lyrical sense, by rejection, by the breaking of vows, by the lending and withdrawal of my beauty. If only it could have happened and been concluded in that instant, when it was still in a state of lovely plangency, because murder isn't lovely as it is in that poem, it is hideously ugly, unspeakably shamefully ugly; in vain do the poets try to disguise and excuse and purify these things, in vain do they try to dignify their own rejection by dignifying cruelty and scorn. They suffered, they bled. But nevertheless, I prefer to think of Malcolm, innocent, passionate, singing of murder, than to think of him with his fingers and thumbs sunk into my shoulders, beating my head against the bedroom wall.

After the recital my tutor, Miss Jones, who was responsible for the occasion, had invited the performers and several dons and a few students, including myself, to have a drink with her in her rooms; it was not an easy occasion, as nobody had anything to say to anybody else, and I stood for some time with a glass of sherry in my hand listening to a conversation between two fellow students—a conversation about college breakfasts, which was little better than a defense against silence, and which I could not find the words to join. I was wondering how soon I could decently excuse myself when Miss Jones, on her sherry-replenishing round, came by, and asked how we had enjoyed it: "Very much, most interesting," we feebly chorused, and then I, attempting to salvage my own endured boredom, and my sorrow at the sound of the dull subdued murmur in the room and the sight of her frantic hairpins, remarked that I had particularly enjoyed the songs.

"Very good, weren't they, very good," said Miss Jones, nodding her agreement: and then, rising in her like a memory of some forgotten rule in some submerged and rarely played game, I saw a recollection of her social-duty surface, and she said to me, "Would you like to meet the man who sings?"

And I nodded, having no choice, and she led me over to him. I could see why she had done so, because he was more detached from the gathering than I had been, and less covered, more mercilessly exposed: standing alone, he was, by the corner of her bookcase, gazing at the titles of her books. He looked up as we approached, Miss Jones and I, and I could see in his face a dreadful gratitude for his deliverance, an emotion that I recognized so well and would have disclaimed until my dying day. I can disguise such things, I think, but I can recognize them in others. Anyway, whatever the truth of it, I appeared to Malcolm then as a deliverance, from boredom, and exposure, and social neglect.

"Mr. Gray," said Miss Jones, "this is one of my students, Jane. She was telling me how particularly she enjoyed your singing."

"Ah," said Malcolm.

"It's true," I said, as Miss Jones left us, implying perhaps ungraciously that she might have invented the information as a social lie (a felicitous duplicity that would have been in fact beyond her). "I thought it was marvelous. That Campion song, it's always been one of my favorite poems, but to hear it to music, like that, as it was intended . . ."

And so I went on, with such evident sincerity that he had no choice but to believe me: I did it well, oh so well, basely fortified by his insecurity, that I won from him smiles and speech, his life history, an invitation to supper, his hand in marriage, his peace of mind, his self-respect, his hope of salvation. In vain do I tell myself that there had been no hope, that he like me had been marked from birth for such a fate; the protagonists suffer and are guilty, though the drama is a drama of necessity. If I hadn't tortured him, another would have done so: but perhaps less cruelly, with less finesse? Anyway, however I look at it, it was with no intention of such prolonged cruelty that I talked to him that evening; I meant to be kind to him, to flatter him, to amuse him, to cheer him up. Though I've never been particularly dazzling in conversation, I could usually think of something to say, and Malcolm was not one of those whose shyness and ineptitude drove me into paroxysms of ugly garrulity and nonsense: on the contrary, his reticence encouraged me, it helped me to display a confidence that fails me when there is stronger competition. I managed the encounter well, and was conscious that I was doing so, and conscious also that I had done well to get so much out of somebody who clearly did not talk with ease. I saw virtue in the trouble I was taking, and my interest in him seemed to me therefore to be virtuous: I see now that this was not so.

He lived in London; he had studied at the Guildhall, and was now embarking on earning his living; he was twenty-three, three years older than I was. He told me that he was giving his first appearance at the Wigmore Hall the following month, and even I, uninformed though I was, knew enough to ask the right questions about this significant step; in fact I behaved with such unusual rectitude that he asked for my name and address and promised to send me a ticket. Looking back, I cannot decide why I displayed quite such an interest in him at this stage; it wasn't wholly genuine, I didn't find him very interesting, but I was still clinging to the fact that somehow, out of this rather nervous ordinary small young man, had issued that amazing, relevant, unforgettable tragic note. Perhaps I wanted to see where it had come from, and whether he'd known he'd done it. I believed that he must know, for after all a human being isn't an instrument, made of wood and strings. I wanted to find the source of that sound; I believed in communication, I wanted to believe that what I had heard was true, a true offering, and not in my head alone. Also, the circumstances of our meeting compelled me to take a polite interest in him; perhaps it was his reticence and his total ignorance of my identity, together with my positive though circumscribed information about him, that made me work so hard on him.

Whatever my reasons, I went to the Wigmore Hall. I was flattered that he had remembered to send me a ticket. I could see, from the audience's reception of him, that he was talented; although, ominously, once more I enjoyed the vocal part far more than the instrumental. At this stage in his career he was undecided as to whether he should concentrate on singing or his guitar; singing was his first interest, one acquired in the school choirs of early childhood, and he enjoyed it more, but

I think he took the guitar more seriously, because it was harder work and he enjoyed it less. Most of the program therefore consisted of instrumental pieces, and to me, at least, the few songs that he sang made all the more impression because of the surrounding waste. It happened for me all over again: the pure plaintive notes, that sound of the unendurable made lovely, the loss turned into beauty itself. He could do it so easily: it wasn't just a trick, an accident, it was something he himself could do, and therefore, I thought, it must be a true part of him. After the recital I went around, as he had suggested, to have a word with him: I congratulated him and thanked him for remembering me, but I didn't stay long, as he was occupied with various loyal colleagues and teachers, and also several members of his family, including my future mother-in-law, a small gray silent woman in a mauve coat.

During the vacation, he wrote to me. He asked me if I'd like to go to a concert with him, if I could ever get up to London. I could, quite easily, so I did, and we went to the Festival Hall, and afterward he took me out to dinner. Thus began a prolonged association: one that I did not expect to end until death. That year I left University and came to live in London, in a large flat just off the Cromwell Road, which I shared with three other girls; he took me out regularly, though we went to concerts less as he noticed my lack of enthusiasm, and to the cinema more. Neither of us had much money, so a lot of our time together was spent in finding cheap things to do, cheap things to eat, and walking. It soon became obvious that he had no other girls in his life, and I therefore felt a positive responsibility toward him: I felt I ought to spend time with him. And I enjoyed his company, I liked hearing about the musical world, a world of which I was so ignorant that when he talked of it he

seemed authority itself, although I knew he couldn't be. I liked
having a safe dependable reliable man to go around with and
kill time with. I was so much at ease with him; I behaved so
well, I was so agreeable and even-tempered that he can't possibly have believed some of the dark and airy hints about my
true nature that from time to time I honorably threw about. I
misled him, I gave him a false impression of myself, though
not of course intentionally: the truth was that when I was with
him I felt a different, better, safer person, a person well able to
look any shop attendant or bus conductor in the eye. I remember thinking, as the months rolled by into a year, that this calm
kind person was surely my real self and that the other person
had been a mistake, an adolescent, unhappy mistake, lacking
Malcolm, lacking a man. Thus I cast off more than twenty
years of experience, thinking I could abandon them and
emerge from them as a butterfly emerges from its scrappy
dingy inelegant case.

After a year, we became engaged. I don't think he proposed
to me; we drifted sensibly into marriage, as people do. He
bought me a ring with a ruby and small diamonds in it, and I
used to spend a lot of time watching the refracted lights. At
night, I dreamed several times that the stones had fallen out of
the gold clasps and that nothing was left of the ring but grasp-
ing empty tiny claws. Then, in the morning, I would sigh with
relief to find that they were still there. I was still, I think, a
virgin, and I was relieved rather than disappointed that he did
not make more effort to try to sleep with me: the neglect of
this point was not in any case grossly conspicuous, as neither
of us had a place of our own, and he was too tentative to ma-
neuver a situation in which such an event would have been inevitable. He had been brought up in an ultra-respectable lower-

middle-class home, and I assumed that his diffidence was due largely to his background—as indeed it was, though why I should have thought this irrelevant and lacking in ill omen I no longer know. What faith I must have had to believe that there was any hope of eluding the grip of environment. There was, in fact, a good deal in Malcolm's background that positively appealed to me, though in a somewhat inverted, masochistic way; and I felt that he held the same relation to his as I to mine, and that we met in the middle, both in a sense exiled from our past, united by our isolation, by our artistic efforts, by our lack of identity with our own history. I was ill at ease with his family, as he with mine: but then we were neither of us happy on our own territory, either. I look back now on my early meetings with my parents-in-law with considerable bewilderment, wondering how I could have managed them with such calm and goodwill, and how I could have presented myself so seriously as a prospective wife. There was so much in them that was a positive affliction to me, and yet I managed to accommodate these offenses—in fact, I embraced them willingly, telling myself that they were not real offenses, not moral flaws, or defects of anything other than manner and custom— trying, in a sense, in my own way, to deny the distinctions I had been reared in, the Jane Austen distinctions of refinement and vulgarity, of good and bad taste. I was not fool enough, even then, to imagine that the Grays represented, even by reaction against my own parents, the coziness and warmth of working-class life: their way of life had none of the warm virtues, and they were, in their own style, as pretentious as anything I had known. Their style was arid and unlovely in the extreme, but I forced myself to think that it was not therefore fit only for rejection: I labored to see its good points, to discern

the features beneath the blank face. They lived in a house on
the outskirts of Croydon, one of those houses which one passes
in cars on every journey one takes: semidetached, half brick
and half wash, a house in nothing land, a land that is the legitimate butt of all sophisticated mockery, the legitimate scare-
crow life for all those afraid of the void. And yet I know that
it is not the void: those acres of suburbia are populated by dense
passions, by stoic fathers, by bitter grandmothers, by raging
adolescents, by tender mothers enraptured by their first-born
babies and their new chrome prams. Faces, they have, those
suburban people, faces and identity, despite their mortgages
and their alarms; and there are few emotions more ignoble,
more contemptible, than the terror that seizes such as myself
when we drive, quickly, past their net-curtained windows. Fascist sentiments, fascist evasions.

It was this land that my parents-in-law inhabited. Sometimes
I think that I sought them out through social masochism,
knowing that only by sinking could I avoid the deadly, human, incriminating impulse to rise—an impulse which had
been displayed to me throughout my childhood in all its
squalid gracelessness. And so in revenge I hugged to my bosom
the tray cloths, net curtains, luster vases, querulous accents,
pastry forks, and antimacassars of Malcolm's impoverished
genteel past, the lifeless chill of which was as far removed again
from the cozy beer-drinking neighborly bonhomie of the
workers I aspired to admire. Never could I have found a working man to marry me: and pride, inverted pride prevented me
from acknowledging my own kind. So I found Malcolm, like
me an exile, like me cold to the marrow. And yet, even now, in
full view of the consequences, I cannot entirely disown the
motives that impelled me: ignoble and unchosen in many ways

they may have been, and yet there was some virtue in them. I did in some manner negate a false distinction or two: I did manage to avoid the more simple forms of discriminating social competition, and in this much at least I escaped the fate of being my parents' daughter. I declassed myself to an extent. I know, too, that by the end I could see my parents-in-law as people, as real people, not merely as symbols, or as pawns in some game of my own playing. I remember one evening that I spent there, during our engagement, when we sat in the small neat lounge after supper drinking tea, and the conversation turned to immigration—then a hot topic, owing to some smallpox scare in the press. One of Malcolm's aunts, with her husband, had been summoned in for the evening to meet me, and we sat there, discussing Asians. Mr. Gray and the aunt and uncle took a hostile though overtly sensible line, insisting that the country could not possibly assimilate the numbers of immigrants, and that such scares as the smallpox one could merely aggravate the situation: immigration control could only be for the good of the immigrants, they said, with every appearance of reason. Malcolm and I said nothing: we sat quietly and listened, unwilling to rush in, unwilling to declare our interests. I have a feeling that the line of argument was toned down for our benefit anyway, and would have been more virulent and outspoken had we not been there. But as I have said, we were unwilling to provoke, comforted by the knowledge that our protest was mutual though silent. The aunt, an irritating and very stupid woman, encouraged by lack of opposition, eventually started to argue that the immigrants were ruining the health of the country, giving true British people not only smallpox and tuberculosis but also other diseases that she did not like to name. I could see that Malcolm's father agreed with her

in spirit, though he was too finical and logical a man to support
her shocking reasoning; but Malcolm's mother was becoming
increasingly distressed. She was a strange little woman, Mrs.
Gray: gray-haired, listless and yet nervous, and horribly restless. Like me, she could not sit still, and her every word was
accompanied by painfully excessive movements of throat and
eyes. She suffered from what she called migraine, and was very
sensitive to drafts. She also went to church regularly, despite
the mockery of the rest of the family. Somewhere, somehow,
inside herself, she kept herself safe: there was identity there
and on that evening I remember that I saw it and knew that I'd
been right to believe in its possibility. She spoke, about the
Asians, with much coughing and self-disparaging swallowing,
in a voice so watery one could hardly hear it, and finally said,
"I don't suppose they much like having smallpox either, you
know." And as this remark fell into silence, she bravely followed it up. "All the Eskimos died, you know," she said,
"when the white people got to them. They all died of common
colds." Silence continued. "The red Indians, too," she said,
gently, almost inaudibly. Malcolm's aunt could not make the
connection: I saw her eyes goggle and her jaw drop. Poor Mrs.
Gray: such bird-like frail defiance. The human spirit, maintaining its ridiculous liberal faiths. I always liked her, after that
evening, but I don't suppose that she knew it.

(That tatty neglected family I saw in the playground when I
went to the race track with James, the dirty children that play
with Laurie in the street. Images of happiness, images of content. Fanny Price's Portsmouth squabbles. James as a child in
bed with his wicked mother. Throw away choice, emancipation, distinction, selection, friendship, in favor of enforced,
compulsive, abrasive familial ties. Organic ties. Five children,

whose ages added up to thirty-seven. A man so tied to me that he cannot get away.)

After a year of engagement, Malcolm and I married. We had known each other for two years, and had never given each other any nasty surprises. Safe, one would think: prudent. A responsible marriage, not rashly undertaken. My mother liked him, as I had thought she would, because he was likable and deferential: he did not threaten her, and she enjoyed his appeals to her authority. The difference in class went down surprisingly well, as I had suspected it would: my parents enjoyed condescension and drew a great deal of pleasure out of their attempts to make Malcolm and his parents feel at ease with them. The social gap between the two families was not, of course, spectacular, and to a detached observer the acute consciousness with which both parties observed it would have been ludicrous: but then I was not detached. My father was, I think, distinctly relieved that I had managed to find a father-in-law so much his inferior, a mere income-tax official, so unmistakably, in his eyes, a member of the lower middle class. There was no need to produce, for Malcolm and his parents, those familiar references to famous dignitaries: he did not have to try to put them in their place, so he was all ease and affability. This was a relief to me, though I would not have liked to think that I married Malcolm simply (or even partly) for such relief. Fortunately, Mr. and Mrs. Gray were well aware of their good fortune in meeting with such an easy parade of graciousness: they acknowledged that the equality offered to them was not true equality, but some amazing indistinguishable counterfeit of it, that would not pass for true coin in any other transaction. They did not presume on the acquaintance. What curious meetings we had, during our engagement, sitting at home in our drawing room, talking of wedding plans and begonias and parking meters. We never talked about the most dangerous topic of all, which was Malcolm's career and his prospects therein: as it happened, neither family knew much about music, and Malcolm was therefore able to confuse them very easily with professional chat about various aspects of his intended life. I expressed faith in him, and he in himself, and that was it.

My father said he would give us some money as a deposit on a house and I found a house that was so decayed and damp that the deposit more or less paid for it; it was a large house and everybody said that it was a ridiculous choice, but I defended it by saying that with a musician for a husband we would need a large house so that I could get away from the noise of his practicing. I used to say this as a defensive joke, not realizing what good reason there would have been for such a motive, had it been truly mine. I did not know anything about the private lives of musicians, because he was the only one that I knew and I had never lived with him. I don't know what I thought our life together would be like. God knows what I expected. I thought perhaps that marriage, that mysterious state, would somehow bestow itself upon us because we had undergone the rituals of invocation. I had no image of a mutual existence, no domestic skills or interests, no views on curtains or wallpaper, no knowledge of my own body and its unpenetrated depths. And yet I must have hoped for something: I cannot have been as unwilled as I now, recounting it, appear. I would not have married any man who asked me: so what was it that made me take that particular and fatal step? Love, maybe. I did think that I loved him, but I don't like to think that love might die: so I prefer not to believe that I married for love. I felt protective toward him, responsible, as I had done from that first moment

when I rescued him from loneliness at that party. I felt in a way
that having accustomed him to my company and taken away
that loneliness, I owed him myself. I was hopeful; but I admit
now that I was also afraid, and I knew then that in marrying
him I was denying something. I thought then, oddly enough,
that I was denying myself tragedy, that I was choosing companionship and safety and dignity, and avoiding thus the
bloody black denouement that I had been sure, as a girl, would
be mine: the lyric note, I thought I had chosen in Malcolm,
not those profound cries that I was later to hear issuing from
my own throat in childbirth and abandon. Often, in jumping
to avoid our fate, we meet it: as Seneca said. It gets us in the
end. What treachery to all that I had been, to think that I
could evade it. Needless treachery. We walked to the altar,
Malcolm and I, a hopeful couple, waiting for time to unite us,
poised delicately together, hand in hand. At the wedding reception Malcolm's father, in a carefully written speech, said
that he trusted we would live together in harmony, creating
one sweet melody, I the words and he the tune, I the verse and
he the musical refrain. It was a lovely image and he worked it
out well, hindered only by the fact that it would have been
more appropriate to our respective sexes had I been the musical
and Malcolm the verbal element. I was moved, I wept.

It is a curious business, marriage. Nobody seems to pay
enough attention to its immense significance. Nobody seemed
to think that in approaching the altar, garbed in white, I was
walking toward unknown disaster of unforeseeable proportions: and so I tried to emulate—I emulated successfully—the
world's fine confident unconcern. Such an emulation had paid
off so well on so many other alarming occasions (anaesthesia,
for instance, or diving off the top diving board, both events

which, I was assured, despite a natural reluctant fear, would not harm me) that I was prepared to take the world's calm view of marriage too, distrusting and ignoring the forebodings that even then possessed me: in such a mood, assured that it is a normal event or a commonplace sacrifice, one might well lay one's head upon the block or jump from a high window. Such images are not wholly retrospective. I found the same was true of childbirth, an event so terrifying that a stoic calm was the only way of enduring its universal trials. Had anyone whispered in my ear, during that ceremony or the reception after it, that I was mad, that I had sacrificed my whole life quite needlessly, my heart would have been unable to deny its full assent. But nobody spoke. Just as, while I was expecting my first miscarried child, nobody said to me: this will surely kill you, you will die for this. I connived at the world's silence, hoping that nobody would ever guess at my alarm and my dissent.

James and Lucy came to my wedding. They had their baby with them and it shouted during the service; the noise consoled me. During the reception, which took place at home, I did not have much time to see them: they got very drunk, approaching the champagne with a serious professional attitude. At the end I remember looking out of the French windows of the drawing room and seeing Lucy standing by the rockery with the baby hooked carelessly under one arm: it was squirming and crying, and she was laughing as she talked to a college friend of mine. And I remember thinking: she, though married, is not dead, so perhaps that service was no more fatal than gas or ether or deep water, and I will wake up in some real other world where I shall know why I did it, and what other people do it for.

But it was not so, of course. From the very beginning, from

the first day, I could not imagine what I was meant to be doing. I had, until this point, had a job—an undistinguished, temporary job, it's true, for with characteristic passivity I had taken the first thing that offered itself on leaving college without bothering to lay more serious plans—and I had lived in a flat full of girls, whose chat about sex and food and clothes and books had given me an illusion of life and company. Now these things were lost to me, taken from me by my own choice, and nothing presented itself to replace them. Malcolm shut himself up at the top of the house practicing, or went off to work, and I sat there in those dusty rooms like a ghost, like a shadow. Somehow the fact of being married took all life from me, it reduced me from the beginning to inactivity. I had meant to look for another, more convenient job, and I now see that there is absolutely no reason why I shouldn't have found one, but once the necessity had been taken from me I lacked the confidence to do anything about it: it would have seemed a mere evasion of the dreadful Medusan image at which I knew I must force myself to stare. My descent into inactivity was so abrupt that it seems hardly credible to me now, because until this point in my life I had managed to cope amazingly well with practical affairs and social contacts: I'd never found daily life easy, and had always done the simplest things with an excessive expense of anxiety and apprehension, but nevertheless I had done them, I had not sat at home and evaded them. Once married, I gave up; or rather, I began to see activity as evasion, and inactivity as an obligation. In a sense I suffered not so much from a lack of confidence as from a conviction that I was uniquely gifted: perhaps I wished to evade my gifts by leveling myself, by handicapping myself, by withdrawing myself from the race, the competition, the sphere of operation; or perhaps I said to myself that I would confront those gifts more bleakly, with less palliative, less chat, fewer friends, less distraction. I was a poet. I am a poet. I do not like the notion of unique blessings, unique gifts. I would put them to the test. When I try to formulate to myself the reasons for my withdrawal, I always find myself describing my certainty of survival, my indestructible certainty. As a defense, as a fact, I do not know.

Some might see the abrupt decay of my life after marriage simply in terms of my first encounters with sex. And indeed they were pointless and painful enough, though I have no intention of elaborating this theme. I conceived almost instantly after marriage, out of what I pretended to myself was laziness, but which I knew to be a deep terror of the disgusting contraceptive techniques that I was told that all sensible women employ: I tried to obey the rules, but there were some sacrifices I could not make, so I conceived instead. At three months, I miscarried. By this time, frigidity had set in relentlessly: I was relieved to lose the baby, I had been scared out of my wits at the thought of having one, and I found the miscarriage a convenient excuse for my subsequent lack of interest in sex. Malcolm and I tried to be kind to one another about it, but I felt all the comfort drain so quickly out of our relationship as it transformed itself into the very things I had sought to escape—loneliness, treachery, hardness of heart. I know now that the fault was partly his, because having got me he did not really want me: he did not want a woman at all. It took me so many years to discover this that I feel oddly light-headed, to be able to write it down, simply, in an ordinary sentence, like that. It never occurred to me then, in those first years of marriage, that he didn't want me: I thought that all the not-wanting, all the failure and guilt, must be mine. I thought that he wanted me and I, through some obscure corruption of my own, didn't want him. I didn't even suspect the truth, though I would have been so much happier had I done so. Always more willing to cast myself as wronged than as wronger, I didn't suspect it until, after four or five years of silence, he began to suggest, in a kindly concerned and pleasant way, that I might be a Lesbian. Oh, yes, I said humbly, glad of any excuse, so I might. I was surprised that he had heard the word. Malcolm, as a child, was a choirboy. His happiest days were spent in a white surplice. I should have known, but I was innocent, I never saw the obvious, I was too sophisticated in my trust, I believed what I was told and not what my own eyes saw. Malcolm said he wanted me, so I ignored that tremulous mouth, that thin and delicate neck, those evident signs, that slight shrinking from my own more desperate attempts.

It was a fatal conjunction. I never managed to find any point in living with a man and cooking his meals in return for housekeeping money: the secret was never revealed, the door into the garden never opened. I would gaze at other couples and wonder if they knew what they were doing, whether I alone was shut out and excluded from joy. I was an impossible wife. My only conjugal virtue was an extreme enthusiasm for my husband's work, which I quickly realized that I did not understand at all: my level of response to music was abysmally low and unsubtle, and yet nevertheless I liked to hear the thin notes in the air, the scales, the exercises, and I rejoiced in each success, each good notice, each discriminating compliment. *I* never complained when he went out to concerts, or when he went on tour: perhaps it would have been better if I had. Because unfortunately Malcolm's chief conjugal virtue was an acute consciousness of the fact that his work excluded me, that he was forever abandoning me, both in the house and out of it I did not complain, but he was so sensitive about his constant desertions that he imagined that I did: he never went upstairs to work, in the end, without some crack about my miserable jealousy and my constant nagging. It was his guilt that spoke. I never nagged him about his work: on the contrary, I was delighted that he cared about it, that he continued to care, because his passion lifted the weight of my own guilt, it meant that he was, for hours of every day, inaccessible to my sorrows I wanted him to be immune: the last thing that I wanted was to contaminate him with my grief. I admired his work: although I could not share it, I admired it, I did not want him to stop. But he could not believe this. He blamed my unhappiness upon his absences; he ruined, as far as he could, his enjoyment of his work and his unquestionable success by convincing himself, with some generosity, but without foundation, that I grudged it him. We are undone by our virtues. In the end his conviction that I resented each moment of his working life—which in the early days we could joke about, from time to time—reached paranoid proportions, and he would break off an hour's rehearsal to storm downstairs and shout that I was a mean destructive grudging creature when all I was doing was sitting quietly drinking a cup of coffee and staring at *The Times*. Then he would blame me because the fact that he had shouted at me had put him out of voice.

I do not judge him for this behavior. What else could he do? How could he, in that situation, see the truth, which was that his work was the one thing in him that remained to me pure and beyond abuse? The rest had sunk so quickly into the mire, and the only way I could recall my original sentiments for him was by remembering the emotion I had felt the first time I had heard him sing—a fact that remained untransmutable. But he had no means of knowing the crazy, precarious foundations for my love. I cared so much for his singing that I could not even resent it when he shouted about the baby and the noise it made: I sympathized with his complaints, because Laurie was a dreadfully noisy child, he cried incessantly, his yells shattered the house and dislodged the plaster. I could not blame Malcolm for disliking this disturbance. I did not blame him at all: I blamed myself. He behaved far better than I did, throughout our association; I didn't behave like a normal person. Almost from the beginning I gave up: I would sit for hours in the evenings staring at the wall without speaking, and in bed at night I would lie there like a lump of wood. I think that I expected that my complete dreariness, apathy, and misery would finally drive Malcolm away and free me from him, and him (more significantly) from me. As it did, but after more years than one would have thought possible.

When I look back over my marriage, I wonder how much that first miscarriage accounts for its course. I can see, now, that I could fairly make it bear the whole weight of blame; but I also remember how much I resisted such an interpretation at the time, and how inadequate and unchronological an explanation it seemed. I did not take it well, of course, neither in the conception nor in the loss; but then I took nothing well, I was equally disturbed by missing a bus or breaking a fingernail. I cried all the time when I thought I was pregnant, because I knew I couldn't face bringing up a child, that I wasn't fit to bring up a child, that having a child with Malcolm would bind me to him and my empty destiny forever. I even felt quite normal womanly emotions—irritation at the prospect of a ru-

ined figure and no more cinemas and no more possibility of
work and no more freedom. Then, when I lost it, I cried because all the crying had been wasted, and because I had already,
at three months, managed to accommodate some, at least, of
the impossibility that faced me: and all that effort was gone.
Such an experience, I suppose, could be seen as the root cause
of all my subsequent malaise. But I persist in seeing my reactions to it as symptoms, not causes. I don't know what the
cause was. It's true, I can admit it now, that I didn't like anything to happen to my body, and so much happened to it that
was disagreeable that naturally it upset me. But other women
have miscarriages and babies without suffering such ludi-
crously misplaced anxiety and self-pity as I did.

When I had Laurie, three years later, I went through exactly
the same cycle of resentment and nonacceptance while I
was expecting him, having learned nothing, nothing at all
from my preceding experience: my mind was just as unwilling
to accept the events of my body. But my body, strangely
enough, seemed to take the affair more calmly; I had assumed,
from having lost one child, that I would find the next difficult,
that I was in some way physically neurotic, as I clearly was
mentally. But Laurie was born with considerable ease, and I
took to him without any problems. The strange confidence
with which I found myself able to handle a baby could, perhaps, have given me an identity, could have rescued me from
inertia: I could have turned myself into one of those mother-
women who ignore their husbands and live through their children. But with me, this did not happen; my ability to kiss and
care for and feed and amuse a small child merely reinforced my
sense of division—I felt split between the anxious intelligent
woman and the healthy and efficient mother—or perhaps less

split than divided. I felt that I lived on two levels, simultaneously, and that there was no contact, no interaction between them: on one level I could operate well, even triumphantly, but on the other I could only condemn myself, endlessly, for my inadequacy and my faults. My body, healthy, indestructible, said to me, look, you can do it, you could do that other thing too; but my mind hovered somewhere near it, shut out, restlessly unattached, like a bird trying to return to its familiar cage, like a living soul trying to re-enter its dead habitation. I don't put it well. I sound as though I am trying to describe a classic schizoid state, or a state of alienation, but I know that it was not this that I suffered from; it was something less severe, less acute. Less certifiable. I felt, all the time, a possibility of reconciliation; my mind did not reject my body, nor my body my mind, and indeed these two words ill describe the states or levels on which I lived, for the bodily level was in many ways more profound, more human, more myself. I didn't feel lack of identity, really. I felt an unacceptable excess. And in my second childbirth, as I bore Bianca, I think I could feel (though perhaps I say this in hindsight, and certainly wrote it so) that I was coming together again, that I could no longer support the division, that my flesh and mind must meet or die.

Malcolm was pleased to have a child, I think, and got on well with him; but this relationship too was ruined by his too great awareness of his other absences and other preoccupations. He worried that he was away too much, leaving me with the child alone; he worried that the child would not know him. Sometimes I think that this undue degree of responsibility and anxiety must have been nothing more than a mask for his violent personal ambition: he always claimed to be unassuming, unambitious, but his attitudes toward success were so ambiguous, so confused, that I became suspicious in the end. He always claimed to despise the world of professional competition, and affected nonchalance about such matters, laughing off any disasters or criticism, pointing out the circumstantial, invalidating qualities of praise and good luck, studiously avoiding the company of the highly distinguished, avoiding name-dropping, and bargaining, and well-frequented pubs. But I came to see that in doing this he was merely making elaborate efforts to conceal his true, voracious nature—good efforts, praiseworthy efforts, efforts that I applauded. We were very like one another, in dissimulation: we avoided the showy and the spectacular, as though it might corrupt us. But gradually, as time passed, he began to transfer his own frustrated expressions of desire to me— only the expressions were frustrated in him, for in reality he received a good deal of acclaim and publicity—and to imply that I was suffering from the retired and quiet life I led. He began to insist that I had always wanted a gay and colorful ex-istence, and that I resented him and the child for depriving me of it; he accused me of denying my nature by so ignoring the world. He even said on one occasion that I must envy Lucy, whose work took her out, and gave her a status in the literary world: and in a way I began to worry lest he might be right, even though I knew at the same time that he himself did not believe it of me, and was merely accusing me for his own hy-pocrisy.

Luckily for both of us his career prospered, despite his ap-parent lack of diligence in pursuit of any of the more corrupt ways of furthering it: perhaps, like me, he wanted to know that he was good enough to survive the worst of self-imposed handi-caps. Success crept up on him, and he was able to smile and spread his girlish deferential unsoiled hands in amazement at

this unexpected good luck. It changed him, though only gradually: probably I was the only person who could see the stages
of change, because he remained to the end modest and almost
irritatingly unassuming. The change was most marked in his
appearance: he developed, as his income rose, a curious weakness for camp and slightly theatrical clothes. When I first
knew him, both he and I dressed so protectively that we
merged into classless, unidentifiable nothingness: he wore cor-
duroy trousers and heavy jerseys and pretended to look like a
student, and I wore unmemorable skirts and light jerseys and
hoped I looked like Lucy. But as the years passed he began to
purchase slightly more outré garments: flowered shirts, oddly
buttoned jackets, boots. The final confession was made in the
last year of our marriage when he started to wear one of those
navy blue caps popularized by certain pop singers: it suited
him all right, he looked perfectly presentable in it, but for
some reason I hated it, I despised him for wearing it, and I despised myself for having noticed it. I, by this time, had taken
to dressing deliberately, provocatively badly: my clothes were all
worn out and I refused to buy anything new. And yet my face,
indestructible, looked back at me from the mirror in mocking,
flourishing complicity.

I still can't think why we stayed together for so long, in
view of the little pleasure that our association gave either of us.
I have tried to describe, out of justice, our similarities: we were
traveling the same course. We were locked together by our
knowledge, the one of the other: our knowledge of what lay
hidden in our unspoken thoughts, our knowledge of that small
house in Croydon with the querulous mother and the Sunday
church choirs, our knowledge of the house in Surrey where
my parents ate their hearts out in bitter desire for the forbid-

den fruits of prestige. We were alike, and we could not find any
other people who bore the same relation as we did to our past
and to our desires. We had few friends in common; social
contacts could perhaps have saved us, or at least have alleviated and distracted us from our mutual guilt, but it was the
guilt itself that isolated us and kept us from such relief—
through fear of discovery, through fear of seeing sights that
would arouse in us envy and sorrow, through fear of seeing
sights that would confirm a universal desolation. As I said long
ago, I've never been able to seek extenuation; I've never believed in helping myself. I realize that I make it sound, improbably, as though we lived in a dank and crazy solitude, like
mad people, like outcasts—but so, improbably, it was. Whom
should we have known, whom should we have seen, to whom
should we have turned? We were separated by class and by
profession, and too *tentative,* each of us, to brave these sepa-
rations: diffident toward each other as toward life, we did not
like to inflict our friends upon one another, and a too con-
scientious delicacy stranded us entirely. I had had friends,
once: friends forced upon me by circumstance, by proximity,
by institutional life—even a friend or two of my own choosing,
people who resembled me, a girl who wrote poetry, a man who
edited a literary magazine, a man who wanted to write plays—
normal people, real people with roots and branches, fed by the
outer world. But I dropped them, I lost them, suspecting that
Malcolm would not like them; and he in the same way protected me from his musical acquaintances, thinking they
would bore me by talking about music. I did make slight efforts at contact, later on, for the child's sake, as I became aware
that he too would suffer for my shortcomings, but by then I
was so unnerved by years of disuse that the effort was pain-

fully apparent and out of mercy to my victims I desisted. So I sank into solitude, as though it were my natural element. All women are isolated, to some extent, by marriage and small children, but in my case the tendencies of the situation were fulfilled with grotesque elaboration; for weeks, while Malcolm was away—and he was away often—I hardly spoke to a living soul. I still don't know, I can't assess the incidence of such a condition; others like me must bravely hide it when chance drops an inquisitorial visitor upon the doorstep. Sometimes I would tell myself that I must pull myself together, ring up a college friend, join some society, take up a new interest in life: but what wild fancies were these to one who could hardly force herself to walk along a street or ask a grocer for a pound of sprouts? Once, late one night, I was reduced to such a state that I rang up that organization that dispenses sympathy to potential suicides. A man answered me and asked me what was the matter with me and I heard my own voice replying, calmly, thin and possessed, "Nothing much." "What brought you to ring me, then?" he inquired, and I said that I was lonely; so he asked me why I didn't call round to see him in his church or wherever he was, and I explained about the baby. So he asked me about Malcolm and about my mother and about other people who might have been expected to be of use, and I said that it was because they were of no use that I was ringing him. He couldn't think of anything to say to me, that charitable man, but he continued to talk to me, asking me idly about this and that—the baby's name, my name, how old the baby was, whether I enjoyed reading or not, and if so, what books; and I politely answered, but after a while I could detect in his voice the same note that I could hear in my own—a note of diffident, hopeless, anxious concern, striving with im-

mense effort to sound detached and unconcerned. I felt so sorry
for him, poor useless man, I knew that he was like me, equally
afflicted, and that that was why he was there on the end of
that line at one o'clock in the morning, and I did not want him
to know how irrelevant his questions were, and how inexpressible my true complaints, so I tried hard to sound more cheerful to cheer him up so that he could ring off thinking that he
had done a good job with me; I tried to humor him, I told him
I felt better already, that the sound of his voice had in itself
consoled me—trying to fulfill my suicidal obligation, trying to
say the right words of response. "I'll go to bed now," I finally
said. "I feel better now, I'll go to bed." "That's right," he said.
"It'll all seem much better in the morning, it always does." So
I rang off and went to bed, wondering if he, poor fool, had
known how vain his efforts were; and then realizing later that
his efforts had not been in vain, it was merely my own arrogance that had thought them so, for I had in fact gone to bed
consoled by the sound of his voice, just as I had told him I
would; and that he had probably never set himself up to understand, had never claimed to say the divine words of comfort,
he had been content to play the holy humble role of service, he
had been content to provide the sound of his voice to distract
me from the crying of the silence, he had not cared whether I
should mock him for his stupidity, whether I should shriek at
him for his inability to save me from my complicated state.
He had been willing to use himself without credit to save me
and those like me from the glamor of the gas oven and the selfish corrupt pleasures of despair. He had humbly asked me boring questions so that I could be distracted from my anguish
by my contempt for his inadequacies: he had used his voice

without pride. I was the only one that held out for significant words. My meekness, my silence, my passivity, were merely a sign of my appalling faith, of my disgraceful arrogance.

There were moments when this faith seemed justified. Few enough, but enough. The only thing left to me to want to do was poetry: I wrote constantly, badly, with passion, and with flashes of alarming satisfaction, flashes that seemed to shine back at me, reflected from another, brighter source of light. The more unhappy I was the more I wrote: grief and words were to me inseparably connected, and I could see myself living out that maxim of literary criticism which claims that rhyme and meter are merely ways of regularizing and making tolerable despair. As nursery rhymes familiarize pain and cruelty and death, so I acquainted myself with the end-stopped patterns of my solitude. My verse was flawlessly metrical, and it always rhymed; I think that I tried unnaturally hard to impose order upon it because I was unnaturally aware of my own helpless subjugation to my gift, my total inability to make a poem at will, my total dependence upon what seemed like fate or chance which would drop into my mind one afternoon as I was pegging out the washing, a phrase that weeks of effort and discipline could never have produced. I resented this helplessness as I resented a woman's helplessness with a man, and yet at times—in those moments of felicity—I was grateful for it. If only I could have been sure of it, sure that it would descend upon me again, that capricious muse, but there was nothing one could do to invoke it, it did not belong to one, it was not a personal quality or possession—one could merely stand around and wait for it. Perhaps this is why I was so unwilling to distract and console myself; I did not want to be distracted when an immortal syllable was hovering, unclaimed, just beyond my reach. This is fanciful, neurotic. I deserve whatever bad things come my way.

I told a really shocking lie at the beginning of this narrative, when I said that I told James I wasn't writing any more—I did say so to him, but it wasn't true, though I allowed the narrative to imply that it might be. I don't know why I said it to him— perhaps because I thought he, a garage man, would not like me to write poetry, perhaps to arouse pity, perhaps because I wished him to think that my abandonment and desertion had destroyed my work, perhaps because I was ashamed that I was *not* destroyed entirely, that in the midst of such apparent misery I could still work, that I was in no way too fragile to work in such conditions—for the truth is that after Malcolm's departure and before Bianca's birth I was writing more copiously, more fluently than I had ever written before, the ink was pouring on to the sheets like blood. My sublime blood, my sublimated blood. I had not published for years, having lost all contacts, and all desire to see my treacherous words in print, but there were still pieces of mine current, pieces that I had written at Cambridge and in the year immediately after, which had been anthologized and reproduced. Great hopes had once been held out for me, and I kept a secret faith with them. Until James. It was after James that I stopped writing. I did not know how to write about joy, I could find no words or patterns for the damp and intimate secrets of love.

I lied, too, about the circumstances of Malcolm's departure. In fact I have already told two lies about this event, and who can tell if I will now risk a true account? Malcolm didn't desert me: he was driven away from me by my bad housekeeping, by my staring at the wall, by my too evident frigidity. I didn't want him: my body refused to accept him, it refused the act, it developed hysterical seizures, it shut up in panic, it grew rigid with alarm. I tried to cure myself, I tried to read the right books, but the very sight of the diagrams made me feel ill. When I was a girl I fainted once, while trying to read the instructions for the first time in a packet of Tampax. So what had I expected to do with a man? I've never understood why I found childbirth so easy, why I didn't refuse to operate on that level also. There must be some reason for these things, but I've never found it. When Malcolm married me, he didn't want me, either, he didn't know what to do with me. Had we never married, had we endured a perpetual courtship without union, as respectable couples are said to have done in history, we might have been together, faithful and affectionate, and delicately balanced, to this day. But we could not survive knowledge. Or rather, I could not—for although Malcolm did not want me when he married me, he came to want me in the end: out of defeat, out of pride, out of revenge. Perhaps merely living with a woman, the shapes of a woman, had bred desire in him where it had not been before: the edge of unfamiliarity and ignorance removed, he began to desire me, but by then I was gone from him, shut to him, though I was still a good shape, a good womanly shape, as I lay there beside him at nights, remote, and inaccessible, and his. I destroyed him, by taking him, by making him through proximity want me, by rejecting him. I destroyed him. That's what he shouted at me, that I'd destroyed him. Then tell, O tell how thou didst murder me. I destroyed him by closing up against him, by wearing ragged old cardigans and laddered stockings, by weeping feebly when he tried to touch me. He was too kind, too gentle a man to survive my rejection and abandon me with impunity.

A crueler man would have hated me more and suffered less. I forced him into cruelty, and it was unnatural to him, and he could not forgive me for it.

The night before he left me for good, I was lying in bed—I went to bed early, I was unwell, I was seven months pregnant—when I heard him let himself in downstairs. I decided to pretend to be asleep so I wouldn't have to talk, and I shut my eyes, and kept them shut when he came up into the room. He stood there looking at me, and I tried to breathe evenly, but I couldn't, for some reason, by some premonition: I couldn't because I was afraid. How quickly, when it happens, one senses the unforeseen truth. That was my moment of true shock, for which I can find no forgiveness. My mind may forgive, but my body will lie there forever, terrified, breathless, vainly assuming the refuge of sleep to fend off its surprisal.

After a while, he said, "You're not asleep, are you?" and I made a sound, and moved, and pretended that he had just woken me.

"What time is it?" I said.

And then he crossed over to the bed and yanked me out by one arm, and hit me very hard across the face with the back of his hand. I can't remember what I did; I think I just stood there. Then he took hold of me by the shoulders and shoved me back against the wall, and started to beat my head against the wall, and I started to struggle and kick. He was shouting at me, about how I'd taken everything from him, and ruined his life, and been unfaithful to him, and I knew at that instant, at the sound of that extraneous word "unfaithful," that he had been unfaithful to me. He didn't go on for very long because he got frightened by what he was doing, as he wasn't used to violence; he hadn't even the strength for it, let alone the aptitude. When he let go of me I didn't say anything, I just got straight back into bed and lay there, waiting for him to go away. I couldn't think of anything else to do. I shut my eyes. In the end, he went; he must have slept downstairs on the sofa. In the morning I was covered with bruises. I looked at them with alarm and some pride, as though I was glad that my flesh had made some response to so desperate a statement.

Anyway, that was the end, because in the morning he left me. He went to live with his new woman, whose existence I had not even suspected before that night; she was a pianist, and I had seen her on the television, and heard her, but never met her. I remember hoping that he would be happy with her, and feeling amazed that he had managed to create any kind of new relationship, and feeling ashamed of my amazement. Such was his guilt or his inflexibility that he did not try to communicate with me after his departure; he rang, once, to see if the baby had been born, and he paid money into the bank for me, and that was all. I did not think of protesting, or of trying to communicate with him; I did not even want to know where he was. I was not surprised that it had happened, but I was surprised that it had happened so suddenly and violently; he must have required the violence to sever our disgraceful knot. I felt guilty that I had driven him not only into adultery, but into unfamiliar cruelty. I was ashamed of my technical impunity, of the strength of my position; I wished that he could have deserted me for more dramatic vices in me. I search in vain for the more comprehensible or alleviating aspects of this disastrous affair, which surely sheds on human nature a light too ghastly to endure, but the only relief I can find is in the fact that both he and I for months pretended to both sets of parents—and quite successfully, too—that Malcolm was still living at home with me. We embarked on this pretense simultaneously, but without collusion, thereby betraying some character trait at least in common; and our false marriage after death was as real, perhaps, as our real one. There were, of course, some tricky moments, but on the whole I was amazed by the ease with which one can construct a whole self-contained, self-explaining world of deceit. From time to time I discovered that he and I had told an identical lie: by accident, without consultation, we chose the same alibis, the same excuses. I wondered if he was lying to protect me, or I to protect him: it seemed sinister, this inability to admit the truth about ourselves, this reluctance to cause inevitable pain. And yet sometimes our mutual weakness seemed like the last vestige, the last bond of love.

I had a bruise down the side of my nose for weeks: I, who had never quite known what a black eye looked like. I kept thinking it was dirt and trying to wash it off.

How easy it is to betray the texture of a life. I found the other day a letter that Malcolm wrote to me from Middlesbrough, where he was on tour; it was written only a year before our parting, and it said:

> *Dearest Jane,*
> *Thank you so much for your lovely letter, glad to hear that all is well. Give Laurie a big kiss. Don't worry about the shirt, I must have left it at Bill's. This is an odd place, rather posh,*

with big smart houses and leafy roads, and a thing called a
transporter bridge that we went over last night.

Look after yourself, darling, don't be lonely, why don't you
go to the cinema with Brenda one night, you ought to get out.
I'll see you Sunday. Meanwhile, all love,

M.

What more could one require? Endearments, domestic solicitude, parental affection, the mention of two distinct adult
acquaintances, even a little landscape? And I have no doubt
that my letter, which solicited this response, had been of equal
tenderness.

I could look at it another way. I could look at it from
the point of view of Lucy.

Lucy was, if you like, my sister: more nearly my sister than
my own sister was. I never knew either of them well—my sister Catherine was three years younger than me, and she was
my parents' favorite, which alienated me from her from the beginning, from a time before memory. She was much less reserved than I was, and also slightly more intelligent, quicker
off the mark, more easily responsive to ideas. She was much
more committed to being the daughter of our parents, a fate
from which I withheld myself. The more I withheld myself
the more they suspected me, and the more they turned to her.
I don't blame them. She didn't get on with them easily—
such a thing would have been impossible—but at least she

tried. She quarreled with them bitterly, in fact, but at least she remained in contact: she remained a whole person because she managed to accommodate protest in her manner toward them, which I could not do. I split myself, I went underground, but she had the courage to show them what she was. But then, I say for myself in extenuation, she had this courage because she knew that she was acceptable, which I was not. I had inherited some hereditary streak that had mercifully escaped her. We have, as well as those admirable admiral relatives, great-uncles in asylums up and down the country, and my father's father killed himself. Catherine, despite all these facts, appeared to be normal. She was a nice girl, she hardly affected me; I did not bother to envy her superior adaptability, I did not waste time wishing I were like her: her interests were not mine, her friends were not mine, we inspired in each other nothing but a nervous mild suspicious middle-class boredom.

With Lucy, though, it was another matter. She was my sister, my fate, my example: her effect upon me was incalculable. Perhaps it was merely the significance of her identity that diverted my attention from Catherine; had she not existed, Catherine might have affected me more. As I said, there was only a fortnight's difference in age between Lucy and me, and I suppose that in view of this, and in view of the similarity of our temperaments, we could have enjoyed a true intimacy—and God, how I have always desired and envied intimacy, with what jealousy have I heard its language and listened to its exclusive laughter. But the war divided us: we were one of its least significant casualties. Lucy spent the war in America, removed there by oversolicitous parents, and she was little more than a name to me until her return in 1946. We were both seven. By then it was too late: we never became close enough, and yet we were too familiar to become friends. I remember our reunion, upon her return, and I think that maybe, even then, I knew that we were embarking on a drama that would be played out not over that one summer afternoon but over the years, over a lifetime: a concept strange enough to a seven-year-old child, but perhaps not beyond the reach of hazard. Perhaps I could sense something from the reunion of my mother and her mother. I remember sitting in the drawing room of our house in Surrey and awaiting their arrival. I remember the old black Ford car coming up the drive, and Aunt Bridget getting out, and my mother kissing her on the cheek— my mother, who never kissed anyone—and both of them bursting into tears as they walked toward the front door, along the weed-thick pebbles of the drive. I watched them through the window. I watched Lucy, neglected, forgotten, jump out of the car after them, and follow them, swinging her straw hat, to be remembered at the doorway, and included in embraces and exclamations. The two boys, Lucy's brothers, weren't there, I can't remember why: perhaps Lucy, significantly, had been brought merely because it had been decided that she could play with me.

I don't know what expectations I had formed of Lucy. I think I did not much like the idea of her, largely because during the war Aunt Bridget, suffering from the universal American fear that all the British were starving and clad in rags, kept sending us parcels of American food and clothes, which gave me a very strange idea of what American children must be like. The clothes were not at all what comparable English children would have worn, and indeed, even in those desperate days, my mother, whose taste was not of the most sensitive, considered some of them too outré to inflict on us, and put them away in a drawer with mothballs. I can't now see quite what was wrong with them, except that they were all rather coy and girlish and heavily frilled and flowered, whereas most English girls at that time were dressed in boyish garments remarkable only for their utility. Also, I think the Americans had a tendency—still current, I believe—to make pointless, useless, nonclassical mock-up inventions, such as frilly dungarees, matching shirts and trousers, odd-shaped playsuits, dresses with braces, and so forth. I did not like these things that kept arriving in these parcels, and I was relieved when I was not compelled to wear them. It took me years to realize that in some sense they must also have reflected Aunt Bridget's taste, as well as the American nation's, and she certainly was capable of greater lapses than my mother, as well as of greater felicities.

I think I had expected Lucy to stroll down the garden path wearing some embarrassing and unsuitable garment, and I was not far wrong. She was wearing an embroidered white shirt under a red pleated pinafore dress, and she looked (as my mother said, in a vain search for idiom) cute. She looked cute. Imagine the ferocious dignity and integrity of a child that could survive such a description. Because survive it she did. She stood there, in the corner of the room, and when my name was mentioned to her, in introduction, she scowled at me with such poise that I was afraid.

"This is Jane," said my mother.

"Yes, I know it is," said Lucy, not moving an inch.

She had an American accent, which I had not foreseen: it was the strangest thing of all. From time to time our mothers had made us write letters to each other, and I had always read her dull epistles out to myself in pure King's English, and it amazed me to hear her speak like the child in the only film I had ever seen—some haunting saga of hospitals and saintliness and reunited parents, I recollect.

I had always disliked writing to Lucy.

"What on earth should I write to *her* for?" I used to say, crossly, chewing my pencil, denting the soft wood angrily with my teeth.

"Because she's your cousin," my mother would say. "Because you'll see her again, when the war's over."

"What shall I *say* to her?" I would say, groaning, bored by my own boredom.

"Oh, I don't know," my mother would say, losing interest at this stage, as she always did. "Anything. Tell her what you've been doing."

And I would, under duress, compose laborious sentences, saying, I went fishing today, I caught two minnows; our cat had three kittens; it is my sister's birthday; knowing that these trivial scraps could hardly merit a transatlantic journey, knowing that she would read them with as little love as I composed them.

And suddenly, there she was, American, strange, my own cousin. I despaired, as I stared at her, of ever bridging that gap, that separation, that enforced distance of relationship, of ever making good those halting childish phrases on the blue air-mail paper. She stood there, demure as her name, self-possessed, detached; whereas in myself I could feel only panic. It took me years to realize that my panic was so great that I rightly knew that I must never, never show it, and that the front I presented was her own front: demure, self-possessed, detached. We looked alike. Adults, seeing us, thought we were alike. Cold, they said we were. Cold fish.

From the first, we treated each other with great delicacy.

Our parents flung us together, crudely, without finesse, as parents do, as we had known they would.

"Go and play with Lucy," my mother said, when we had encumbered the drawing room for ten minutes with our small silent presences. "Go on, take Lucy up to your room and play with her."

I had always considered this command as indelicate as I now would consider it if, when introduced at a party, I were instructed by my hostess to go off and make love: playing then, as love now, seemed to me no easy matter. But I had grown used to suffering such social moments, and Lucy and I both turned and left the room quietly together. She followed me without speaking up to my bedroom, and I opened the door and let her in. Then we stood there, surveying my bed, my threadbare wartime carpet, my touching collection of austerity toys.

I have always had a highly sophisticated sense of the difficulties of communication, a sense of audience so acute that it silences me before I have spoken. It was this that led me, perhaps, to that most rigid, incommunicative art, where the passion and the impossibility exist most nakedly, side by side. A minority art. Poetry, an obdurate form, speaking obsessively, unpaid, to the select ear.

I did not know what to say to Lucy. How could I demean myself by speech? How could I offend her with the barrenness of my amusements?

After a while, I said, my voice thin and high and cool in my own ears, "I collect marbles."

"Do you?" she said, courteously. "Could I see them?"

"If you want to," I said.

And I got down the box in which I kept them. It was a black

enamel box with faded scratched painted flowers and butter-
flies. I have it now, though the marbles are all lost, all dispersed—
though still, presumably, like atoms, still intact. I often wish
I had kept them for Laurie, for he too is a collector, he would
have felt a bond with me in those three hundred small round
spheres.

Lucy liked the marbles. Any child would have liked them.
Some of them were very old, with whorls and spirals of differ-
ent-colored glass inside them; some were worn and gritty and
pitted from combat; some were smooth and new. I knew each
one, as it were, by face and name. I don't think that I minded
showing them to Lucy: I was not a secretive child, merely un-
hopeful. Lucy looked at them for some time, picking up first
one and then another, and then she looked at me with something like suspicion, and said, "Do you *do* anything with
them? Or do you just collect them?"

"I just collect," I said, and started to put them away again
into their box. But her question, although I did not show it, had
filled me with unease, because it was something I had always
worried about: for what, after all, did one do with things when
one had got them? I always felt myself, with those marbles,
to be on the edge of some discovery, some activity too delight-
ful to bear, and yet I could never quite reach it: it always eluded me, and whatever I did—laying them out in rows,
looking at them, not looking at them, adding to them, pretending to lose some of them—never quite fulfilled the glorious expectation of having them. I felt there was always something left undone, some final joyful possession of them, some
way to have my having of them more completely. I felt this
with all games—there was a particular one that Lucy and I
used to play, later, with ration books and an old handbag of

my mother's, a game of shopping, that at the outset seemed to
promise each time bliss beyond belief, some violent orgasmic
moment, perhaps, where we would *become* adults, where we
would *be* our mothers; but the moment never happened, it
would fade and drop away from us, leaving us with the old
rituals, the cutting out of the coupons, the adult magic shopping chat, leading us nowhere, each time bypassing its rightful end. And so it was with sex. Ah well, it is too clear to state.
But what, at the age of seven, had I done wrong, to suffer so in
later life? And how could I refuse James, who gave to me that
moment, who gave to me this impossible arrival, condemning me, by that gift, to an endless ritual of desire, to an endless repetition of phrases and gestures, all redeemed, all beau-
tified to me by impossible, impossible possession?

I think our parents were quite pleased by the way that Lucy
and I got on together. We certainly never quarreled, never
squabbled, never argued, as I did, childishly, with my sister,
and she with her brothers. I always looked forward to seeing
her, but could never quite tell what to do with her when she
was there, and I think she felt the same about me. In a sense,
we had too much respect for each other: neither of us would
take the initiative. We were both old for our years, both un-
demonstrative. And as we grew older, we talked not more but
less. We were both predestined from birth, by ambitious parents, for University, and I remember there was at some point
some discussion about whether we ought to go to the same one
or not, but the question remained academic because she got a
place at Cambridge and no place at Oxford, and I got a place
at Oxford and no place at Cambridge. Through family affilia-
tion in part, need I say. The old stale air of patronage. Neither
of us did brilliantly—Lucy got a very bad degree, because she

was unbelievably lazy and never did any work at all. I got a mediocre degree, and I was rather disappointed not to do better. I don't think Lucy cared at all. She always persuaded everyone that she was highly intelligent, through her limp enigmatic manner of speaking; and a reputation for intelligence, unsupported by examination results, was quite enough for her. Even after all these years I couldn't say whether she was intelligent or not. It's not something I can ever tell about people.

She spent all her time at Cambridge sleeping around. When I first realized this I was amazed, because she didn't look that kind of person at all. She looked rather like me; if anything she looked even more modest and innocent. I have always thought her beautiful, but I am surprised when others think her so because it seems of so personal, private, and unrhetorical a nature—a beauty full of defects—the kind that one would imagine could be perceived only by eyes of love. She has nondescript fine floppy brown hair, a soft-featured oval face, thin shoulders. She has nice skin, lovely pale-brown skin. I love the slight stoop of her shoulders under her jersey, and the way her thick neck grows. But I'd never expect other people to notice these things as virtues. Nor did I expect her to be so confident of them.

She did not put herself out much to make people fall in love with her—she dressed carelessly, never wore any make-up other than a pale lipstick, never had her hair cut. But at Cambridge, where there are ten men to every woman, effort was not required. A backward glance, a reported word, a passing smile—any of these could accomplish the fatal work. And a reputation, once acquired, will work for itself. By the end of her first year, Lucy was established as a *femme fatale*, of a kind familiar to that small world—not cheerful, not even casual about her affections, but emotionally promiscuous, faithlessly intense, universally sincere. People fell in love with her to suffer, to share her exploratory sufferings, to share a share of her bed. She collected them. She liked their devotions, their pain. She thrived on them, she grew strong on the arousing of unrequited passion. She sat there in her room in Newnham, a pale queen, and they gathered around her, seeking destruction: tenderly she wept over them as she pulled off their wings, tenderly she drank coffee with them, and discussed their grief.

I visited her once, at the end of her first year; it was an accidental visit, I had not intended to see her at all. I had gone to Cambridge for the day, just for the outing, with a friend who was going to see a friend. We had lunch in a pub, and I drank too much gin. As we ate our Scotch eggs Lucy's name came up.

"You're Lucy Goldsmith's cousin, aren't you?" said Nicholas, one of the accumulated friends of my friend's friend, and when I nodded my head I could see that it was significant to him. He sighed, and said, "She sometimes talks about you."

"What does she say?" I asked, rashly, fortified by alcohol, but he would not tell. But I could see that the fact of our connection was a solace to him: he liked me to be there, as he would have liked to have held one of her gloves, one of her books. I, who had never been in love, envied his preoccupation.

After a while, he said, "Let's go and see her. Let's go and see Lucy. Take us to see Lucy."

"I don't know," I said, hesitating but weak, reluctant but curious. "Do you think she'd like to see us?"

"She'd like to see *you*," said the young man called Nicholas. "She says you're the only person who knows what she's like.

She says she's afraid of you, because you know her too well."

And I, hearing this quite gratuitous and false account—issued by Lucy surely in some moment of highly dubious and false mutual confession, when the names of innumerable third parties had been dragged in to thicken some already potent emotional brew—was fool enough to allow myself to be interested by it, thinking drunkenly that it might contain some dregs of truth—as no doubt, no doubt it did—and we set off for Newnham, through King's, and along the Backs: my friend, my friend's friend, Nicholas and I. I went largely, I think, in the faith that she could not possibly be in on such a fine afternoon, but she was. Nicholas led us straight to her room, through some side door, and up a wide shallow flight of stairs; at its threshold he lost heart, and said to me, "You knock."

So I knocked. Lucy called, almost instantly, "Come in," so I pushed open the door, but as soon as I had done so I thought she could not have meant it because she was sitting, half undressed, on an unmade bed, with a young man. I stopped there in the doorway, and she stared at me, and took me in, and smiled, undismayed, and said, "Good Lord, it's you."

"I came to visit you," I said, "but perhaps I ought to go away again."

"No, come in, come in," she said. Her hair was all tangled up and untidy, and her cheeks were pink, but her coolness was such that I could not believe that the scene implied what it seemed to imply. "*All* of you come in," she said, seeing the other three at the door.

We went in and sat down on the floor, on the bed, on the one chair. The resident young man, when I dared to look at him, proved to my relief to be fully dressed, but he was just as disheveled as Lucy, and the air of the room was heavy with closeness. Lucy got up off the bed and put the kettle on for us, to make us some coffee. She was wearing a jersey, but she had no brassiere on underneath it, and her long legs were bare. She was wearing a pair of dark-blue regulation school knickers: she looked, though I did not realize it at the time, and could not place the inappropriate association, as though she had just finished a gym lesson at school. The jersey was long, a flecked fine dark pinky-gray lambswool. She was, in fact, perfectly decent, I suppose. Round her neck, on a thin silver chain, she wore a pendant—a piece of mother-of-pearl, set in an intricate wiry oval silver mesh. She always wore it. She told me once that it was half of a buckle off an old belt of a dress of our grandmother's and I asked her where the other half was, and she said it was lost. I liked the look of the silver on the soft flecked wool. I liked the way she bent down and lit the gas ring, the way she sat down again on the bed, her knees together, leaning hunched forward, her legs splayed from the knees in a diagonal.

The resident young man was, thank God, quite well able to deal with the situation. Perhaps he felt he was in a position of strength. He had a young, wide-eyed, vulnerable face, and very black hair. I still see him, from time to time; he is a lethal child, he has been through two marriages already, and innumerable high-quality women. A dangerous person. No wonder he put the coffee in the cups and handed them around to us with such complacency. He did not last long with Lucy: he was too like her, I think. While we were there I kept glancing at Nicholas to see how he was taking it, telling myself in vain that he had brought it upon himself, feeling myself responsible. When we left, Lucy put some jeans on and came out with us, and walked into town to our parked car, and waved us off. I cannot forget the way that the silver pendant slopped around, as she walked, on the low hills of her unsupported breasts.

It was a shock to me, that visit. Before then I had heard whispers, I had heard rumors of Lucy's way of life, but that visit was a vision to me, a total revelation. I saw it all, in that crumpled single bed, that half-drawn curtain, that tangled hair, that too-easily opened door. It frightened me, it made my heart stand still, my blood run cold. One could diagnose jealousy, no doubt: a passion for Lucy, unrequited, betrayed? Such a notion, I must confess, did not occur to me, but it may nonetheless be true. At the time, I thought I was shocked for other reasons. It seemed to me that Lucy was behaving badly, wantonly— not so much by sleeping with people as by demanding them, taking them seriously, encouraging them when they had no hope. For years she had several perfectly serious candidates for her hand in marriage, hanging helplessly around, reduced to a state of beggary and cold scraps. It seemed to me that she was taking more than her share. To enjoy or to encourage a one-sided passion in another seemed to me corruption. Myself, I could not do it. I was always so afraid of being unable to return emotion that I never dared to arouse it, and it amazed me to see somebody who did not care if she did not return what she was given, who handed out destruction with such lovely pitying smiles. While I was there she looked at Nicholas several times, with such glances of complicity, such sincere and generous sorrow. I could not have done it. Any meanness, any coldness, any hardness would have seemed more honorable. I could take no pleasure in being loved, I could draw no warmth from it.

Lucy was taking more than her share. I could not get over this impression, I could not reconcile myself to it. In vain did I

tell myself that young men like Nicholas probably enjoyed
an unrequited passion; for I knew it was not so. The principle
of natural selection has always haunted me: each day—truly, I
am serious, each day—I try to batter out for myself some principle of equality that might apply to the savage and indifferent
world. I fail, of course. The game of sexual selection seemed to
me, as I embarked upon it, to be the most savage game in the
world. I did not see how anyone could in conscience enjoy it.
One is trained up to it by all those other games—nursery games
first, games of selection, games where children dance round in
rings, singing:

> The farmer wants a wife,
> The farmer wants a wife,
> Ee-eye, ee-eye,
> The farmer wants a wife—

and woe to the poor children who are never chosen, never
elected, who dance round endlessly in the common outer circle, never admitted to the inner circle of choice. Then comes
school, and the choosing of teams—Mary, you be leader, you
choose a team for netball, for rounders—and who was the last
to be chosen, who was left each time, she who could not see
the ball, she whose thick glasses prevented her, she whose
short breath forbade her to run? And then the dancing part-
ners for dancing lessons, and the new girls, the misfits, the late
arrivals, those who arrived at the wrong time of the year, the
wrong stage of the term—wallflowers, drooping by the walls,
haphazardly paired off by an impatient dancing instructress—
ill-matched, flung together. And sometimes the numbers were
odd. Sometimes the numbers were not even even.

And when it came to sex, what then? There was no dancing instructress left to supervise the pairing off, no interceder to stop those pale extended hands of Lucy's from choosing all. I choose you, and you, and you, and you, and you will all come. And you I reject, I don't like the look of you, I don't like your face, go and stand by the wall until it is over. You can watch, if you like, but you can't join in. Well, perhaps, if you're very good, I'll dance one dance with you. You will be good? All right, then, one dance. But only one. And don't come bothering me next time. Next time, I choose to suit myself.

Lucy's lips were pink, and soft, and dull, and animal. Her mouth had a gentle outline, a soft curve. She did not look voracious.

Why should I have suffered so from the terrible knowledge of inequality? I must know, I must find the answer. If I don't find the answer now, what shall I do? Was it through fear that I wouldn't be chosen? Did I protest against the game in case I was the game's victim? Were my scruples nothing more moral than a selfish terror, born during some period of instruction in the art of the Viennese waltz, when I was the twenty-ninth child out of twenty-eight? It's possible, for my blood still runs cold at the notion. Did I marry because monogamy, cruel though it may be in its initial selection, seemed safer, more honorable, more innocent, than endless choice and endless realignment, in which the victims could merely lose more and more often, and the takers more often, more surely, take all, take each other, take all? Better a bad match and stick to it than to form a part of the endless snatch and grab. Better to be nothing, better to weep by the wall, the twenty-ninth child. Better to lose than to endure the guilt of winning; better to lose than to be a capitalist of the emotions, staring down from one's guilt-constructed office tower at the hurrying throng below. This is what I thought. I protest the virtue of my renunciations: I could have chosen, I was a reasonably endowed woman, not a natural pauper, I could have chosen the other way; and perhaps after all I only allowed myself to lose so badly because I knew that I held in my concealed hand a trump card, and that at the end of the game I would fling it down, the ace of hearts, gaping red, and that James would fall into my arms and die there?

It defies explanation. I do not understand. The twenty-ninth child, so terrified of rejection that it shut its eyes and never again dared to open them, cringing there in the corner behind the dusty piano as the dance continued without it. Go on, now, weep now, weep if you can. Such pointless injuries, such cherished sufferings, such irrelevant formations. Such pointed neglect of more happy pairings, more significant successes. When the murderess chooses the role of victim, when she arrays herself in shabby clothes, slopping down to the shop on the corner in her slippers and her apron, what disasters is she inviting, what massacres, what inverted cruelty, what blood will she not see flow?

My own sheets, warm with my own blood, where James slept with me, in chaste, incestuous desire.

When Lucy had finished with Cambridge, she took a job at a publishers. She has it still. The competition of the real world, where there is one man to one woman, should have subdued her a little, it should have cramped her style, but she was too well established to be subdued, she had too many men, reared on her strong insidious diet, already waiting for her: she never felt the pinch, the rub, the cold exposure, or if she did she never showed it. I felt sorry for her men, the helpless drones of her love. I remember having lunch with one of them once, so that he could have the dubious pleasure of talking about her, and he was a truly sorry spectacle, groaning over his chicken curry.

"I can't see what you *see* in her," I said, to condole. "I mean, she's not all *that* marvelous, is she?"

"I don't suppose she is," he said, glumly. "I mean, she's not even as attractive as you, is she? Objectively speaking, I mean."

"Isn't she?" I said.

"No, she's not," he said, "but it doesn't matter. I wish it did."

"We're neither of us *spectacular*," I said.

"No, I suppose not," he said, shaking his head.

"It's not relevant," he said. "I wish it were. Do you know what I do, I try to think about her looking dreadful, when she's got a bad cold, when her hair needs washing, things like that."

"That's treacherous," I said.

"No, it's not," he said. "It's self-defense. And anyway it doesn't work."

"One wouldn't expect it to," I said.

When Lucy said that she was going to get married, I wasn't surprised, because I have too little grasp on probability to be surprised by what people do; and therefore what they do seems always right. It seemed immediately that of course she had always been about to get married, that it was of course the right thing to do, for her to do, for everyone to do. And when I first met James, it was easy to see her motivation. Lucy and I,

let me admit it, are no more than average, it takes goodwill to
see the virtues of our features, but James is beautiful, like a
tree, like a flower, like an angel. I mean that I love him. When I
met him I shook hands and coldly turned away. That's what
one gets, I said to myself, if one keeps in condition, if one rejects enough people, if one litters one's path with enough
corpses, if one's strong enough to lie and make love on that bare
deck with the dead albatross staring from its white accusing
eye.

She was proud of him, I could see that—proud of his absurd-
ities, his thing about cars, his pointlessness, his lack of utility,
proud rather as a man is proud of a lovely woman, so much
more serious a possession than some people think—and yet I
thought I could see that her pride, even then, was tinged with a
slight reservation, a slight dismay. One reason for it became
apparent when, seven months later, their first child was born.
In Lucy I had my first opportunity for observing the transfor-
mations of maternity. I remember that I was amazed by the
domesticity which she and James instantly achieved, for
neither of them looked at all gifted in such directions. They
lived at first in Lucy's old flat at Earl's Court, where they had
been living together for some time before the marriage, and
just after the child was born they bought a house in Wimble-
don—a horrid little house, I thought, but then all married people lived in horrid little houses (and when my turn came I
was no exception, save for the fact that I found a horrid mid-
dle-sized house). I didn't see much of them during that first
year—I spent a couple of evenings there, and one Sunday—but
I made such good use of those occasions, and the impressions
I received sank so profoundly into my heart, that I felt that I
knew the whole story. As far as decor and curtains and car-

pets went, they were both amazingly idle, so their house never achieved an appearance of unity: it had some nice things in it, portable impermanent things that they had picked up while passing, but they did little with the basic structure apart from slapping a good deal of uneven white paint all over before they moved in. But it was their very idleness that created such a feeling of intimacy. They lived there, they lived together, they didn't want to go out, they couldn't be bothered to go out. They watched the television endlessly, night after night, in suburban harmony, speaking with a pretense of fervor about programs I had never seen and could not have brought myself to watch, simulating astonishment at my highbrow ignorance. "Do you mean to say you don't *like* Casino Quiz?" Lucy said to me on one of those evenings as she switched it on, and I watched it with them and I could see that they were happy watching it, but that their happiness was hardly related to what was going on upon that flickering screen, and that I could gaze at that idiot game until I went blind without ever discovering the image of their contentment. I was so painfully entranced by such an appearance of harmony that I didn't think to ask myself if it would last. I inspected their cutlery, their furniture, their bare wooden floors, as though I might find in these things the secret of matrimony, the secret key to being a woman, and living with a man.

Lucy was a marvelous cook. Cooking suited her temperament: she liked sitting in the kitchen chopping things up into very small pieces and stirring things very slowly in saucepans while other people talked to her. I remember watching her slicing vegetables for a chicken casserole. She was slicing them on a white wooden board, with a black-handled knife, slicing them into paper-thin wooden disks, carrots, turnips, onions:

orange, grained, cream, white. James was sitting holding the baby. He liked the baby, and the baby sat on his knee as still as a kitten. I have never had the patience to cook, it seems to me such a hopeless filling in of desperate time, I cannot concentrate, I slice my fingers, I hack wildly at the meat: meat disgusts me, fish disgusts me. Lucy can cook hares, and gut mackerel. I think to myself that such things as cooking are an evasion, they are a wrong use of time, time so pure, so precious, so reserved: for what? for nothingness, for solitude, for boredom, for silence. Comes the blind Fury, while I am in anguish, deciding whether to peel or scrape the potatoes, or whether to abandon them altogether in favor of some more convenient commodity like rice or macaroni.

James, in fact, didn't much care for Lucy's wonderful cooking. He used to make jokes about it and say that he didn't like garlic. She ignored his protests completely, and continued to force him to eat the kind of meals that I would give anything to have given to me—anything, that is, but my own time and patience. And she, similarly, didn't much care for his cars, except at the beginning, though he continued, resolutely, to treat her as though she must. Once I saw him tip a plateful of salad Niçoise, dark with olives, back into the salad bowl and walk off eating a slice of bread and jam. Once I heard her shout at him over the telephone that he could go and kill himself on the track tomorrow if he wanted, but she was too bored to come and watch. But despite these differences, they seemed to get on well. They had complicity.

Sometimes I think that I married because Lucy married. I got a house because Lucy had a house. I had a baby because Lucy had a baby. One should not underestimate the force of example. There were things that she did that I could not do—the cooking, and the collecting of suitors—but I followed her where I could. When I was pregnant (and I took pregnancy badly, I found it almost unendurably frightening) I said to myself constantly that it could not be so bad if Lucy had done it, that it must, if Lucy had done it, be *right*. She was a sanction. Although, as I can see, she operated, in this role, selectively. Though not, now I think of it, as selectively as all that, because when I was first married I remember that I did try for some time to emulate Lucy's culinary skill—I messed around with sauces and puddings and French country cooking for some time before shrugging the whole business off in bored abandon, and resigning Malcolm and myself to a lifetime of hamburgers and sardines.

Lucy. Lucy Goldsmith. Lucy Otford. It couldn't be possible that I wanted James because he was hers, because I wanted to be her. It wasn't so, it wasn't so. I am getting tired of all this Freudian family nexus, I want to get back to that schizoid third-person dialogue. I've one or two more sordid conditions to describe, and then I can get back there to that isolated world of pure corrupted love.

Firstly, and briefly I hope, I don't think I could have slept with James if the house I did it in hadn't been technically mine. I've always worried about women having to commit adultery on their husband's money: it seems hard, to have to betray one's husband twice over, both sexually and financially. It's bad enough having to ask for money to buy inessential articles like stockings and books and toothpaste: and how much worse to spend it on assignations? I must confess that Malcolm did send me money after he left me, and that I did live on it, but then he was by that time doing extremely well and couldn't have missed it, and the children were after all his—

though that didn't much console me, knowing as I did that I had in effect taken them from him. I told myself that he was lucky that my neuroses were the reverse of extravagant: my extreme fear of moving out of the house or employing any domestic help cut down my expenses to a bare survival level. It would have been hard to live more cheaply. At least I wasn't obliged to ask him for money to have my hair done to preserve to myself the illusion of my own attractions, and for the benefit of another man. And the house, as I said, was mine. This mattered so much to me that I trembled before my own meanness, because it couldn't surely be honorable, so much solicitude about so mean and irrelevant a thing. It merely proved that I had never belonged to Malcolm—proof I little needed—if I could pay such revenging attention to the crudities of justice. Thine, mine. I can't take, I can't give, because I know I'm such a rotten offering. What, in our house? as Lady Macbeth said, when true emotion failed her. What a liar I am. I'd have slept with James anywhere, I spent Malcolm's money on him, I slept with him in my marriage bed, with our newborn child as witness. It didn't matter, it was of no importance. The possession of the house was no condition, it was a mere straw of extenuation, and even now I can hardly tell whether it lies on the side of credit or discredit. I have no more credit, I am penniless, I am bankrupt, I no longer care for such things, I am a receiver of free gifts.

I began the last paragraph with the word "firstly," so I must have been intending to begin this with "secondly," but I can't remember what it was or if I can it was too embarrassing and I've repressed it. Anyway, I'm tired of all this. It has a certain kind of truth, but it isn't the truth I care for. (Ah, ambiguity.) Perhaps I meant to brave the subject of my children, my shame at involving them in these unsuitable distresses, my inability to deny myself for them, my casuistry on my own behalf—better for children, I would say to myself, to see their mother improperly saved than virtuously mad.

One last concession I will make to facts, before I return to them entirely: I said that James was reading *Thérèse Raquin,* that night in my bedroom, when he sat with me, just after the child was born. Well, it was so. He has an odd taste in books, by which I mean that he reads good books, though not very often. It must be a habit inherited from his cultivated mother, because he does not enjoy them at all, they bore him to distraction, in fact any distraction suits him better than the sight of the printed page. *Thérèse Raquin* is the story of two lovers, who conspire in passion to murder the unnecessary husband, and find, when free, that they have murdered instead their own love: love thrives thus secretly on living guilt, and dies with the dead.

Zola was an unforgiving man. But I read somewhere that he used to walk about the Tuileries with his mistress and their babies and the perambulator. In his novels, he has an old-fashioned artistic view of decadence. He likes to turn his characters into corpses. But in his life, perhaps he was more charitable to the flesh?

As she sat there, waiting for him, waiting for the telephone to ring, waiting for the sound of his car, she thought that it had perhaps been for this that she had emptied her existence, for this dreadful, lovely, insatiable anguish, for these intolerable hopes. She wondered if other people had ever suffered so, and how they had found time to suffer through lives so full of occupation, so full of jobs and work and cooking and society. She vainly believed, with the arrogance of all lovers, that she was the only woman who had waited as she waited. She grew expert in the tones of the engines of cars along the road outside. For the first time she noticed when her neighbors left for and came back from work, for sometimes she would mistake the gleam of sun on metal for a promise of his arrival, only to find it shining merely from the blue Cortina of the man next door. She would say to herself: is it more likely that he will come if other cars go along the road, or if the road is empty till his arrival? Which is a better portent: silence, or the wrong noise? Her ears strained so for the telephone that she could hear it in the clink of a teaspoon, in the rustle of paper, in the baby's sighs, in the creaking cartilage of her own neck as she moved her head. From an upstairs window she could sometimes see the reflection of an approaching car cast around the curve of the corner against the windows of the houses on the street opposite—the first possible intimation, this, of arrival—and when he was late for an appointed time she would permit herself to go up there and watch for him, watching with aching eyes for that faint prophetic insubstantial gleam. Madness, she would say to herself as she stood there, her head pressed against the glass. She knew it could not last. But it did not seem to end, and she felt herself helpless, ill with longing, quite unable to do anything about her state except to conceal its more grotesque manifestations from her child.

She was amazed by her inability to do anything to bridge the absolute difference between his presence and his absence.

While he was not there she suffered so acutely from his absence that she thought the suffering must continue into the times when she was with him: and when he was there he was so close to her that she thought she should be able to preserve some shadow of him to keep her company when he had gone. But there was no way, no adequate way. She tried the classic means: she stole things from him, she kept his cigarette packets, his copies of *Autocar,* she begged photographs from him and locks of his hair, and when he was gone she would gaze at these objects as though they were magic relics, as though they could hold him in them. But they merely dulled pain; they did not remove it. When in the throes of labor, she had thought of the absolute gap between pain and absence of pain, a gap that the body can in no way bridge, for no amount of foreknowledge can prevent pain, and nothing can shorten the times of its endurance: and yet when it has gone it has gone entirely, beyond recollection, far beyond imagination. So, when he was there with her, she would think idly that he would be gone in an hour, in two hours, but such thoughts could neither hurt nor protect her: the cycle had to be endured, in her body, passively, as he came and went. When she was waiting for him, as the minutes ran down to nothing before his arrival, she would feel her knees start to tremble, her hands to shake. She laid out for herself charts of reasonable expectation, knowing that she could not expect him before the time he had named, yet beginning to hope, in her heart, five minutes before—telling herself, as the hour struck, that he was always late; starting to expect, reasonably, five minutes after the hour; awaiting him with some anxiety after a quarter of an hour; and when, as on one or two occasions, the statutory fifteen minutes of anxiety lengthened into thirty, into forty, into sixty, she was almost out of her mind with grief, had almost resigned herself to despair, by the time the car screeched into the curb before her. And then it was over, instantly over, as though it had never been: like the pangs of birth, so soon forgotten, so lightly undertaken, so bitterly endured. Once, he was ten minutes early; as she opened the door to him, she felt herself cheated of that habitual addictive pain.

She never questioned his arrivals or departures, never asking him why he came so often, or, as it at other times and by another scale seemed, so rarely: she feared that the wrong question would reveal beneath them depths too sinister to investigate, so she asked no questions. Unacquisitive—for what could she hope to take without losing?—she waited. Mariana at the moated grange: he will not come, she said, but he did come, he continued to come, he continued to put an end to those hours of waiting. When he was there they did not talk to each other much, they had not much to say to each other. She felt that she was taking part in some elaborate delicate ritual, and that if she broke some small unknown rule of it, by a false word or touch, by a treacherous mention of Lucy or Malcolm, by a murmur of indignation at his leaving, by a too willing acceptance of that same leaving, then he would be taken from her, she would forfeit him for her unwitting transgression. At times something in her would attempt to defy this entire subjugation; she would hear within her a mute and reasonable voice, another woman's voice, raised in protestation, asking him what he thought he was doing, where was Lucy, did Lucy know what he was up to, why on earth wasn't he at work like everyone else, whatever did he think he wanted her for, what did he intend to do with her now that he had got her; but these crude questions never reached the air, she silenced and suppressed them, afraid to disturb love by doubt. Once, one afternoon, she did ask him why he never did any work; she asked him almost without thinking, in her most daytime voice, a reasonable voice, that spoke out by itself, sick of its prolonged disuse: "Why don't you ever do any work?" she said to him, as she sat there, the baby on her knee.

"So that I can be with you," he answered, the courteous answer of the role that he had for some reason chosen to play. But she persisted, stepping dangerously out on to the unmarked squares of real life, of the outer world. "What rubbish," she said. "If you had some work to do, you'd be doing it. Why haven't you any work to do?"

"My partner does all the work," he said.

"Why don't you go and help him, then? It isn't fair, for him to do it all."

"Of course it's fair," he said. "It was never meant that I should do any work. Anyway, I do do some, from time to time. But it's not my job, doing work. I'm what's called a sleeping partner."

"I see," she said, amused, almost ready to retreat once more into those dull, repetitive exchanges; but before she did so, she said, in a tone that belonged to neither world, a tone that could be taken to request any answer, "But why do you waste so much time with me?"

And he smiled at her, ambiguously, gently, and said, "It's because of boredom, you know. Because really, I've got nothing else to do."

And she, too, thought of nothing else. She devoted her life to this preoccupation. It sucked, obsessively, all other interests from her: they were pulled into it and engulfed like dry leaves or bits of straw. As she fed the baby or washed the clothes her body was remembering him, it was fainting and opening for each word, each touch, each gesture, each one relived a hundred times. Much of the time she was half dead with exhaustion: her mind grew thin and dizzy, her limbs were light from lack of sleep, her hands so slow and weak that in the early mornings she had to struggle helplessly to fasten a safety pin or to put the teat on the baby's bottle. Its rubbery obstinacy defeated her weak grip: she spilled milk on her nightdress every morning, and her clothes were constantly marked by the faint pink stains of black-currant-flavored water. The baby was a placid baby, but nevertheless she needed feeding in the nights, and Laurie would wake too, in jealous sympathy. When Jane got to bed in the evenings she would fall asleep as she touched the pillow, and James had to keep her awake for him by violence, a violence which she received with tired gratitude, for she wanted him more than she wanted sleep. "Hit me," she would say as she lay there, her eyes involuntarily drooping shut. "Go on, hit me, hurt me, wake me up," and he would do so, gently, carefully, nervously. "I could do it to you while you were asleep," he said to her once, overcome by a passing guilt at the sight of the circles under her eyes, but she smiled at him drowsily, and said, what would be the point of

that? Sometimes she hardly managed to get to sleep at all before the baby woke in the early hours of the morning. James,
penitent, would bring her tea and try to give Laurie his breakfast, but he had to leave her in the morning, and when he had
gone she would drag down to the shops with Laurie perched on
the edge of the pram, and the very sound of her feet on the
pavement came to her muffled by fatigue. Weariness and desire
walled her in, like invisible glass, keeping the cold air from
her, protecting her from the cruel inquisitions of salesgirls and
neighbors, so that she moved in her own element, clouded by
a perpetual hangover, isolated as though by drugs or drink.

Her only contact with the outer world was Laurie: he alone
could reach her. The baby was still a part of her, still within
those glassy walls, a mere innocent, easy receiver of the embraces and smiles that she found inexplicably easy to give; but
Laurie was another matter. He was three, now, able to talk,
able to perceive. She had feared, after Malcolm's departure,
that he would miss his father, and make her pay for his absence, but he appeared not to notice it: he asked no questions,
he hardly mentioned him. He slept badly, but she put that
down to the separation before the baby's birth, but the arrival
of the new baby. He accepted James without question, and just
as James liked to claim her in public as his cousin so she liked
to hear her son address James as uncle. It gave the situation a
permanence, and sometimes she wanted James so badly, with
so little sense of dignity, that she would have clutched at him
and claimed him in any way, even as the uncle of her child. She
told herself that it was better for Laurie that there should be a
man in the house from time to time, even if it was not his own
father; and she could never tell whether this argument was a
sophistry, covering some morass of vicious neglect, or whether

it was instead the simple truth. The answer did not lie in her
own motives for desiring James's presence, but in the effects
of that presence. But who could say what those effects might
be?

She worried most, however, not about James, but about the
fact that Laurie lacked companionship; meaning by this that
he lacked friends of his own age. He played from time to time
with children in the street, but they were not what she, a
woman of her class, could consider as suitable companions, and
she lacked the confidence that might have had faith in them
and encouraged them. She looked at Laurie, sitting in a corner making neat elaborate structures with building blocks and
toy cars, and it seemed hard that her own solitude, a self-in-
flicted decontaminating isolation, should be inflicted upon him.
But she did not know how to free him from it, she did not
know how to break the fatal hereditary chain. She had per-
severed, until recently, with taking him out to tea with other
mothers, so that he could play with their offspring: thrusting
him crudely into a corner with another child and a pile of
broken plastic rubbish, as she herself had been thrust with
Lucy, while she and the other mother sat and surveyed and observed and exchanged dim hostilities and pleasantries and cups
of tea. But when Malcolm left her the strength that carried her
into such engagements had deserted her and she had declined
Laurie's invitations in selfish dread, pleading her own health,
and Bianca's imminence. But her weakness tormented her: she
knew that some effort was demanded of her, some heroic sacrifice.

And in the end she made it. She decided to send Laurie to
the local nursery group. She had had his name down for a year,
but she had never thought she would get around to sending

him. It was not losing him that she feared: it was the confrontation with the other mothers, the daily task of delivering and collecting the child, the daily greetings, the daily partings. Such a trivial decision became to her something momentous, terrifying, impossibly difficult. And yet she knew it was trivial: madness did not offer the solace of its own exclusive faith. She knew, as she walked him along, at a quarter past nine one May morning, that what she was doing showed perhaps the bare minimum of maternal care, and that all her utmost effort could do would be to conceal from the child, and from the world, the extent of her panic. She remembered how she had panicked once, some months before, when she had been unable to decide whether or not an invitation to tea with another mother and child had been offered in earnest: as the hour approached, she sat in her own house, paralyzed, unable to move, unable to risk arriving unexpected upon that doorstep, unable to ring, unable to offend by nonarrival: inert, sweating, suffering. Watching the spectacle of her own lamentable passionate anxiety until Laurie had come and tugged at her skirt and asked if he could see Johnnie, he thought they were going to see Johnnie, why weren't they going to see Johnnie, when were they going to see Johnnie. Terrified, she turned on him, and she saw him wince from the indecision in her eyes, and she thought, oh God, all his life he'll suffer for me, all his life he'll wince from me. And she went over to the telephone and dialed, as though her life's dignity depended (at the point of death) on such heroism, the other woman's number, and listened to her own voice saying, "Denise, hello Denise, this is me, yes, Jane, I was just ringing to check if you *were* expecting us . . . oh yes, of course, I was a bit held up, but we're setting off right now . . . yes, yes, we'll see you soon," and replacing the receiver she looked down to see the small wise face, fooled, entirely fooled, gazing up at her, anxiously reassured, saying, "Can we go now, Mummy?"

The nursery group was a private one. It took place in a church hall, and it was run by one of the women with whom she had attempted those painful afternoon teas. She lived within ten minutes' walk of Jane, in a large converted house, the top two floors of which were let off to students. Her husband was an economist, and he had been at school with Malcolm. These were the sole connections between the two women. They had given it a try, they had made an effort, but they both had suffered: they had sat there in their respective chairs, dutifully throwing out hopeful scraps of information, attempts at jokes, chat about children, but each remark had dropped, deadly and pale, in the vast wastes between them. They judged each other: Jane condemned Brenda for her loud false laugh, for her wallpaper, for her choice of newspaper, for the bored authoritative way in which she subdued her child, and Brenda condemned Jane for her vicious reticence, for her insulting uncontrolled jerks into communication, for the yearning anxiety with which she watched Laurie play. They did not dislike each other; they were afraid of each other. Jane, clinging desperately to some hope of two-way perception, knew that the fear did not come from herself alone, that she was not merely trembling before a woman more competent, more brusque, more womanly than herself: she knew that the other woman was afraid, that she sensed in her something fearful— her perception, her sensibility, her intellect, one of those things, perhaps, one of those things that so sets itself up against the ways of others. This knowledge that she was not mad, not paranoid, not seeing doubt and persecution where there were none, in some way absolved her, but it also immobilized and transfixed her, for what could she do, if her terrors were well placed, well founded, and also trivial? Brenda did not lie awake at night, worrying about Mrs. Jane Gray, she was sure of that: so why should she lie awake, why should she feel her throat dry up and her knees weaken, as she approached her? Perhaps it was simply a question of the degree of apprehension. She apprehended so keenly that she could not bear it, that she had to withdraw herself. She wept when she irritated telephone operators and bus conductors by foolish requests. She wept at the bitterness of their irritation, at the sheer quality of irritation and bitterness loose in the world. She feared human nature. In herself, in her children, everywhere.

When she reached the church with Laurie and Bianca, at half past nine, she did not know which entrance to approach, but was fortunately rescued from the humiliation of public indecision by the arrival of another mother, pushing a pushchair and child. The mother was wearing trousers and a long cable-knit jersey; she was a pretty woman, thin and pretty, but her face was pallid and gray. She saw Jane, and gave her a watery half-smile of acknowledgment, and then began to push her child around to the back of the church, along a pathway. Jane followed her. At the door, the other woman paused: she tried it but it was locked. She turned to Jane and said, "She's late again, with the key."

"It's my first time," said Jane, apologetic, as though accused.

The other woman did not respond: she did not say, "I thought so," or "Nice to see you." Instead she yawned. Then, after some moments, she said, "Getting out of bed is too much for me."

And Jane, looking at her covertly, could see that she was indeed still half asleep: her face was gray because it was still gummed up with a night's rest, her hair was unbrushed, and her child had egg around its mouth. Oh God, she thought, with sudden shock, her faith shaken, perhaps all the world's as bad as me, perhaps none of them get up and clean their houses. And then she looked down at herself, and she could see that she herself was neatly dressed, that she was wearing stockings, and that she had cleaned Laurie's shoes for the occasion expressly. She was confused by such implications, by the fact that she looked better and knew she was worse than the yawning woman who displayed her lamentable sleeping indolence so unashamed, who did not make even the faintest pretense at shame when Brenda and her child, and various other mothers and children, arrived: she continued to yawn, and handed her child over without another word. When she had gone, Jane, hovering anxiously, trying to introduce Laurie to the tricycles and jigsaws, found time to notice that she had been unrepresentative, a felicitous introduction. The others were more what she had expected, a collection of insincerely cheerful middle-class women with the usual constituents—the dark-haired, wide-mouthed girl in well-assorted artistic clothes, the pinched varnished blonde, the sensible subdued woman with healthy clean hair shining evenly and short around her square face, the tall classy girl with a loud voice and an expensive dress, the bad-tempered graduate, the fat blowsy hypochondriac, embarking instantly, this last, and with no sense that she was betraying and branding herself, upon some tale of rheumatoid arthritis, some saga of the treacherous disbelief of professional men. The bad-tempered graduate's husband was a doctor, and trouble appeared to be staring up between them, amid the push-chair handles and the smell of plasticine: and trouble of so predictable a nature that Jane could see the others turn away as they listened with comfortable superiority to this degrading ritual. Proper people, the people of the real world, seemed to claim their identities so easily, to step into them with their professions, to wear with defiance the uniforms and voices and faces of their selves, but she felt herself to be nothing, nebulous, shadowy, unidentifiable. And yet she saw that this could not be so, that she was defined as clearly to these others as they to her, and that some of them might flutter uneasily inside borrowed garments, as she did. Perhaps each such group, each such collection, had a woman like herself, a woman with her features, playing her role. She shivered for them, frail ghosts. What vanity, to think oneself chosen to be nothing, to think oneself selected by fate for nonentity. And yet what cruelty, to condemn others, with egalitarian passion, to such a fate.

When the time came to leave Laurie, he did not want her to go. Characteristically, she had not warned him that she would be leaving him there: weakly she had evaded the issue, flinching before those sensible orders of separation that she had obeyed so meekly in her own childhood. She had hoped that she could retreat without his noticing, and when he was sitting engrossed at last, the round fronds of his unbarbered hair drooping earnestly over a large wooden elephant jigsaw, she started to back out; but at the door Brenda, loud and cheerful, said, "Bye, then, Jane," and Laurie, hearing his mother's name, sensing treachery, looked up and caught her in the cowardly act of departure. He jumped up, scattering pieces of elephant as he ran, and clung to her knees, the angry tears starting up in his eyes. She tried to comfort him, to explain to him that she wouldn't be long, that she would be back for him soon, but he wept loudly and stamped his feet.

"Don't worry," said Brenda, "he'll be all right in five minutes, he'll be all right as soon as you're out of sight," as though it were somehow the sight of his mother that affected and corrupted him.

"They all do this," said the professional lady in charge as she swam up from the background, summoned by an evidently familiar sound. "Don't worry, he'll be all right."

"Yes, yes, of course," said Jane, trying to prize his fingers off her skirt, trying to wipe his eyes. "Don't you worry, Laurie, I'll be back."

And he looked at her, already sobbing less violently, bravely facing her cowardice.

"Darling," she said, as he unclenched his fist. She had to go: she could hear Bianca starting to scream in rivalry from her pram. The conflicting claims tore at her: hooks in her flesh.

So she left him. He was still crying as she left, and she herself, shaking with emotion, once she had rounded the corner, felt her nose prickle, her eyes fill. She wept, as she walked along the street, for poor Laurie, abandoned, and for the sad way she had handled him, compact of all maternal crimes—indecision, duplicity, lack of confidence—and she wept because she had meant to do the right thing, she had taken him there for his own sake, so that he should have the friends that she had never had. It was the right thing, but she was the wrong mother to do it. There was no way out, she said to herself, as she walked the dirty streets of Paddington: she could not save him, though she knew the meaning of salvation.

But when she went back for him, just before lunch, he was playing quite happily. She stood in the doorway, unobserved, and saw him, with her own eyes, dancing round and round, laughing: they were playing "Here we go round the mulberry bush," that innocent noncompetitive game. She felt sick with relief for this mercy, although he burst into noisy tears once more when he saw her, and was to weep daily, for weeks, at the moment of parting, so that each time she had to endure the same cycle of anxiety, despair, self-justification, relief.

That afternoon, James came to see her. She had been expecting him. She was doing the ironing when he came and she pretended to herself that she had not heard him when he opened the door; she continued perversely, not looking up, smiling to herself. She was ironing the baby's nightdresses; amazingly careless about most aspects of her domestic life, she attached herself passionately to the ironing of baby garments as though such entirely thankless labor could protect her from the guilt of neglecting more useful jobs. And when she did look up, he was there. He sat down at the large kitchen table, and watched her: he asked her politely about Laurie's nursery school, and she asked him politely about his garage, which she knew he had visited that morning. As the weeks drew on they had learned what questions to ask each other: they had asked each other these things at first out of a merely hopeful faith in the communication value of words, any words, though their thoughts were on quite other subjects, inarticulate, inexpressible. But already she was beginning to understand his answers, they were more to her now than representations of speech and symbols uttered as in another language; she was beginning to acquaint herself with his daily anxieties, as he with hers. And sometimes she could even glimpse a time when she would ask him these questions not only because she loved him and wished him to know it, but also because she wanted to know for herself, for interest's sake, whether Bert had managed to deal with the Maserati order, and what had happened to Garret at Silverstone. These things, that had seemed at first beyond the grasp of her imagination, were becoming familiar to her: the thin papery structures that they had built between them, faint shadows and airy bridges, would one day perhaps bear the weight of quite ordinary feet. This, in her better moments, was what she hoped. It seemed almost to promise a kind of future.

This time, as he sat there watching her, she even remembered to ask him if he wanted anything to eat, and he, who had on occasions starved himself rather than distract her by admitting a need for food, said that he would. She offered him bacon and eggs but he said that he would have a sandwich, and started to make one for himself: the bread, a sliced loaf, had been standing on the kitchen table since she had bought it the day before. He discarded the top slice and started to butter the second, but she saw him lose faith in the second slice too.

"What's the matter with it?" she said, amazed to detect in her own voice a very faintly querulous note, a note of wifely resentment.

"It's stale," he said. "It's as hard as a brick."

"I'm sorry," she said. "Does it matter?"

"Of course it matters," he said. "If there's anywhere I draw the line, it's at stale bread. Why on earth don't you ever put it away in a breadbin, or a tin or something?"

"I've only had it two days," she said.

"Two days, two days—for God's sake, you must be mad. Really, darling. If you leave it standing around like that it's inedible within a couple of hours."

"I'm sorry," she said, once more. "I'll make you some bacon and eggs instead. I said I would."

"Actually," she said, as she started to fry the bacon, "I have got a breadbin. But I never use it. Why do you think I don't use it? Can it be because it's too much trouble to open the lid?"

"That sounds like a good reason," he said. "Laziness is a good reason for most things."

"But it's not only that," she said, attached now to the topic, and beautifully redeemed by the readiness and sincere sorrow with which she had started to provide him with an alternative meal, "it can't only be that. Because every time I look at the bread lying around, and biscuits going soft and cakes drying up, and stuff like that, I feel something quite specific about it. I feel—I don't know, I feel a *positive* reluctance to putting lids on things. It's not just laziness. Is it Freudian, do you think? I think that really I think it's immoral to impede the course of nature by a tin lid. I mean to say, if things are made to go stale, it hardly seems right to stop them, does it?"

"You're mad, my darling," he said. "You're like a boy who used to be at school with me who thought it was wicked to interrupt God's work by cutting his fingernails or hair. You can imagine what trouble it got him into."

"I'm very sympathetic toward that kind of madness," she said. "I see exactly what he meant, that boy. Don't you?"

"One can't surrender to these sympathies," he said, taking the plate of food from her and settling down to eat it.

"And what about that thing I read in the paper the other day," she said, "about some place in America where they're using real corpses in experiments on the effects of car crashes, or something like that? Did you see it? Don't you think it's disgusting?"

"I can't see the connection with breadbins," he said, wiping up the egg with half a stale slice.

"People have no respect for the organic," she said. "That's what's wrong."

"*I* respect the organic," he said, leaning over to touch the back of her hand, "and if anyone starts using my corpse in any experiments, even if it's only to re-create the crash I died in, I shan't think much of it. When my body reassembles on the Day of Judgment. Because bodies do, you know. They all come together again. Did you know?"

"What about slices of bread?" she said, and started to laugh. "Do they reassemble too? Or only those like mine that die a natural death?"

"You're crazy, my love," he said, but she could see that he did not think so.

Later, Laurie came in from the street where he had been riding his tricycle, and persuaded them to play picture dominoes with him, a game that he had recently mastered: they played with him until they could bear it no longer. The child himself, despite the famed lack of concentration of those under five, would have played forever. Watching him, Jane wondered if she had been like that herself. She was sure that she had: she remembered her collections, her private rules about the use of cutlery and the ascent of the stairs, her dreadful persistence. He whined and groaned, when deprived of his dominoes, until James, to divert him, asked if there were any cards in the house.

"Cards?" said Jane.

"Playing cards," said James. "I could show Laurie some lovely card tricks."

"He's too small to understand," said Jane, but she went, just the same, and found a new pack; there had been one lying for years on the top of the bathroom cabinet. She and Malcolm had played poker, before they were married, and a penniless flute-playing friend of Malcolm's had given them the pack as a wedding present. She wondered, as she brought it down, how it had got into the bathroom. The cellophane paper was soggy with damp. Once they had married they never played cards. They had not cheated; they had not alleviated their discontent, they had not varnished over the cracks between them, they had sought no alternative occupations or diversions. She had not permitted it. Ruthless, she had stared at the old walls and the damp plaster, and she had made him stare with her until he could not stand it any more. Nothing but the worst, she had said to herself. Inhuman. Cruel.

She handed the packet to James, and watched him strip off the paper as though he were opening a box of cigarettes. He took the cards out, new and smooth, shiny bright canvas.

"Lovely, aren't they?" he said.

"They smell nice," she said, sitting by him, reaching for his knee under the table.

He spread them out, suddenly, into a fan, with an even dexterity.

"Choose one," he said, and she smiled, and chose. It was a five of diamonds.

"I can't think of a more insignificant card," she said, as she stared at it, and laughed. "You choose."

He chose. It was a three of spades.

"Spades are bad," he said.

"But three," she said, "there's nothing wrong with a three. An ace or a queen, that's another matter, but there's nothing wrong with a three."

"I suppose not," he said. And smoothly, with a lovely gesture, he striped the cards across the table, in a perfect, evenly spaced row. She and Laurie gaped.

"That's *marvelous*," she said, once the shock of perception had worn off. "Do it again."

And he did it again, faultlessly.

"However do you *do* it?" she said, deeply impressed by this extraordinary talent.

"I've spent years of my life practicing it," he said, doing it again for them, and again, and then embarking on variations—circular roses, airy shuffles, concertinas.

"I saw a film once, when I was a boy, and there was a man in it who could do these things. It was a Western. I can't remember what it was called. The man was sitting in a corner of the saloon, doing these things with cards at a table. So I went away and practiced. Anyone could do it, if they put in as many hours as I put in. But who would? Who'd think it was worth it?"

"I love you," she said.

"The things I do aren't worth doing," he said, "but I like to do them."

"I like to see you do them," she said. "I like you to do them to me."

"It oughtn't to be a serious matter," he said, "but it is."

"It has always been thought to be so," she said.

He splayed the cards again, and this time he slightly misjudged the edge of the table, and some of them fell on the floor.

"If one's going to do it," he said, as he bent to pick them up, "one has to learn to do it well. There's nothing worse than doing such things badly."

"Not everyone has the talent," she said.

"No, that's true. But some that have don't care enough, and they do it badly through not caring. It's a question of priority."

"Do you care enough?" she asked him.

"I care for you," he said. "I care enough for you."

"My mother told me," she said, "when I was a girl, that one didn't need sexual experience, one would do it right if one was in love. Is that what all mothers say?"

"Not all," he said, "but most, I should think. They are right, too. But not many people care enough, and heaven help those who do."

"What do the others do?" she said. "Those who don't care?"

"They practice," he said. "They practice, those who haven't got inspiration."

"Do they get better, those who practice?" she asked.

"Some of them do, I should think," he said. "I wouldn't know. Would you?"

"Perhaps some of them get worse," she said.

"When I was a boy," he said, "there was a master at my school who could do a marvelous thing with a cigarette—throwing it in the air and catching it in his mouth. It looked lovely. I could never manage it. I could never get it right. I spent hours on that, too, but I could never do it."

"I think it's the symmetry I like," she said, gazing at the new card pattern that he had just nonchalantly created. "I find it—significant. But I don't know why. It's like rhyme in verse. It's no good, you know, rhymes in verse are a trivial matter, as trivial as playing cards, as pointless as fast cars. It's no good, any of it. It doesn't do any good. I try to justify it, I try so hard, but there isn't any justification, there isn't any meaning. It can't be important, poetry."

"Your poetry rhymes," he said.

"You noticed that much of it, then," she said, smiling faintly and distrustfully.

"One can see that from the way it's set out on the page," he said, disclaiming knowledge, or impertinent biographical curiosity. "One only has to skim one's eye down the last words of each line to see that."

"If I practiced poetry," she said, "do you think I'd ever be as good at it as you are at those cards?"

"I should think that poetry requires a native gift," he said.

"Just as your skills require a certain elegance," she said.

"Dexterity," he said. "All they require is dexterity."

"You're left-handed, though," she said.

"Ah well," he said, "it's a perverse talent, then, mine. A sinister gift."

She gazed at him: he amazed her, sometimes, by such inappropriate verbal felicities, of which she had always thought herself to possess a monopoly, and she wondered whether they came to him as they came to her through the consciousness, or whether they might not rise in him unsought, naturally, almost by accident, or from some unrevealed natural accord.

"You're lovely," she said. "You're lovely."

"I find you so too," he said.

She raised her eyebrows at him.

"Look," he said, "I'll show you my *coup de grâce*. Although the trouble with a *coup de grâce* is that it doesn't always work. But if I warn you now that it might not, you won't be too disaffected if it doesn't?"

"No," she said. "I'll take it on trust, that it might have done."

"You love me enough, then," he said. "Do you?"

"Of course," she said, wondering if it was so.

"There was a time when I might not have risked it," he said. "One can't take these risks too early in a relationship, you know."

"Of course not," she said, watching him as he divided the pack once more into two piles, and then held them, at a height, one pile in either hand, above the table. She watched his fingers, holding them, and the look on his face, the tightness of concentration in his mouth, and then, suddenly, when she was not expecting it, not knowing anyway what to expect, the cards fell, in an amazing careful rhythm, interleaving, dovetailing, one by one, joining and melting as they fell into one pack.

"Oh, no," she said, in a kind of polite disbelief, and he said, calmly, not showing his satisfaction, "It worked."

"Yes," she said.

"It's pretty, isn't it?" he said, gathering the cards up again. "It's called a waterfall."

"Oh, God," she said, "if I could do a thing like that I'd never feel incompetent at anything else ever again."

"It doesn't always work," he said. Though it didn't matter, this warning, it was irrelevant; since it had worked, in fact.

Later, in bed, when she turned to him after the long delays of the day, she heard her own voice cry out to him, inarticulate, compelled, from such depths of need that it frightened her. How could it not be serious, this matter? How could it be taken so lightly, and so dismissed? It was like death, like

birth: an event of the same order. Her cry was the cry of a
woman in labor: it broke from her and her body gathered
around it with the violence of a final pang. She had known it
would be like this: dreadful, insatiable, addictive, black. How
wisely she had avoided this destruction, with what self-preserv-
ing foreknowledge had she avoided it: and now it was too late,
she had let herself be led here tenderly by the hand, garlanded
with kisses, a sacrifice. And he would never be able to kill her,
she would thrash on there alone forever, and he would hate her
for it, he would hate her for having shown herself willing to
die, for the ugliness of the near lethal wound. Malcolm hated
her for it, and how much blacker would this hatred be, for the
desire that had preceded it. She had no faith, she had no faith:
he had taken her too far, and she would never get back to the
dry integrity she had once inhabited, she would be exiled forever in this painful space between desire and arrival. There
was nothing to do, no way to help herself: she lay there a victim, helpless, with the sweat standing out all over her body. In
her head it was black and purple, her heart was breaking, she
could hardly breathe, she opened her eyes to see him but she
could see nothing, and still she could not move but had to lie
there, tense, breaking, afraid, the tears unshed standing up in
the rims of her eyes, her body about to break apart with the
terror of being left alone right up there on that high dark painful shelf, with everything falling away dark on all sides of her,
alone and high up, stranded, unable to fall. Then suddenly but
slowly, for the first time ever, just as she thought she must die
without him forever, she started to fall, painfully, anguished,
but falling at last, falling, coming toward him, meeting him
at last, down there in his arms, half dead but not dead, crying

out to him, trembling, shuddering, quaking, drenched and drowned, down there at last in the water, not high in her lonely place: and she sank her teeth into his shoulder and then turned her head into the pillow and bit it and choked on it and wept and wept and finally, faintly, gently, shivered into silence.

He seemed to take it calmly, at the time, not wishing, perhaps, to disturb her by showing her too soon the degree of uncertainty that had led him there: he smoked a cigarette, and held her in the crook of his arm, and stroked her wet hair. But later, as she was falling asleep, he suddenly began to weep himself, and he held her to him, shaking, desperate to communicate, and what he was saying was, "You'll never know, how can you ever know how much I wanted you."

But she did know, for in his voice she caught the echo of her own desperation. He could not choose but want her: he had been as desperate to make her as she to be made. And he had done it: he had made her, in his own image. The throes, the cries, the pains were his; and he could no more dissociate himself from them than from his own flesh. She was his, but by having her he had made himself hers. She had feared, in that blackness, that it would have nothing to do with love, this place that he had brought her to, that it would be a cold and mechanical victory, the releasing of some spring in her body, as dry and accidental as loneliness: but how could he have brought her so far without some kind of passion? He wanted her, he too had sweated for this deliverance, he had thought it worth the risk: for her, for himself, he had done it. Indistinguishable needs. Her own voice, in that strange sobbing cry of rebirth. A woman delivered. She was his offspring, as he, lying there between her legs, had been hers.

I did not, even at the time, think myself born into happiness forever. It seemed, rather, like some inevitable doom, better known than unknown. I was never to find it easy; it wasn't easy. It was harder than that card trick that James had worked on for so many years, and I saw him fail with that more often than he succeeded. I was too old to find a state of innocence in such acts. My sexual salvation—for as such I saw it—merely stressed for me the dreadful, sickening savagery of what, for want of a better phrase, one could call human nature. What right had any deity to submit mortality to such obsessive, arbitrary powers? The meaningless violence of the world—the Lisbon earthquake, the *Titanic,* Aberfan—has given thought to better minds than mine, but at least these disasters are external, and can be ascribed to a hostile, ill-ordered universe: not so the violence of our own bodies, as unwilled, as foreordained, as the sliding of mountains, the uprooting of trees, the tidal waves of the sea. This violence is us: is me. Who ordains that one woman should die, and one be saved? What fatal conjunctions condemn people to torture each other for a lifetime? I saw myself saved, but at what a price, after what wrongs inflicted, while inflicting what wrongs? I had thought I had the grace to die quietly, but how I had misjudged myself. It had merely been a question of not wanting: and all my pride in not-having had been nothing, nothing but a defense against not-being-given. I had thought

I had behaved more honorably than Lucy, and now I saw that it was I that had been guilty: the crimes had been mine. When offered a chance of salvation, I had taken it: I had not cared who should drown, so long as I should reach the land. And yet I do not accuse myself of weakness of will. There had been nothing else to do. There had never been a question of choice. There had been nothing in me capable of choosing. I had done what I had to do, I had done what my nature was, what I would have done anyway, I had done what was to be. It is not myself I condemn, it is the nature of man. A fine evasion.

I wanted James so badly that I did not know what to do about it. There was only one thing to do, and that was to have him. Sometimes the grim logic of this made me feel quite cheerful, I must confess: the confrontation of my own total lack of volition was a comforting sight. For long stretches of time I would cease to think, I would submit myself to desire. I loved him, I loved everything about him, and I would tell myself that such love, being the only credit in the situation, must not be distrusted: that there was nothing to do but to endure it, until it died of its own accord. For I still, naïvely, expected it to die at any moment: I did not think we could keep it up. I was unfamiliar with the body's subterfuges, with its natural persistence, with its defense of its own ends. Sometimes—once a week or so—I would get myself into a total panic about the extent of my subjugation, and I even went so far as to look it up in a sexual textbook—an old-fashioned one, Havelock Ellis, I think—where I found the word "bondage," which seemed quite elegantly to describe my condition. I was in bondage. Having discovered this, I flipped through the rest of the book, gazing in amazement at all those curious masculine perversions, wishing I could attach myself to something more easily attainable than a living man. Perversions are cruel, but surely love is as cruel: it is too selective, too exclusive, too desperately mortal. It was James I wanted: nothing else would do.

There didn't seem to be very many female perversions in that book. Perhaps that was because it was old. Perhaps women have developed these things more recently as a result of emancipation. But love is nothing new. Even women have suffered from it, in history. It is a classic malady, and commonly it requires participants of both sexes. Perhaps I'll go mad with guilt, like Sue Bridehead, or drown myself in an effort to reclaim lost renunciations, like Maggie Tulliver. Those fictitious heroines, how they haunt me. Maggie Tulliver had a cousin called Lucy, as I have, and like me she fell in love with her cousin's man. She drifted off down the river with him, abandoning herself to the water, but in the end she lost him. She let him go. Nobly she regained her ruined honor, and ah, we admire her for it: all that superego gathered together in a last effort to prove that she loved the brother more than the man. She should have, ah well, what should she not have done? Since Freud, we guess dimly at our own passions, stripped of hope, abandoned forever to that relentless current. It gets us in the end: sticks, twigs, dry leaves, paper cartons, cigarette ends, orange peel, flower petals, silver fishes. Maggie Tulliver never slept with her man: she did all the damage there was to be done, to Lucy, to herself, to the two men who loved her, and then, like a woman of another age, she refrained. In this age, what is to be done? We drown in the first chapter. I worry about the sexual doom of womanhood, its sad inheritance.

In the summer, James went on his summer holidays with his family. Nothing could have been less surprising, I suppose, nor more to be expected, but I am afraid that nevertheless I took it very badly. I didn't see how I was going to get through two and a half weeks without him. Without him, what was I expected to do? As it was the summer—August, in fact—there was no nursery group, so I lacked even that distressing counter-anxiety. I knew that he would go away, that he had to go away, and yet I didn't see how I could possibly survive his absence. At times it seemed absurd to me, that something as innocent and apparently optional as a summer holiday could inflict on me such grievous wounds, and yet at other times it seemed equally absurd that an event as unreal and unacknowledged as a love affair could threaten to curtail a summer holiday. Neither event has much priority in the scale of eternity, I imagine. Looking back, it's hard now to remember that I speculated so little about the real, the significant, the imminent future: I thought only in terms of days and hours, of presence and absence. What did I care that I knew that James would never be mine, that I would never be able to claim him and have him, that he would never have me? I wanted him near, I did not want him to go away to Italy. If he had said to me that he would leave me for a month and then return to me forever, I would have died at the prospect: I had lost all foresight, all view of any end, I wanted him to be there, and I did not care what I lost in the future, so long as the present could be mine.

I got into such a lamentable state one afternoon about his projected holiday that he said he would see if he could shorten his absence by pleading evidently nonexistent work; this offer called out a little of the Maggie Tulliver in me, for with infinite self-sacrifice I protested against such a notion and swore that I would be quite all right and that he was not to worry. He was in a bad position, of course, because it was quite obvious that he had to go, and I was still sane enough to know that he probably wanted to go—for who would turn down a couple of weeks *en famille* in the sun?—and yet he could not plead to me the true and inexorable reasons for his departure. I didn't force him to do so: I didn't want to hear them any more than he wanted to say them. And yet I think he was glad to see that I would suffer, so I had to present him with an all-too-genuine assurance of my suffering. I wouldn't have liked him to think that I didn't care; I trusted him enough to think that he would like to know that I did.

They were going to Italy, to a place near Lerici. On the evening of their departure, Lucy rang. I had not spoken to her for some time and the sound of her voice made me feel slightly faint. She told me where they were going and for how long, information that I little needed, and then she asked me if I would be all right while they were away. It seemed such an odd inquiry, in view of the tenuous nature of our contact, that I wondered if it were fraught with implication. I said that of course I would be all right: what else could I say? Then she said, "You should be coming with us, you probably need a holiday as much as I do," and her light, inexpressive tone seemed full of meaning.

"Another year, perhaps," I said. "I'll come with you some other year."

"I'll send you a postcard," she said and rang off.

I assumed from this conversation that she knew something, if not all, of my feelings for James, and what his departure, even so briefly, would mean to me. I could think of no other reason why she should have rung. A postcard from her I might have expected, but nothing more.

The next morning, at the time when I knew they would have

left England, I felt so full of loss that I could hardly see. The air turned quite dark with it. I do not exaggerate. I had known in advance how long the time would seem—for what else had I to do with my time, what other distractions—but I had not foreseen this sensation of physical absence, this terror at the thought of the widening space, the hundreds of miles of land and water between us. It made me feel sick. On the first evening, I got down my atlas, and stared at the size of France and Italy, and then went off to the bathroom and vomited. Then I came downstairs again, and looked through the atlas until I found a page—a map of the whole of Europe, it was—that made Lerici look quite on London's doorstep, and that made me feel much better. He was, after all, less far away than he might have been. Less far than Tashkent, or Syracuse, or Athens. I thought of what he would be doing, and wondered if I felt any jealousy. I didn't. If he wasn't with me, I didn't care what he was doing. It was the lack of nearness that hurt me. The lack of proximity. It was so pure, my passion for him. Dazzling. White.

I had a calendar in the kitchen. It had a big picture of Woburn Abbey, signifying August; it was a calendar of the Stately Homes of England. The numbers of the days were down the right-hand side of the page, and there was a little red plastic box, clipped onto the page, that one would move downward, framing each day as it came. They departed on the fifth: they were due back on the twenty-second. I counted, on the evening of the fifth: I made it eighteen days. I counted again, trying to make it less, but it came out the same. So I said to myself, I won't include today, or the day they get back on, because the day they get back he'll surely ring: and I tried again. This time I got sixteen for my answer, and I felt quite clever.

The next morning, the first thing I did, as I was making my coffee and Laurie's cornflakes, was to move the red clip. The sixth looked considerably nearer the twenty-second than the fifth had done. It cheered me. But it left me with nothing to do for the rest of the day. So the next morning I made myself leave it until after breakfast. I became obsessed by that calendar, by its relation to time, by the way that red mark descended, eating up the hours, the long days. I tried infinite ways of counting. I counted the hours, I multiplied by sixty and turned it into minutes, but the result of this last sum came out so astronomically high that even the consolation of watching it diminish on the face of my watch did not reassure me. I assessed the numbers of Mondays, the numbers of Tuesdays—appalled when it was three, cheered when it was two. I told myself how much better it would be when I was past the halfway mark: after the dangerous thirteenth, the watershed, it would be easier, it would be half endured, the time would have been dignified by my mere survival. In my sleep, I saw that calendar. It was imprinted on my vision. It must, in some way, have satisfied me, to see my sentence so embodied: there is something consoling in representation, in analogy. In that calendar I saw the abstraction of time delivered to my eyes, just as in James's card manipulations I thought I saw some precarious embodiment of symmetry. I have seen it too, this sense of abstraction made visual, in a speedometer of a car I once was driven in, where speed was measured by an extending diminishing red line, like the line of mercury in a thermometer. Measurements of health, of time, of speed: an assertion against infinity, a cutting down of limitless extents.

It was at the end of the first week that I suffered most

acutely. I had, on the fifth day, received a card from James
with tinted harbor and boats and blue sky; it said:

> *This is where Shelley died, my darling, but I trust I shan't
> follow him. When I get back I will take you away with me
> to some cold northern place. If you still remember me.*

It was the first of his handwriting I had received, and I gazed
at it with such ardor, rereading it a hundred times, taking it
with me wherever I went: I thought it would give me enough
to think about for another week. But in the morning I under-
went some kind of reaction, because when I looked at the position of the day upon the calendar (the tenth, it was, oh God,
I'll never forget those dates, they were marked on my brain
and retina too dangerously, sometimes I knew I'd live to hate
him for all the love I'd spent on him; it seemed that I had made
no progress, that there was still an eternity to be endured. I remember the feeling of threatening chill that overcame me. I
spent a long time washing up the dishes from breakfast and
supper the night before, handling each knife with care, and
then with equal care I made the beds and washed the nappies
and made a custard for lunch: but despite my care I could not
prolong these activities, and by eleven I had left myself nothing to do. Laurie was playing with two black children in the
sandpit in the garden; the baby was asleep. I stood at the
kitchen sink, my hands still wet from my last chore, and I felt
it take possession of me: blind terror, nothingness stronger
than myself, blackness. It must be thus that I shall surrender
to long-defied death. I tried to weep, to deafen that silence with
my own cries, but I could not do it. I stared at the face of my
watch, and the hands did not move. They had ceased to move.

Time had stuck. One hears of the eternity of delight experienced by saints and visionaries: I would swear that I have experienced an eternity of nothingness. An eternity, when the thought of five minutes more of time to endure, let alone a lifetime of it, seemed an impossibility beyond the reach of effort. I believe that such states must be common: in my waking moments. I tell myself that they must be common, that all are subject to them, though I cannot see the signs of it in their faces, but when I am alone there I know that it is not so, that I suffer uniquely, incommunicably, without a hope of parallel. Those who go there will know where it is that I mean: though I, not there, writing calmly in recollection, can no longer, mercifully, recall.

I forget what rescued me from that occasion. The milkman perhaps, or Laurie with sand in his eyes, or the baby's cries. I know that for the rest of the day I was subdued with alarm lest I should walk suddenly into nothingness once more. I tried to occupy myself with small distractions, looking at my watch every five minutes, hoping each time that by some miracle an unsuspected hour might have passed. As children, Lucy and I used to play together the game of naming our worst fears: I, prophetic, usually chose solitary confinement; she, more evasive, chose rats. It seemed that I had done my best to invoke for myself a suitable punishment for whatever crime it was that I had unwittingly committed or inherited. I suppose that I was glad of my children, for at least they provided me with jobs that had to be done and words that had to be spoken: and yet in other ways they accentuated my distress, for I knew that I had no right to impose my states upon them, that I had no right to allow them to see me in such a grim light. At least those who are truly isolated can suffer for their isolation in innocence. I felt that mine was intimately and harmfully revealed, and to those that I would most have liked to preserve from it. As I went to bed that night I felt so bad on their account that I resolved to take action: I said that the next day I would take them out, an enterprise so alarming, this, to me, that I hoped that it would not only amuse them but would also do me the service of terrifying me so much that it would drive out that other terror, that it would prevent me from gazing so foolishly and endlessly at my motionless watch face and my accusing calendar.

Some mothers, I know, take their children out frequently, and without ill results. I was not one of them. I used to be quite brave, as a girl, and not averse to fairly dangerous pursuits such as climbing and riding, but my first pregnancy bequeathed me a physical timidity so acute that I could not shake it off: I was afraid of strain, afraid of transport, afraid of unfamiliar places. James knew this, and when he took me out he took me out as an invalid. I was so grateful to James, for Laurie's sake, for those compulsory excursions, because although I deceived myself a good deal of the time into thinking that a child of Laurie's age did not need variety, I knew that I was wrong. He would grow too like me, I knew, living too close to me, pacing the same yard, infected by my diseases. James took us out in his shiny fast car: out of our unnatural nearness. And in a sense his example had given me a little courage: without him, without the impulse of his loss, I would never have made the efforts that I made.

I took them to the zoo. I had been promising the zoo for months, ever since Laurie had learned to say the word. He had a book with animals in, a zoo book, and he knew all the names—giraffes, elephants, camels, panda bears, monkeys. I thought he ought to see them, but I could not think of a way to get him there. I could not face taking him on a bus, with the baby and the pushchair, and he himself still in need of a helping hand. I told myself that people did not take babies and pushchairs on buses, although naturally even I had seen plenty of evidence to the contrary. I spent most of the morning worrying about this carefully constructed anxiety, dwelling on its disagreeable possibilities: it made the time pass quite quickly. And then, as I was giving the baby her lunch-time feed, I hit upon the solution: I would walk. It was not, after all, so far: I could go along Bishop's Bridge Road and through St. John's Wood and across the top of the park. I looked at the map; it looked a long but perfectly possible walk. It would have a double advantage: it would get me there without involving me in any human incident or contact, and it would tire me so that I would sleep better at night. Boredom had been driving me to bed so early of late that I found it hard to sleep when I got there.

A walk would do me good. And then I could come home in a taxi. It must be possible, I said to myself, to put two children and a pushchair into a taxi, although I had never tried it before. Lucy, I knew, used to take her three children all over the place, dragging them into town, into shops, into restaurants, on trains to the seaside, to Battersea funfair, and none of them seemed any the worse for these excursions. I must make the effort. I must subdue my nature and make the effort. There is something so ludicrous about efforts to subdue trivial phobias, unfounded fears: even the most heroic victory on this field has a quality of the pitiable. When we see a woman walk along the street, how do we know she is not some brave agoraphobe, flinching from the brutal sky? Some people are afraid of insects, of water, of green leaves. Of the very air. They fight against unseen impediments to perform the most simple human acts—speaking, hearing, making love. They expose themselves to their own ridicule, in efforts to avoid a stammer or a fit of impotence. And yet we dare to judge each other, we dare to suppose a norm. We continue to live, as though life were a practical possibility, as though we could know something of one another.

I had a double pushchair. I put the children side by side. Bianca, now seven months old, was as yet hardly able to sit, so I had to prop her up and wedge her in with pillows and secure her with straps. Luckily she had the most mild and placid nature and she sat there smiling proudly, unperturbed. I supplied Laurie with some Dinky cars, hoping he would not amuse himself by running them too violently up and down her fat legs, and at about two o'clock we set off. I began to feel uneasy as we emerged from my familiar span of territory, but not sufficiently uneasy to prevent myself from glancing still, every five minutes, at my watch, to check upon how near I was getting to James's return. My anxiety about the unfamiliar had become secondary, it seemed self-induced, artificial, less engrossing than it once had been: it was hardly strong enough to counteract my hopeless, hopeless need for absent James. Threatened suddenly by a slow but fatal illness, or transported magically to the Taj Mahal, it would still have been at my watch that I would have glanced, for reassurance or dismay. Obsessive by nature, I had merely replaced one obsession by another; though the word "merely" is unjust, invidious, for some obsessions are salutary, and I knew as I walked past the iron-girdered half-moons of the bridge that I was saved, I was released from my enclosure, I was able to go out now with the children into the sun, because I was no longer bending upon these trivial fears and excursions the whole force and weight of my ridiculously powerful passions. I had found, in James, reciprocation: I had found a fitting, unrejecting object for desire. One is not saved from neurosis, one is not released from the fated pattern, one must walk it till death and walk through those recurring darknesses; but sometimes, by accident or endeavor (I do not know which, in writing this I try to decide which), one may find a way of walking that predestined path more willingly. In company, even: one might find a way of being less alone, and thus confining the dangerous outward spreading of emotion, the dark contaminating stain, which when undirected and unaccepted kills and destroys all around it—children, shopkeepers, parents, husbands, all. My need for James had not saved me from myself, but it had perhaps saved others from me.

We reached the park in the hot middle of the afternoon. I had not been to the zoo for years, I had no idea it would be so expensive. And as I waited in the short queue I noticed that there was a turnstile, and I did not see how I was going to get the pushchair through it. My heart started to thump quite violently, awaiting crazy official exclusion, but of course when I got there they opened the gates for me as though it were something quite natural—as it was, for as soon as I calmed down and looked around I could see that the place was swarming with pushchairs, that every other member of the queue was possessed of one, that I was in no way uniquely encumbered. Logic might have indicated that this would be so, but I have little faith in logic. I await the impossible, the irrational, the grotesque, a zoo without children, love from an empty heaven.

I must say I had forgotten how unnatural some animals are. If I had remembered, I might have been more chary about introducing Laurie to them, but luckily he took them in his stride—all except the elephants, whose sheer size drew from him screams of horror. I passed them by in haste. I do not like the zoo. I still feel sorry for the animals, as I used to feel as a child: I feel they are caged and bored and lonely. This may be a pathetic enough fallacy, but I can't get rid of it. And this time, pausing in front of the gorilla, I noticed that it was sitting on its small square floor idly tossing up and down, up and down, a piece of straw from its bedding. From time to time it sighed. It was sick with true human boredom, that animal, I would swear it. The crowd was laughing a little at these familiar, recognizable gestures, but nervously, without pleasure, without amusement. After the gorilla I had had enough: I escaped into the peaceful dark aquarium, and watched the soulless fishes, ignorantly, happily unaware of their glass confines. In the aquarium I looked at my watch. It was five o'clock. It was time to go home. The afternoon was over. It was only seven hours until the next day. As I walked back toward the exit, from the far end of the aquarium, my arms heavy from carrying the baby, past the small illuminated watery windows, I felt a sense of curious shaded peace, a knowledge that the time would pass, and with it my pain, a knowledge that I could not stop time any more than I could hasten it, that I had merely to wait once more to submit myself to deliverance: I was through, it would be better, it could not get worse.

I caught a taxi home with no difficulty. Getting the children into it was rather a problem, as the driver had clearly no intention of helping me. I put Bianca on the back seat while I folded the pushchair, but Laurie, in his eagerness to help, unfortunately managed to knock her off it, and she cried very angrily all the way home, for once she had started to cry she could no longer distinguish pain from approaching hunger, and she would not be comforted until I got her into the house and fed her. But this fit of crying did not too much distress me: I was thinking about the afternoon post. And when I got back, there, like a reward for bravery, was another postcard, with another view of the harbor, saying:

We'll go North, you and me, and have a look at the midnight sun. The weather here is too good by half. You and I will suffer together, darling.

The rest of the time passed. It was never as bad again as it had been on that sixth day. As the red mark dropped into the late teens—eighteen, nineteen—I even began to worry about the shortness of the time left, and wondered if I could bear to see him again, and what it would be like. I continued to search my small segment of the outside world for signs and portents that would bring him nearer to me, and I was horribly affected by news of a coach crash on the road between La Spezia and Genoa—a stretch that I knew James and Lucy were shortly to cover. There were fifteen dead, all from Lancashire. I knew that their death had rendered that stretch of road, at least, innocuous, for statistics would not permit any more British deaths upon it in the month of August, but what about the remaining 805 miles? As the true countdown started, I tried to follow their conjectural homeward route upon my atlas, reproaching myself bitterly for not having demanded from James each detail of his journey, each inch of his intended way. I should have foreseen my meticulous anxiety, my earnest desire to gaze at the printing of the names of the towns through which he passed. On the day of their return to England I found myself ringing the car-ferry service at Victoria to inquire the times of all possible crossings: as I spoke to the woman at the other end it occurred to me that I had forgotten the question of European Time, and that a whole hour's grace had been added to me in my calculations: I had been given a whole hour for free out of two and a half weeks of penal expectation. It felt like a reprieve.

I recount these things as proof of my madness. In extenuation. As indictment. Perhaps merely as a record, in case I should forget. And it was worse, it was worse than I can ever say.

That night, at about nine, he rang. He rang me from a public call box, and at the sound of his voice it seemed that all was absolved, all past, all over, though I knew that I would bear the scars of such severance forever, as I bear on my body the scars and patched wounds of maternity. We exchanged soft words, familiar names, silences, assurances, eternal vows: vows that could have been made as easily, perhaps, over several hundred miles by Subscriber Trunk Dialing, but we had never thought of that palliative to separation, and anyway it was not so much the sound of his voice that I wanted, it was the knowledge that he was standing there, in a small red kiosk of which I knew the exact location, less than eight miles from where I was. He said that he would come to see me the next day, and I said to him, drive carefully, don't die before you get here; and he laughed and said what about that coach crash on the road to Genoa, and had I too interpreted it as a portent of safety. What an irrational, superstitious world we inhabited: I see it now but I cannot even now repudiate it.

◆ The next morning he came, as he had promised. He was wearing sunglasses and a fancy Italian shirt and he was brown, dark brown from weeks of sun, the skin of his chest burned into an ancient-looking blackness. She stood in the doorway and watched him as he got out of his car. She had feared perhaps that at the sight of him her love would in some way fail her, or that he himself would be disfigured, visibly disfigured by the marks of her unnatural passion, because she had always known her own emotions to be destructive, disproportionate, a menace to their object: she had feared that she might have destroyed him by too much love. But he had survived her attachment: he stood there, quite whole, not yet maimed or blinded by her need, and when he touched her, taking her hand, taking her into the kitchen and sitting her down, she could tell from the touch of him that he was still within her reach, that his restoration to her was entire, and not merely a sign that he had in some less evident manner escaped her.

All that they could do was to talk, because of the children. "I've thought of you so much," he said to her, when they had become used to the sight of one another again. "I've thought of you sitting there, exactly there, and I hoped you were being pale and good and thinking of me. I did so hope you wouldn't manage to distract yourself by getting out into the sun."

"What would I have done in the sun?" she said.

"I'd have liked to have locked you up in here," he said. "I'd like to put you under a stone, to make sure you'd stay where I wanted you."

"Cruel, you are," she said, smiling.

"You're not allowed to go out except with me," he said.

"I didn't try to," she said.

"You had to sit here and wait for me. You had to sit here and miss me. I hope you were sad enough, while I was away?"

"Oh God," she said, laughing. "I was so sad, I don't think even you would quite like it if you knew. You'd think I was mad."

"Don't you believe it," he said. "The sadder the better, as far as I'm concerned. You couldn't do it enough, for me."

"I don't know how you could put up with it," she said, amazed at his acceptance of her dreadful tribute.

"I like it," he said. "It's what I want."

"It's all right," she said, "having what one wants."

"It's worth waiting for," he said, and touched her cheek.

Then, when they had had a cup of tea he went back to the car and brought her a bottle of Campari, which they could not resist opening, and a battery-powered jeep for Laurie. It would run up a gradient of forty-five degrees, and they sat there drinking and watching as it climbed over books and over plates and saucers. She did not like to ask him about Italy, in case he tormented her by telling her, and she did not think she could take it, so instead they talked of the symptoms of their separation, a subject that could be neatly abstracted from the surrounding facts. "I missed you so much," she finally said, laughing, slightly drunk. "I missed you so much, because of all the things you do for me. The iron broke, I dropped the iron one day, and there was nobody to change the plug for me. I need you so badly, I can't get on without you at all." And so he changed the plug on the iron for her promptly, frowning slightly at the wires, bending earnestly over it, his hair bleached from the sun, as the jeep ran over his foot. "I love you, I love you, I need you so badly," she said.

"I wish it were nighttime," he said, not looking up, slightly clumsy with the screwdriver from the Campari. And she, who had never had the courage to ask him such a question before, who had always waited for his unpredictable dispositions of his time, said, as though it were the easiest question to ask, "Will you stay?"

"Of course I'll stay," he said. "How could I leave you?"

"You left me for three whole weeks," she said.

"That was different," he said, looking up at her, the job concluded. "Look, I've done it now."

"Thank you," she said, politely, and tried to embark upon the last week's ironing, but it was all parched and dry, and she burned a hole in a nylon shirt of Laurie's, and abandoned the task, and sat down again, to do nothing for the whole of the rest of the day. In the middle of the afternoon, as they sat there still immobile, still transfixed, he said to her suddenly, "Will you let me take you away, some time?"

"Of course," she said.

"I'll take you to Norway," he said. "How would you like to go to Norway?"

"Why Norway?" she said, not thinking he meant it.

"I don't know. It seemed a good place to take you. We could go and see my grandfather. It's my ancestral home, you know, it's a place I ought to go to, I've never been in my life. It will probably speak to me, it is my soul's country after all, I shall probably have a lovely revelation of myself amongst all those fjords and conifers. Say you'll come, you've got to say you'll come."

"You know I'll come," she said, weakly shrugging her shoulders to demonstrate her servitude.

"I like the idea of those long winter evenings. Like that night when your baby was born. It pulled an ancestral heart string, the sight of you sitting in that bed, and the snow falling outside. That's why I'll love you forever."

"Liar," she said.

"Anyway," he said, "it's bound to be better than Italy. Italy's dreadful. It's full of idiots like me flashing around in their stupid cars just like I do."

"Too many Maserati?"

"Too many Maserati by bloody half there were," he said, smiling at her gently with that ironic gentle defeated smile of self-knowledge, presenting his weakness as a gift, a shared gift. "Crawling with them, it was."

"And it won't be like that in Norway?"

"Certainly not," he said. "It's a serious place, Norway." And he looked at her, with calculation, and said, "And I have to go, anyway. On business. So you see how convenient it would be."

And thus he offered her the theme of their conversations for the weeks to come. She raised objections to this projected journey—how could she not?—but he overruled them, calmly, persistently: of course they could not leave the children behind, they would take the children, it would do them good, it would be their summer holiday; of course his grandfather would not object to her presence, and anyway they could pass her off as Lucy, it was so many years since he had seen Lucy that he would never be able to tell the difference; no, of course his grandfather wouldn't write to tell James's mother about it, he only wrote to her once a year at Christmas and by Christmas he would have forgotten, and anyway he wrote in Norwegian, which his mother had forgotten how to read. When she expressed doubts about Norway itself, he purchased her a Baedeker and read it aloud to her in bed, trying to arouse enthusiasm for the rain and wooden houses and the scenery and the fish soup. She in turn attempted frivolously to dismay him by news of the prohibition laws and the driving regulations and the alleged danger (on account of wolves) of solitary walking. They lay there, reading these details as though they were some manual of love, envisaging a dozen appropriate ends, and laughing so much that from time to time she had to bury her head in the pillow to prevent herself from waking the children. She took it as a theme for fantasy: a dud project, delicately introduced by him to disguise their immobility, their lack of progress, the impossibility of their ever sharing a journey or a life or even a common interest; an extension of their wholly speculative connection. How could he think that he could take her so far away? How could she ever have him for a whole fortnight of time?

"You're coming with me, aren't you?" he would say.

And she would say, "Yes, of course, where you go I have to go."

"Would you come with me to Australia?" he would say, and she would nod, and smile.

"It will be so lovely," he said, "going to bed with you, and waking up with you in the morning. We do that so rarely now. Will you like it too?"

"Yes, yes," she said. "That's what I would like."

But amazingly enough, he really meant it. I don't know how long it took me to realize that he really meant it, seriously, in earnest: that he was really going, and that he meant to take me with him. I had been so careful with him for so long, so reluctant to try to exchange any of the promises that we pledged each other into the currency of real life; but now it seemed that he was asking me to trust him, to redeem those pledges, to see what they would purchase in the transactions of the world. No more toy money, but chips, worth five-pound notes: those dialogues in bed were going to be coined, I was intended to see the conifers and the grandfather and the midnight sun.

I think that I first became sure when he asked to see my passport. I found it, finally, and it was out of date.

"You'll have to do something about this quickly," he said, and he stood over me, while I rang the Foreign Office to see how long it would take to renew it. Mad he was, but not so mad. He took me straight down to the bank on the corner to get a renewal form, and I filled it in as he stood over me. We were both seized with a fearful panic when we saw that we had to obtain the father's consent to include the two children, and I would have given up at this point, had it not been for his insistence, as I had given up over the technicalities of sex, but he made me ring Petty France again, and when I had explained my dilemma, in tears of distress, the girl at the other end said that I had been given an out-of-date form, and that the ruling had been changed exactly two months earlier, and that maternal consent alone was now considered adequate. I thanked her as though it had been arranged for me alone.

The next day he showed me the booking. We were going on the ferry from Newcastle to Bergen. I gazed at the piece of paper: it was a real document, not a forgery, not a figment of my imagination. He really meant us to go. Fantasy had somehow solidified into fact. I looked at the date: the twelfth of October, it said. Evidence. Commitment. When one books a berth in advance, he said, one has to go and sleep in it.

Clearly, I spent a good deal of time worrying about his true motives for this journey, once I had accepted it as a reality: he said he wanted the time to be with me, and yet he also said that he had to go anyway to deliver a car to a friend, so I could not tell whether love was a cover for business, or business for love. Perhaps he did not know himself. He was taking a new car, an Aston Martin, to a friend of his in a place called Voss, and he told me some fairly convincing story about the financial benefit that would accrue through the saving of purchase tax or export duty or something of the sort. I could tell, innocent though I was, that the transaction was fairly dishonest, but I could also see that unless he and his friend had arranged some system of splitting the profit the advantage would be less for James than for his Norwegian customer. I couldn't think what anyone wanted an Aston Martin for in Norway, where the roads are all mountainous, and the maximum speed is something like fifty miles an hour, but I had learned to accept the fact that cars have virtues which are quite unrelated to their practical utility. On balance it did seem that James's determination to go must be in some way connected with me, and that the business arrangement, if not subsidiary, would certainly not have been undertaken had I not existed: I wondered why he wanted to get me away, and what significance the actual destination had. I found it hard to believe that he had never been to Norway before. I had some dim impression of knowledge that he had, which I finally connected with the fact that I knew that Lucy had once been to Bergen because she had sent me a postcard of it, years before, and I had assumed that she must have gone there with James. I looked for the card, not without hope, because I never threw away anything that Lucy wrote. I did not consciously preserve her rare letters and cards, but I did consciously refrain from discarding them, with the consequence that my desk drawers, kitchen cupboards, and dressing table all contained sacred scraps of her writing. I found the postcard with revealing ease: it was underneath a pile of old petticoats in the bottom of my bedroom cupboard. And it was of Bergen, but it was not with James that she had been there. It was with a man called Richard (unidentifiable, one of many Richards) and the card said:

> Can't think what we're doing here. It's all wooden, and it rains all day. Would you ring James Otford for me, FRE 6654, tell him I'll be home on the third. Love, Lucy and Richard.

I stared at this historic piece of card: its postmark showed a date in the year before her marriage. Lucy, when there were no observers, no possible knocks on the door, sent postcards to advertise her lapses, her passing passions: a true collector, proud of quantity as well as quality. James Otford. I recollected that I had tried once to ring him, and that he hadn't been in, so her message had gone undelivered. Thus did I miss my first encounter with James.

I wondered what erotic journey of hers James wished to re-travel with me, and why he wanted to present me to his grand-father as his wife. I could not tell if these tricks of impersona-tion and misrepresentation had significance, or if they were merely moves in a game, arbitrary, in themselves meaningless, forced upon us by the confined area of play: just as I could not tell whether James's desire to see his home country was a frivol-ity or an emotion too inarticulate and serious to impart. The pattern was so clear, its meaning so obscure. I suspected, being suspicious, that the role I played might lack dignity, but I did not care, I did not care what wrongs of possession he made good on my body as long as it was I myself that was there, my own self that he was holding. I loved him. I did not care what use he made of me: I wanted to love him, love was what I used him for.

At moments, naturally, in the time before our departure, I was overcome with horror at the thought of the folly of the enterprise: suicidal, I thought it, and whatever would the children do on the boat? I confessed these fears to James and he laughed at them. He was right, too. Nobody had dragged me across Northern Europe in a sports car with my mother's lover when I was a child, and I hadn't turned out too well despite such protection and restraint. A wreck, I was, an innocent wreck. "They'll like it," James said. "The baby won't even no-tice, and Laurie likes cars, he'll think it's fun."

"Of course," I said, soothed by his sophistries, too willing to be persuaded. I had worried for long enough about shutting them up with me in a house alone: should I now worry about taking them out of it? I remember one evening that I suddenly, half asleep, gripped hold of James's shoulder and started to shake him and said, "Darling, I can't go, what about Laurie's nursery group?" but by some miracle I heard the ludicrous earnest note in my own voice, and I was able to laugh with him because it all seemed so pointless, the true barriers between myself and what I wanted being so low, and the artificial ones so laughably fragile and inappropriate (I'm so sorry, I can't marry you tomorrow, it's the day the laundry van calls; I'm so sorry, says the dying woman, gazing down at the red spilling from her, I'm so sorry, I'm making an awful mess of your ambulance). What harm would it do Laurence and Bianca to visit Norway? If it wrecked their small minds forever, could I be answerable? Since there's no winning, I said to myself, lying there, I might as well lose after my own fashion.

I did not, of course, tell anyone that I was going away: there was nobody to miss me. All that I had to do was to take the phone off the hook so that my parents or parents-in-law would think that it was out of order, and I would evade all possible detection. As the time drew nearer, I grew sick with expectation: I wanted so badly to go that I imagined all possible causes of prevention, inspecting the children hourly for illnesses, throwing myself into torments of apprehension by the discovery of a small unidentifiable spot on the back of Laurie's neck, pondering nervously each twinge of my own back, each clearing of my throat. I was so far from rational behavior that I think I would have gone on that journey in no matter how poor a state of health: I would have taken my children had they been covered with measles. So, since I was going anyway, I prayed that I might be spared this final confrontation with my weakness, that I might avoid the guilt and the risks that I was prepared to confront, if need be.

I wonder, now, if I had foreseen the hazard that so nearly prevented us, or whether I had, in all my calculations, re-

pressed this one anxiety. Because, three days before we were
due to sail, when even I had begun to count on our departure,
Malcolm rang. I was so little expecting to hear him that at first
I could not think who he was: his voice sounded strained and
strangely altered, as well it might. So, in my own ears, did my
own voice in reply. He asked me how I was, and how the children were, and I answered coldly, monosyllabic, unable to
think of what to say, unable in any way to manage the conflicting flood of emotion that swamped me, unable to grasp the
implications of his call. I could not tell what he wanted of me,
or why he had rung. I could not think of any possible response. And then, suddenly, across the halting silence, I heard
him say that he was coming home, that he had been meaning
to ring me for some time, and that he was coming home that
very night. I listened to what he said, and then I heard myself
say, very flatly,

"You can't."

I think he must have been glad to hear this familiar note
of opposition: he felt himself on familiar territory, he knew
what to say.

"Why can't I?" he said. "It's my home, isn't it, I pay for it,
they're my children, aren't they, you can't keep me out of my
own home."

"It's not your home, it's mine," I said.

"It's mine, too," he said, and he embarked then upon a long,
amazing, and quite uncharacteristic speech about his regrets
about leaving me and neglecting the children (interspersed
with odd remarks about his guilt at having left Laurie with me
because I wasn't fit to look after him or any child) and how he
recognized his duty to me even if I didn't recognize mine to
him. Although aggressive in tone he was clearly conciliatory

in intention, his kindly instincts deformed, as so often in the past, by our mutual guilt. I found myself, selfishly, in self-protection, wincing from each kind word and generous sentiment, attaching myself passionately to each moment of cruelty and offense, storing up each dangerous phrase as armament, waiting for him to offer the final condemnation from his own mouth, waiting for the unforgivable, so that I could avoid any painful, exhausting, impossible threat of forgiveness. I wanted his cruelty: I did not want him back, the last thing that I wanted was his return, and I tried to deafen my ears to the note of ugly, resentful pleading that informed even his worst abuse. I could not bear to acknowledge that I had done this to him, that I was the object of this appeal, so I hardened my heart to him and the years we had endured together. I hardened my heart: a crime for which there is no forgiveness. I dismissed his appeal: I extended him no credit. He did not plead well but the lack of skill in his arguments was irrelevant, for I knew, even in my cold heart, what he was asking, and I knew that he had a right to ask it, whatever ill-chosen words and tones he found to ask with. Though I may say that there was one argument he could have used effectively, and had he thought of it, had he himself had the tenderness to think of it, I would have been lost, I would have surrendered: he could have said that he wanted to see Bianca, and I would not have been able to refuse. I could not have kept him from the sight of his own daughter. But he did not say it, he did not even think of saying it as blackmail. What bastards men are to care so little for their own children, to neglect them even to the extent of forgetting to use them in an argument. I kept thinking, as he shouted at me, that he was about to use her name, and I prayed that he would not: I prayed that he would prove himself inhuman, that he would commit this technical offense so that I could cherish his neglect and hide myself behind it.

When he had finished shouting at me, all that I thought of was to defend myself. I could not have him back, no matter how great his desperation (and he sounded desperate, I cannot deny it) because I had to have James, I had to go to Norway with James. But I did not know what to say, I did not know how to hurt him so badly that he would not want to come near me. However, inspiration was lent me: I heard my own voice speaking as though I were another woman, a woman in a play, with lines that had to be spoken, in phrases that I had not known I knew.

"I suppose your new woman's got tired of you, then?" I aid. "I suppose she's as anxious to get rid of you as I was? Perhaps you gave her as good cause, the same cause to kick you out?"

"Don't let's drag her into it," he said, in a feverish effort to remain calm.

"*I'm* not dragging her into it," I said, my voice rising in volume, "it wasn't me that dragged her into it in the first place, was it? What's the matter with her? Has she deafened you yet with her piano?"—and so on, and so on, in a tone of nagging, petulant bitchiness that I was ashamed to find so accessible to me, so easy, so simple to reproduce. I went on for a long time, progressing from the childish and ridiculous to the horrific, flinging at him the most dreadful insults, the most appalling language and sexual abuse, saying in fact all the things that I had not said for so long, that I had kept myself from saying and thinking. I managed to curb myself only when I realized that he might think I had gone completely mad and feel compelled therefore to come and rescue the children from my clutches,

which proves that I still had an end in view and was not abus-
ing him merely because I could not prevent myself from doing
so. Though which would have been more honorable, restraint
or complete abandon, I cannot say. I was dishonored, I could
tell it, beyond hope of recovery. How could I have hoped to be
spared this confrontation with my offense? In the end, when I
had said everything I could think of, he yelled at me that I had
done my best to destroy his whole life, but that I hadn't succeeded and I never would, and then he rang off. Ten minutes
later, before I had stopped shaking with fright, he rang once
more, and went through the same revolution of concilia-
tion and abuse, and reached the same conclusion, in the same
words. When it was over I left the phone off the hook, unable
to take it again, and I went to bed. I was terrified by my suspicion that my violence of reaction had not been motivated
wholly by my need to preserve my future—my nonexistent,
brief future—with James, but in part at least by real sexual
jealousy, a real anger at the thought that Malcolm had managed to escape me to live with another woman, and a musical
woman at that, a piano-playing woman. I was ashamed of myself for these ignoble emotions, and alarmed, too, at the
thought of my increased responsibility for Malcolm should
he ever find out about James. How could I take him back when
I had so betrayed him? What passions would he suffer when he
found that I, who had seemed already removed from him beyond any human reach, had removed myself and defected yet
more completely, had extended by yet more miles the frozen
wastes between us? It would have been as though he should
discover that one long dead to him, unconscious, vegetable,
merely breathing, had died the second true and final death; or
worse, had been revived, restored to a new life where there

was no memory of the old, no recollection of those who had sat by the bedside by the mute flesh, administering to its un-responsive cells, feeding continuation into the senseless veins and money into the disinterested bank account. What right had such a corpse to wake, and breathe, and walk? How could he endure the sight of my ghostly resurrection? I had thought that I had done him all the harm that was in me, but now I could see that there was yet more that could be endured, yet more that could be inflicted. I had hoped that he would never know, but how could I keep the knowledge from him?

In the morning, he rang again. He rang, on and off, all day. During that day we must have exchanged every remark ever exchanged by such a couple in such a situation: after so many speechless months we left nothing unsaid. We even had moments of *attendrissement,* when, appalled by the words we were saying, we choked into silence. But I did not allow the silences to last: I forced myself into hostility, because I could not risk losing James for a moment of regret, for human-ity, for kindness' sake. I told Malcolm that it was no good, that I would never see him again, that I would divorce him, that if he came near me I would kill myself; and at nine o'clock in the evening, worn out by his dreadful persistence, I once more took the phone off. I did not want to do this, as I was expecting James to ring, and quite apart from the fact that I could hardly for any reason however serious forgo the hopes of speaking to him, I was worried about the ways in which he might inter-pret my unavailability. Perhaps he might think that I had taken fright at the thought of our projected journey; perhaps he might think, rashly, impossibly, that I had deserted him. I sat by the disconnected instrument for an hour, biting my nails, and then I replaced the receiver: it rang, as though human and responsive, as though it had been waiting, within a minute of my putting it down, and it was not Malcolm, it was James. He asked me who had been talking to me for so long, and I said my mother. He asked me how I was, and whether I still loved him, and such idle things, and then he said that he would see me the following evening, and rang off. He was to spend the next night with me: we were to set off the morning after, for Newcastle, whence we were to sail. I had hardly replaced the receiver from James's call when Malcolm once more rang. I disconnected him without speaking, and went to bed. But when I got to bed I could not sleep: I lay there, ill with anxiety, wracked by remorse, obsessed by neurotic calculations of the quantities of children's clothes, bottles, nappies, and medicaments I would have to pack, and tormented by some vague and doubtless hysteric pain in my left leg. I was afraid, as I used to be afraid as a child on Christmas Eve, that I would not live until the morning: desire would kill me, I thought, without external aid. I kept repeating to myself that line from *Romeo and Juliet* that says, These violent delights have violent ends. I could not get it out of my head.

In the morning, with the children around, I felt better, and started to pack. I was soothed, too, by the silence of the telephone, which I had reconnected, unable to endure the suspicion that if I did not do so I would miss some final plan or final rejection from James. If he had rung at lunch time to tell me that the whole thing had been a mere dream, with no more reality than a children's game, that he had never intended to take me anywhere, that I had been mad to believe we were to go, I would I think have accepted his words as the truth, and condemned myself as the insane victim of my own desires, so confused was I by the intensity of my emotion. But he did not

ring to say these things, nobody rang; and at six o'clock, just
as I was giving the children their cereal, he arrived. I had to go
out with him to admire the new car: it was a black Aston
Martin convertible, "specially designed," James said, "to let in
all that Norwegian rain." Laurie thought it was lovely, and
made James take him for a ride around the block: he was very
enthusiastic about the idea of the trip, never having been anywhere except to his grandmother's in his life. The back seat
was so small, it was just the size for children; it was a
pity Bianca was too small to sit neatly by Laurie's side.

When we had put the children to bed we sat down together
to eat our fried eggs and to look at the maps. I stared at the
names of the places we were to go through, filled with rapture
at the thought of all those unwinding miles. We were to go up
the A1 to Newcastle, but I found a better-looking road on the
map, a green road called the M1, but James said that it wasn't
completed and that it was dangerous and that anyway it wasn't
as interesting and would encourage him to drive too fast for
the new car, which he hadn't yet finished running in. Then we
looked at the map of Norway and made some bad jokes about
it. His alleged cousin lived at a place near Bergen called Voss,
but we were rather taken with the idea of visiting Oslo, and
driving up to the Arctic Circle, and crossing to Stockholm,
and making other peripheral, unnecessary detours before delivering the car. We were just in the process of looking Trond-
heim up in Baedeker when the phone went. The phone was
in the hall, just outside the kitchen where we were sitting, and
I was so sure that it was Malcolm that I started to tremble as
I rose to answer it. I couldn't let it ring, without explanation,
and yet I couldn't trust myself, hearing his voice, not to speak.

But when I lifted the receiver, it was not Malcolm: it was worse, it was Lucy.

"Hello," she said, in her flat, even voice.

I answered, like an echo. I don't know what I expected her to say: to ask for James, perhaps, or to embark mildly upon unbearable recrimination. But all she said was, "How are you? It seems ages since I spoke to you, I thought I'd better ring to ask how you were. How are the children?"

"We're all well," I said, wondering if James from the kitchen could identify her voice. "How are you?"

"Not too bad," she said, with a sigh, "not too bad. I'm a bit tired, that's all. Simon's got something wrong with his ears, he keeps waking up all night."

"Oh," I said.

"James has gone to Norway," she said, "so I'm on my own. Perhaps I'll come over to see you one day."

"Gone where?" I said, dully.

"Gone to Norway," she repeated.

"Whatever for?" I asked, trying to assume an inflection, trying to react.

"Oh, God knows," said Lucy, "some bloody stupid notion of his . . ." and then she started to explain where and why he had gone, a story not dissimilar to the one he had told me, but reported by Lucy with such bored dismissive disaffection that I hoped he could not hear a word she was saying. Having explained his objective, she embarked on what I can only call a long complaint about his irresponsibility: "He's such a fool," she said, "I mean to say, you've no idea what the financial position at that garage is, we've been living on bread and cheese for weeks, and yet he thinks he can indulge in philanthropy

toward cousins he's hardly ever set eyes on—have you ever
heard of such a thing? Driving all that way just to do someone a favor? They'll probably catch up with him at the Cus-
toms and then we'll all be ruined. The garage hardly pays anyway, you know, and after that dreadful smash-up they had at
Illingworth Castle it's all been very dicey . . ." And so she
went on, filling in the background to chance remarks of
James's that I had never hoped or wished to hear explained. I
wanted to tell her to stop, to preserve my ignorance, but I had
to listen, and the things that she said were anyway no more
than confirmations of already formed suspicions. I knew these
things, but I did not want to face the knowledge of such
knowledge: I had gazed, in planetary obedience, at what I
took to be the bright side of the moon, and I did not
want Lucy, by a casual flick of her wrist, to tilt the heavens
for me and show me the dark and craterous reverse. I knew it
was there, but I did not want to see it. The most sinister revelation of all, I think, was her evident ignorance of the fact that
James was at that instant sitting in my kitchen eating his supper. I had always, until that point, believed that Lucy was
omniscient, blessed with some supernatural awareness and
forgiveness of my theft. But it was not so: she did not know he
was there; she thought he had gone to Bergen the night before.
She had, quite simply, been deceived. (And if she had, would
not I also? Was I not, even then?)

When she had finished her complaints about their financial
situation, and a sad story about a friend of James's who kept a
car engine in his bedroom (I hadn't known he had such a
thing as a friend, and at the word I felt a pang of jealousy), she
introduced once more the dangerous topic of a projected visit
to me. "Should I come over and see you?" she said, and I could

not think of a reply, so I said, vaguely, implying depths of withdrawal, depths that I knew she would honor, "Oh, I don't
know, I don't feel much like seeing people at the moment."

"Ah," she said, wounded, I could tell, by her own offense in
having made an inappropriate suggestion, wounded by her
own lack of omniscience.

"If you see what I mean," I feebly added, trying to rescue her
from her nonexistent error by implying that she alone could
see such fine shades.

"Yes, of course," she said, straining her eyes, no doubt, to
catch that impermanent unworldly hue. Never, I thought,
would she or I be caught out in the crudity of denial: impris-
oned in our solipsist universes, we would never cry to the naked
emperor of our kingdom, but where, where *are* your clothes?

"Well, look," said Lucy, gentle, honorable, delicate. "Look,
if you ever want me, ring."

"Yes, I would ring," I said, knowing that she would not visit
me, that she would not even phone me, until I gave her permis-
sion, knowing that I was safe with her refined sense of my unspoken, indefinable priority of silence, and so full of admiration for that misplaced refinement that when I put the phone
down and went back to James I felt doubly estranged from
him, by my feeling for her, and by a renewed awareness of
my unforgivable duplicity. How had I arrived at this point,
where I could bring myself to profit from the obscure delicacies
of her nature, from the sad deformities of my own?

We went to bed early, intending to leave early in the morning, but I lay awake as I had done alone the night before, unable to sleep. I was thinking of Malcolm and Lucy, and wondering why fate had denied me the technical innocence of de-
parting without a hearing of their rival claims: why couldn't

my solitude have been prolonged a week more? It would make no difference to the event, their intercession, so why should I have suffered the listening of it? I would have perjured myself, I would have forsworn myself, I was beyond the reach of the appeals of justice. I lay there, and I listened to James's heavy regular breathing, and I tried to lie still so that I would not disturb him, I tried not to toss restlessly, from side to side. It seemed hard, the price I had to pay for him: the price in treachery. And he, quietly sleeping, what torments did he ever suffer for me? He had concealed from me so carefully the more ugly aspects of our love that I felt I was betraying him to think of them: and so I was, so I was. Nevertheless, in that sleepless night, I thought of them, and I brought myself to say to myself that in leaving England with me in this way he was not merely seeking, as he so often protested, a greater closeness to me, whom he claimed to want: he was also evading claims the nature of which I dimly guessed—financial? domestic? sexual?— how could I know, how could I want to know? I touched him, as he slept, familiar to me now, and I thought, as I always thought as conclusion to such painful deliberations, that I did not care what wrongs I committed, as long as he and I ended up where we then were, in that same bed, together: that any guilt would be tolerable if I could keep him by it. The romantic fallacy, I suppose.

I must have dozed off, toward the morning, because at about four I was wakened by a noise from downstairs. At first I thought it must be Laurie sleepwalking, but soon I could tell, though still confused by sleep, that it was adult steps that I could hear. So I thought of burglars, and lay there noting the alarming cowardly changes in my breathing and the rate of my heart. And then, as I heard the soft steps ascend the stairs, I realized that it must be Malcolm, the only person besides myself and James to possess a key. I lay there listening, and my heart seemed to groan and beat in me until I thought it must be audible. The bedroom door was open, and the landing light was on, left perpetually lit for timid Laurie's sake, so I could hear the steps quite clearly. I was terrified, but despite my terror I knew better than to wake James for protection, for I knew that my emotions would never survive the scene that would ensue: what cowardice on all parts, what uncontrollable, undignified laments, what ugly gestures, what sickening revelations. There are some tests to which one should not be put. I would come to hate us all, I knew, if I allowed it to happen, if I connived at its happening, so I lay there and did nothing. I lay there and pretended to be asleep; I tried to breathe evenly, despite the deafening thuds of my heart against my rib cage. Malcolm stood there in the doorway and he looked at us: at James, truly sleeping, at myself, feigning sleep, in a disordered bed. I would not have been surprised if he had tried to murder us, but I suppose he was not equipped. I would unmake that vision, if I could: James and myself, entranced in that deliberate sleep from which he would never waken me.

After a few minutes, he went away. He went downstairs, without looking at the children: what had I done, that he would not look at his own children? I prayed that he would go away, and he did go: I heard the sound of the front door as it slammed behind him, and then, a few seconds later, an appalling crash, and a noise of broken glass, and then his footsteps as he walked away down the street. I was afraid that the noise would waken James, but he slept through it, snoring slightly, worn out by his double life, and after a while I climbed out of bed and crept downstairs to see what had happened. It was easy enough to see: Malcolm had broken the big window of the front room, the public window that fronted on to the street. There was glass all over the place, all over the floor, all over the steps outside. I could not think what to do with it, so I went and got back into bed with James and warmed my cold feet on him. As so often, I couldn't tell if I was shocked beyond reaction, numb with alarm, or simply indifferent. I fell asleep almost immediately.

In the morning, when James got up and discovered the breakage, I pretended to be as amazed by it as he was, and asked him innocently if he had heard anything during the night, because I certainly had not, I said. Not a thing, said James. It must have been passing drunkards, I said, reasonably. Probably, said James. I don't know why I was so determined to conceal from him Malcolm's renewed attentions: perhaps I wanted to spare him the anxiety, or perhaps shame silenced me. Over breakfast we sat and stared at the broken glass and I asked him what I ought to do about it: sweep up the bits and nail a piece of cardboard over the gap, he said, so we did. It was quite a simple job.

"Anyone could break in while we're away," I said.

"I don't suppose it would matter much if they did, would it?" he said.

"No, not much," I said, because he was right, it would not have mattered at all. There was nothing to take, in that house. And little left that was worth destroying. Before we left, I took the phone off the hook and listened for a while to the deadness at the other end. I also remembered to put the plant out of the kitchen into the back yard, where, if it did not freeze, it might flourish.

Beyond Hatfield, going north, gazing out of the window at the gray skies and drifting rooks and autumn fields, she said to him, "I could die now, quite happily. I wouldn't much mind if I died now."

"I'd like to get a little further," he said.

"We must mention that we may not get there," she said. "If we show ourselves willing, it won't be expected of us."

"The readiness is all," he said, smiling, and then added, "Did you read, this morning, in the paper, about those two American girls who were killed yesterday going the wrong way round Scots Corner? You must remind me, when we get there, to keep to the left."

"Oh heavens," she said, in a voice like any woman anywhere, in a voice so like a real voice that it surprised her, "oh heavens, I forgot to cancel the papers and the milk."

"I love you," he said, looking at her through the mirror.

"I love you too," she said.

North of Stamford we drove suddenly into sunshine. Both the children were asleep by this time, Bianca in the carrycot on the small back seat, and Laurie wedged in beside her, lulled by the car's motion. I too was finding it hard to keep awake, having slept so little the night before: my eyes were half shut and I was listening to the car radio in a daze. James was driving carefully: the care with which he always drove the children was one of his most human qualities, and when I wondered, as I often did, whether he or I or both of us were mad, I would think of this ordinary grace. He was also, on this occasion, driving carefully for the car's sake. Running it in, the technical phrase, I think. I state these things in advance because it is necessary to prove that the crash, against all likelihood, was in no way his fault. I was never able, in fact, to remember exactly what happened—I recollect that we were driving along quite peacefully at just less than sixty miles an hour, along a fairly narrow stretch of dual carriageway, and that the radio had just started to play a song that we both very much liked, aptly enough an escape song called "Chimborazo, Cotopaxi," which had got a precarious and highly temporary hold upon the Hit Parade. I looked at him as they started to play it, but he did not look at me because he was about to overtake, reasonably enough, a small van. Just as we passed it there was a sudden violent explosion which threw the whole car up into the air; I saw the wheel wrenched from James's hands and then I must have shut my eyes, knowing, of course, that we were going to die, that this was it, so long awaited: trying, even at that dire moment, as the car plunged across the oncoming traffic, to avoid the impact of eternity by pretending that I had always foreseen it, that I had not been taken unprepared, that death had not dropped upon me like a stone out of a blank sky. Though that, in fact, was precisely what had happened: the accident, when reconstructed for me, was so horrific in its ghastly disproportion between cause and effect that it would have shattered any delicate faith; and yet how dreadfully it reinforced my views of providence, of Divine Providence, of the futility of human effort against the power that holds us. We had, I was later told, driven over a brick which had dropped from a lorry, and the front tire on James's side had blown: the force of the shock pulled his hands from the wheel—all I can see of the accident is his desperate clutching, the knots of his hands and wrists as they gave up—and the car veered to the right, across the narrow grass verge separating the lanes of traffic, across the oncoming traffic, to end up crunched up against a tree on the far side of the road. It hit the tree with such force that both front doors flew open, and James was thrown out. I too would have been thrown out, but I was wearing my safety belt—unfastened, as it happened, as I had undone it five miles before to turn around to rearrange Laurie in a more comfortable position, but even in its unbuckled state it had been enough to prevent me from doing more than sliding from the seat to the ground. James's side of the car had taken the worst of the shock; the back of the car was miraculously whole, despite the fact that it had been hit by an oncoming car, which had changed the direction of our trajectory. The oncoming car, in swerving to avoid us, had itself overturned, and the driver was killed. I did not know this at the time, as I lay there, half in, half out of the car, wondering if I myself was still alive.

I don't know how long I sat there: I know that I could not have moved even had I tried because my legs, though painless and undamaged, felt as though they had been severed at the knee by fright, in violent exaggeration of the slight trembling that has all my life affected me in moments of apprehension. My eyes, too, had shut themselves, so I sat there in darkness, until I forced myself to open them; and when I did so I could not see James at all, he had vanished and his door was burst backward.

I did not begin to care: all I cared for was the survival of the children, but I could tell that they like me were alive, for I could hear both their distinct voices raised in unison, wailing and screaming together. Relief at this noise restored me slightly, and I managed to pull myself up onto the seat so that I could turn to the back to look at them: they looked, amazingly, unhurt. I could do nothing about them, I could not reach them, I was too weak and too tired, so I shut my eyes again and rested my head on the back of the seat. I must be crazy, because what I thought about in those few dark moments was not pain and broken glass and broken bones: I thought, instead, crazily, of significance, I thought that I had been cheated, I thought that death had visited me in person, as an angel, as a presence, and had denied me the final vision, the final revelation. Knowledge itself hung so near me then, and had not yielded itself up to me: I have always cherished the faith that at the moment of death I would be immeasurably illumined, that the mystery would be made clear to my astonished gaze, and I sat there cheated, betrayed, done out of wisdom. The quality of one's living will determine the quality of one's dying, and I said to myself as I crouched there trembling that I had had faith, I had believed in the significance of life and that God had no right to deny me the white lights that I had hoped for. My soul, which had labored like my body, for so many years, had labored unprofitably, and at the moment of death, that moment when all should be paid, I had received nothing.

But then, I did not die. The moment had been false, a false warning. God had hidden His face for some later unveiling, perhaps.

After a while my knees began to feel less broken, and I started to try to comfort the children, picking up the baby, reaching for the distraught Laurie with my spare hand, trying to discover how damaged we were. I knew that James, unlike me, was dead, and I wondered whether God had bothered to throw a word in his direction. It was natural that he should be dead. What other conclusion could there have been, to so much pointless extravagance? It was hardly necessary to get out and look at him. I would wait, I thought, until an ambulance came and took him away, and then I would not have to set eyes on him again. I knew that somebody would come soon, on that busy road, that there was nothing I need do but wait. It seemed a long time, but it cannot have been more than a couple of minutes, I suppose, before I heard a car pull up and saw a man get out of it and come stumbling, running toward me: there was an expression on his face of sick alarm. I was glad he did not look efficient and composed, I was glad he did not take it calmly, I was glad he too was afraid of what he might see. He spoke to me, but I didn't hear what he said, and I don't think I answered. He had to shout, very loudly, to make me hear.

"Are you all right?" he kept shouting, louder and louder, standing over me, and in the end I nodded my head.

"You stay here," he yelled at me. "I'll go and ring for help."

And I saw him run back to his car, and tell his wife to get out and stay with me. I saw her get out of the car and stand there, small and reluctant on that empty road, afraid to come near me, afraid to approach. She was a little woman, in a black coat. He drove off and left her there, and in the end she walked toward me, nervously. When she got up to me she didn't know what to say. We stared at each other through the wrecked window. Then she said, "Are the children all right?" and again I nodded my head. Neither of us looked for James, neither of us mentioned James. But I knew that I would have to get out to look for him, although I feared that it was a shadow of her horror at what she had seen of him that was informing her eyes as she looked at me, that had held her there in that reluctant stillness by the curbside. So I handed her the baby, climbed out of the car, shutting my eyes as I did so: James and I had foreseen this moment so often, had tried so often to exorcise it, and in a sense we had perhaps succeeded because it was my memory of those idle premonitions that brought back to me a faint sense of what it had been like to be alive, and reminded me that I owed it to him to look for his corpse. He had told me so many stories of friends and acquaintances dead, smashed, severed, concussed, miraculously saved, stepping from their shattered cars whole and untouched as from a heap of shredded wheat, and I had listened with such admiration, so docile to his fantasies, so willing an audience: the least I could do now was to force open the lids of my eyes to search for his body in that dry and muddy ditch. So I opened them, and stood up, and looked around me, seeing for the first time the overturned car on the central verge and avoiding its sight instantly, for I could see that its driver was very nastily dead. I could see James, lying face downward in the place where he had been thrown, a yard or two from our car and the tree. I stood there and looked at him. I'd lost both my shoes, and the raw surface of the road struck at me. Oh God, I thought, if I feel this, what must he have encountered?

Before I had moved, two other cars were slowing down to see what had happened, and a man in a lorry was shouting at me from the other side of the road. I started to run, not caring any longer what I saw when I got there, wanting to get there first so that I could cover him up. He looked dead when I got there, but there was no need to cover him: the skin had been taken off one side of his face, but there were no other signs of injury. Disgusted by my relief, I knelt down beside him: I would have liked to be one of those women who, fortified by love, could nurse the severed heads of their lovers, but I am afraid of blood and flesh and gaping organs. I was glad he had died intact. I took his hand, his warm hand, all gray and scored with grit, to pay him whatever rites would come to me before we were interrupted, and I stared at him and at the sparse muddy grass and the uneven texture of the road and the cracked, ridged, aged bark of the trees, and at the bright chunks of glass from the windscreen, and all these colors and surfaces swam and enlarged themselves in my distorted vision until I felt that they would suck me in, that I would vanish into those enormous blades and gray valleys and huge rocky grains of glass and grit. They impinged upon me so shockingly that I could hardly look at James himself, and for weeks after the accident I was to remain obsessed by surfaces, seeing the world through some dreadful magnifying lens. There was a building site just opposite the hospital where they took James, and I would wander around it, staring at the colors in a heap of bricks as though it were a whole landscape. Once I came across a pile of strange black stuff, like coal or solidified tar, bricks and seamed blocks of it, and I would stare blindly at its odd formations, receptive, mindless, negated by its varieties. Pitch, perhaps it was. I think, now, that this strange obsession was a result of being flung so violently from distance into proximity: from a fast car's windows all landscapes, however strange, have a fluid solemn sameness, a dignified irrelevance, and from the dazed and drowsing pastoral contemplation of them I had been flung against the rough locality. A distant field with rooks, a spinney, a plowed horizon, had been changed in an instant, without time for the eye to adjust, into grit and mud and the dead spines of the leaf that was embedded delicately, beautifully, on James's face.

I was still kneeling by James when another man came running up to me. I looked up at him, and I could see that his face wore that look of officious, busy investigation that I had been so dreading and expecting from the man with the timid wife, and I said to him, defending my lovely love from his inquiries, "He's dead, you know."

But the man looked at James, and said that in his view he was not dead at all, and had anybody gone for the ambulance. So I found the courage to listen to James's heart, and sure enough he was still alive because his heart was beating. It would have been so much simpler if he had been dead: so natural a conclusion, so poetic in its justice. The readiness is all, he had said, and a brick had instantly dropped on him from heaven. But no, he would live like Gloucester, like Rochester, to drag blindly on, perhaps; and now I came to think of it I did not like the look of the one eye I could see, it was bleeding. I tried to wipe his face with my skirt, but his flesh was so nerveless and unresponsive that I was frightened to touch him, and anyway the officious man who was standing over me like a sentry said that it was dangerous to touch him, that I ought to leave him alone. So I held his hand wondering if he were dying there before my eyes. Laurie had started to call me from the car, and the baby was crying and struggling with the timid lady, but it seemed important to stay with James until the ambulance came, and in an instant I could hear its wailing siren. As it drew up, I knew—and was confronted by my knowledge, for what worse sin is there than treachery—that I would never learn to live again if he died, that my survival depended upon his, and that if he failed it would be a judgment on me for flinching from the thought of his ugly injuries. I would keep faith, I said, as they picked him up and put him on a stretcher: I would refuse to let him die.

The police arrived, too. They told me to get in with them, but I said I would go in the ambulance with James and the children. So they said they would follow me to the hospital. I put the children into the ambulance, where a man in a white overall took charge of them and gave Laurie a fruit gum, which to my surprise he accepted. Then I went back to the crashed car to collect my luggage. It was all crushed up: the suitcase had burst, and my things were lying about all over the place. I gathered up what I could and put it in the ambulance. I seemed to spend hours wandering around the road picking things up (though it cannot have taken more than a minute) and by the end I could not avoid the sight of the mingled blood and oil that was leaking from the other car on to the ground. So liquid we are, inside our stiff bodies; so easily resolved to other elements. In my memory I cannot recollect that people helped me much, though I suppose they must have done. I remember wandering feebly, a basket in one hand, my passport in the other, looking for the baby's bottle, like a crazy person, protesting anxiously, woman-like, that nobody would know what bits and pieces to collect but myself. The car stank of whisky and petrol: James had a bottle of Scotch in the front pocket and it had smashed into a thousand pieces. A policeman kept asking me for the insurance papers, but I did not know what or where they were, and I told him to look for himself. I was glad we had not packed the car with much care. It would have been dreadful to see neat hours of packing undone in such a way.

In the ambulance, there were people who kept saying that I had had a miraculous escape and should be grateful. I did not answer. I watched James for signs of life, and as the ambulance set off his right arm suddenly gave an involuntary, violent, wounded jerk: it terrified me, this gesture, so unlike him, so graceless, so uncontrolled. I began to think that there might be things worse than death, and that my refuge in the knowledge of his death had not been so treacherous or misguided. I thought that he might never recover, and that this violent stranger might inhabit his body until he died.

As we drew up in front of the casualty entrance of the hospital, I suddenly found myself leaning over James, as in grief, and quietly abstracting his wallet from his jacket pocket. I put it in my basket. I must have done this because I knew I had not a penny on me and would clearly be needing some money, but in a way this action of mine seemed as involuntary, as unlike me, as that wounded spasm had been unlike James. It was a warning to me of the things that I would have to do. And already, in the same way, I could feel myself comforting the children, smiling at them, tightening my arms around them. I did what was necessary. Perhaps everybody does on such occasions.

When we got to the hospital they took James away on a trolley. I had to let him go, because of the children: otherwise I would have followed him. Then I and the children were taken off to a different place and examined, and they put some plasters on my face and said again how amazing it was that so little had happened to us. The baby had not been touched, and Laurie had merely suffered a bad bang on the head: they had both been wedged in so neatly and tightly that the crash had hardly shifted them. Then I was asked if I would mind seeing the police. I said that I would see them, and was amazed to find them not overcome with sympathy for me as an escaped victim, not awe-struck at my deliverance, but slightly hostile. Nor had I foreseen the difficulty I would have in answering some of their questions: for instance, I did not know a thing about the car's insurance, and although I said that the car belonged to James I was not sure if even this were true. I had the presence of mind to see the advantages in being taken for James's wife, and did not deny it when they addressed me as Mrs. Otford: I even had to claim Lucy's Christian name as they had found it in James's passport. Some of their questions seemed highly irrelevant, but I answered them all meekly and did not protest when they used phrases like "in the event of death." I wish now, in a sense, that I had screamed and protested, that I had made for James some final glorious scene, but at the time it seemed wiser to stay quiet. By the end of their questions I could tell that their hostility was related to three things—to the broken bottle of Scotch, to the fact that the car was a new and expensive luxury car, and to the fact that they assumed James had been driving in some way irresponsibly. I, knowing nothing of the brick or of burst tires, could offer no explanation for the accident: I merely repeated, dully, what seemed to me to have happened. There were no witnesses: the van we had been overtaking had wisely driven on, not waiting to delay its journey by involving itself in the tragedies of others. The driver of the car whose path we had crossed was dead. The driver of the second car had arrived too late to see anything: all he had seen had been one car against the tree and one overturned in the middle of the road. They questioned me about the speed at which we were traveling, and I told them the truth: that James had been running the car in, that he had at no point, except when overtaking, exceeded sixty miles an hour. They asked if he had been drinking, and I replied, No, no, no. They asked what the Scotch was doing in the car at all and I said it had seemed a pity to leave it at home, which again was the truth: I could remember James saying as he pushed it in the dashboard pocket, well, what's the point of leaving this for the burglars, it's the only thing in the house they'd find worth taking. In the end I told them that it was no use questioning me, that if they wanted to know whether I was lying or not all they needed to do was to go and test the breath from his possibly breathless body, or take a sample of his congealing blood. I am glad I stirred, however slightly, at their inquisition.

They had not finished questioning me when one of them (there were two of them, a big fat wide-faced man, and a man with an acne-pitted complexion) was called away to the phone. When he came back I could tell that he had received exonerating information because he looked apologetic, and said that one of the boys had found skid marks and a brick further down the road, and that my story was quite consistent with this new evidence. However, he said, if James recovered, there would still be a case. It was at this point that, thinking of James's possible survival, I asked them what had become of the car. They said that a local garage had collected it and that it was up to me to decide upon its fate. I did not know what to say about it, and they said that the garage would keep it for us: in the event of recovery, they said, James could decide for himself, and in the event of death it would be left to me.

At the thought of such practical decisions, and all their dreadful implications, I shut my eyes in horror, and they took pity on me, thinking perhaps that I was going to faint. If it hadn't been for the children I probably would have taken refuge in insensibility or hysteria, but as it was I pulled myself together. The fat man then asked me what I intended to do, and whether I would like to phone my relatives or whether I would like to get on a train and go home, or whether I would like to stay there in the hospital to recover from the shock. None of these possibilities seemed in any way possible. I could not phone anyone for assistance: whom could I have phoned? I could not return home and abandon James: I knew that if I left him he would die, and that I myself could not face the horrors that would await me if I returned to that empty house with its cardboard window. So there was nothing left but to stay. They took me to the matron of the hospital, with whom at last I encountered a little indulgence; she gave me a cup of tea and said that I and the children could stay the night if we wished, or if we didn't wish she would get in touch with a hotel for us provided that we returned the next day for observation. She sent a nurse off to make up the baby's bottle, and then she told me that James was by no means beyond hope: his skull, she said, was fractured in two places, and he had a broken arm and a broken pelvis, but worse injuries, she said, had been survived. When I asked when he would recover consciousness, she shrugged her shoulders and said that she could not say. Then I left her reading a book about a teddy bear to Laurie while I went off, limping by now, ostensibly to the lavatory, but in fact to inspect my financial position: I locked myself into her own private pink-tiled closet and looked in James's wallet, closing my mind honorably to its more intimate contents, and there, folded away, in ten-pound notes, I found a sum of three hundred pounds. I counted the notes in astonish-

ment: I had never set eyes on so much cash in my life. I could
not think what he had been intending to do with it. It solved,
in any case, one problem: I stuffed the notes back, buried the
wallet in my basket, and went back to the matron and told
her that I would take a room in a hotel. I heard myself saying,
so calmly, if you wouldn't mind ringing a hotel for me, or telling me whom to ring, I think it would be better for the children to get them away from here as soon as possible, don't
you? And she agreed, glad, I could see, to be rid of the responsibility for me: I could see her eyes flicker over me, and
some of my newly acquired financial status must have been
visible in my bearing because she reached for the telephone on
her desk, saying, "I think the Saracen's Head is the best hotel,
you'd be most comfortable there—" and rang through, herself,
to its reception. Having booked me a double room, she lost
nerve at the ease with which she was washing her hands of me
and started to protest that I had better stay a little longer under her supervision because one could never tell with shock
and its aftereffects; but I was so insistent and so collected and
so evidently determined to have my way—so evidently, in fact,
shockproof—that she once more, willingly, relinquished me,
and accompanied me to the front entrance hall of the hospital,
where she and I awaited the arrival of a taxi. All starched and
blue-uniformed, she was: my eyes were dazzled by all those
uniforms, by the police and the matron and the nurses. She
said that I could ring later about James, and I said that I would.
Too many new people, I said to myself as I lifted Laurie into
the taxi, and handed in my burst luggage: too many new people to be expected to look at their faces. A recollection of their
uniforms would do.

We arrived at the Saracen's Head within minutes: I, accus-

tomed to the vast spaces of London, could hardly believe we
were there so soon. It was a small town, this place where fate
had abandoned me, a small market town, with two streets of
shops, three hotels, a large church, and a cinema. I did not take
all this in instantly, of course, but I came to know it well
enough. The hotel I was taken to was an old and stately building with thick stone walls, a Trust House that had been a
coaching inn. I stood there in the hall on its flowered carpet,
seeing my pale and plastered face reflected, distorted, from the
circular gilt mirrors, holding tightly onto the baby for comfort,
and I could tell that I was entering into something permanent,
a way of life that was like a whole lifetime: so enclosed, so distinct, so regulated, so interminably long.

It did not take me long to grasp most of the implications of my position, although they were so multiple that during that first night, as I tossed helplessly in the wide double
bed, a child on either side, I seemed to hit upon a new one at
each turn of my mind. It was my duty to ring Lucy and James's
parents, to let them know what had happened; but if I rang
them, the whole sad story would be perhaps needlessly revealed. If he survived, then the worst aspects of the disaster
could be concealed, and so to inform them would be merely
an unnecessary introduction of unnecessary pain. On the other
hand, if he died, what right had I to deny those who belonged
to him the spectacle of his end? It would be a fortnight before

his silence became sinister: I had a fortnight in which to make
up my mind, supposing that he remained alive and unconscious for that length of time, which the matron had implied
was more than possible. A fortnight to keep him to myself, and
then I would have to deliver him over to the solicitude and recriminations of others: for which of them would acknowledge
my rights? It had touched me so much, even in those straits,
to hear myself addressed as Mrs. Otford, to inscribe my name
as his in the hotel register. How could I bear it if they took
him away from me, if they denied my right to mourning? And
yet how could I deny them theirs? I had no claim to him except
the claim of loving him, and that seemed so frail, so insignificant compared with the official claims of matrimony and of
motherhood. The accident, it seemed, had given shape and
form to my guilt: I could no longer evade it, I could no longer
evade the dreadful assessments that crowded upon me, the
comparisons, the judgments, the knowledge. Had he died, as
all true fictional lovers die, had we both died, then these things
would have been evaded forever: never would I have had to
measure my claim against Lucy's, never would I have had to
ask myself whose face he would rather see if ever he should
open his eyes in consciousness again. We would, in death,
have been forgiven. But now I had been presented—I could
see it so clearly, it was so painfully clear—with a period of trial,
with every decision to face alone, with every last degree of humiliation to be endured, with abnegations that I could not
bring myself to contemplate. If he were to die, how could I
lose him twice—to Lucy before his death, and forever after it?
And yet how could I take upon myself the risk of his survival
and the crime of withholding him from those who loved him,
from those whom he loved? What weight, what depth had our

emotions, those frivolous exchanges, those violent nights, when measured in this fearful scale?

Being what I was, I at first did nothing. I let day run into day and I did not touch the telephone: I kept him to myself like a miser. Those days were impossible. How can one amuse a child of three in a hotel room in October? Bianca was all right, she ate and slept and laughed; she even laughed in her sleep. But I had to devote myself to Laurie as I had never done before. I bought him toys, I took him for walks, I took him endlessly to the playground, I sat for hours with him in the dim mustard lounge of the hotel watching the children's programs on the television, I drew pictures for him, I played picture dominoes with him. I became inventive as I had never been in efforts to distract him and to subdue his piercing voice so that it would not offend the other residents of the hotel. Luckily the staff, bored at that time of year, took to the children and would assist me in my struggles; there was an Italian chambermaid who kept an eye on them for me in the evenings while I went to visit James. I spent the days playing snap and dominoes, and as I played my mind attached itself, grimly, like a leech, to its own misery and its own guilt, drawing from them blood and sustenance. It was Laurie himself who thought of the final refinement: as we passed a toy shop one morning he caught sight of something called a snap-together motorized kit for a Formula One Ferrari, and he started to clamor for it excitedly, shouting that it looked just like Uncle James's. So I bought it for him, battered as I was into total indulgence by fear of his boredom, and we took it back to the bedroom, where I tried to assemble it. I had had no idea, as I purchased it, that it would be such a complicated business, and my heart sank at the sight of the extremely complicated instructions and the heap of minute chrome and plastic parts. I have never been good with my hands and the words in the assembly instructions meant nothing to me at all, despite their familiarity: how could I identify such things as rear axles, large gear wheels, hub caps, and exhaust stacks? I nearly gave up at sight but Laurie was so insistent and contemptuous, and said so often that Uncle James could have done it in no time had he been there, that finally I set about it. I spent hours poring over the diagram, trying to fit the right bits into the right places. I was alarmed by the fact that the thing had a battery and a motor with bits of red and white wire. In the end I managed to stick it together, in a more or less correct fashion, and to my astonishment when I pressed the switch it started to emit a ridiculous whirring mechanical noise. It did not actually go, that would have been too much to expect, but when I looked at it more closely I could see that all I needed to do to make it move was to press two small plastic wheel-shaped things more closely together so that they articulated. I did it, and the thing started to move, clumsily, like a beetle, across the carpet. I was filled with achievement, and also with alarm: I am nervous with electricity, I hardly dared to stop it to switch it off, knowing how inexpertly it had been put together. I had hoped that Laurie would be impressed by my perseverance, but he had become bored with the project long before, as he was unable to assist with it: he stared at the finished product with disaffection and said that it did not go fast enough and that the plastic driver did not look very realistic. Motor shafts, axles, king pins, revs, carbs: meaningless language of obsession, the untranslatable language of love.

I used to be glad when it was time for children's television. There were two old ladies in the hotel who always watched it, and I used to dump Laurie with them while I gave Bianca her disgusting tea. One day I came down just as Jackanory was ending, and I heard a man reading the end of a fairy story that I had known as a child, but which I have never since been able to find. There was verse in it that was so profoundly affecting that I stood there transfixed, feeling the hair rise on my head. The serving girl says to the sleeping knight whom she loves:

> For seven long years I served for you,
> The bloody cloth I wrung for you,
> The glassy hill I climbed for you,
> Will you not wake and turn to me?

I could not stay to hear whether he did wake and turn to her because Bianca in my arms started to cry and I had to go. I arrived in time for the beginning of the program the next day but it was another fairy tale altogether: the tale of a princess in China who says she will marry only the man who brings her the blue rose. She rejects a rose of sapphire, and a rose dyed blue, and a porcelain painted rose, and accepts as her lover the one who brings her an ordinary white rose picked from a hedge on the way; turning to her astonished court, she says to them, you are color-blind, this rose is the only blue rose that I have ever seen. I liked this story, but I wished that I had heard the ending of the other one. Laurie was too small for such stories. He preferred cartoons.

When the children were asleep I went every evening to see James. He looked so dreadful that I could hardly bear to see him, and yet it was harder to stay away. His facial injuries, though not deep, were extensive, and his flesh had turned a deadly gray. He was immobile as a corpse: every reflex had vanished, his eyes did not respond to light, his throat had

240 | THE WATERFALL

ceased to swallow, his limbs lay like dead weights. He was fed
intravenously: the final indignity. I sat there quietly by his bed,
curtained off from the rest of the ward, and I spoke to him in a
whisper, endlessly, recalling to him the things that we were to
have done together, the things that we had already done, as
though I could reclaim him by them. I would have given ten
years of my life, twenty years, my right hand, my arm, for a
flicker of life from him, for even an involuntary twitch. (Once
I heard the old man in the next bed wheeze to his neighbor,
she's wasting her time, that one, he's a goner if ever I saw one.)
He was wearing an unbecoming hospital night shirt, poor
James, which I knew, had he been conscious, would have
grated upon his skin and vision. On my second visit they
gave me his clothes in a bundle, and I took them back to the
hotel and unwrapped them, weeping over them silently so that
I should not wake the children, yet at the same time solaced by
memory, glad to possess such relics of the past. His blue shirt
was covered in blood: the hospital had not bothered to wash
it. When I undressed for bed I put it on and looked at myself in
the mirror. I used to put his shirts on, for love, in the days
when he was alive, and we would both sigh and embrace over
the transposition. Now, wearing it, I could see it as a shroud,
as a last rite performed for him, for love itself. I slept in it.
There was nothing else that I could do for him, there was no
other way of getting near to him. I would have committed any
extravagance. In the morning I washed the shirt in the washbowl, and hung it up to dry, thinking that if I did so he would
surely need it again. The bloody shirt I wrung for you: the
plaintive servitude, the meals he had brought me when I lay
in bed, the sheets that he had straightened for me, the feminine endings.

Outside the window behind his bed at the hospital there was a holly tree. It must have been some kind of mutation because its leaves were huge and soft and spineless. I don't know why the sight of it so weighed upon my mind.

It's not possible to say what I felt during those days. The quality of them returns to me now so clearly: the slowness of the hours, the boredom, the anxiety. There was nothing for me to do but to play children's games and watch the modulations of the elements. The town was a pleasant town: old, red brick, elegant, buildings of a deep warmth that glowed in the sun like paradise. Around the hospital, where I would find myself straying like a lost soul, there was an estate of new houses with big shining picture windows and small front gardens and names like St. Helier. It was all very clean, after London. There were playing fields, too, where schoolboys played football. And a signpost to the crematorium. The hospital itself was nothing but a low, sprawling collection of huts and one-story buildings splaying out from a central block: there was plenty of space there, the buildings were all low, and the trees seemed to have room to extend their branches more widely into the wide sky. I watched these things, having nothing else to do. I got to know it all so well.

Sometimes, as I sat on a bench while Laurie swung in the playground, I would say, all I am doing here is waiting for James to die. And I could not think how I had got myself there, I, who would not leave home to go down the street to the grocer's: in a strange place, lost, committing perjury, an accomplice in some unique and indefinable crime. I had done nothing for so many years, for so many years I had withheld myself from action, fearing just such a conclusion: but it had sought me out, it had claimed me nevertheless. How had it found me, how had it known that I was waiting for it? I thought these things over as I sat on the damp and wooden bench, and I could find no answer. What was it in me, what was it in James that had brought us to that place? I had turned from it and avoided it, but now it was there, undeniable, accompanied by faces, uniforms, forms to fill in. Death. Murder. What had I to do with such things, I who had chosen to play the victim? I could not believe that fate was so sensitive to the details of my fears and desires that it had paid more attention to their underlying patterns than to their surface appearances, and yet it was I who had survived, and James and Malcolm who had, in their respective ways, died for me. The shape of my body had ordained it, the construction of my heart, and I had struggled in vain against my dangerousness: I had struggled in vain to lie still and harmlessly. It was my passivity that had undone them: I had ruined Malcolm by rejection, and James, ah James whom I so loved, I had ruined him by my passive helpless acquiescence, by the passion of my assent. The brown blood had seeped out of his shirt into the hotel washbowl like tea, like coffee grounds from a rinsed cup, floating and spiraling in the clear tap water, spreading like faint coils of smoke in the lighter element. I should have kept myself from loving him. Lucy, Lucy who had mocked him and disbelieved him, Lucy had kept him alive.

On the fifth night she lay awake, unable to sleep, unable to bring herself to swallow the sleeping tablets she had been given: restless, hot, oppressed by the central heating, oppressed by remorse, upon the verge of that final encounter, that final trial, that long-dreaded process—the slow death of love, its slow lapsing into insensibility, its ultimate decease. It would drain away from her like water from a sieve, and no effort would restrain it; and with it would go her last sanction and her last defense. How can love preserve itself in death? No hope, no hope of eternal preservation, of an ambered corpse, motionless in its glass coffin as he in his hospital bed, untouched by treachery or fidelity. What do the dead care for fidelity? It is the living who need to keep it, for their own sake, for the dignity of their passion, for the lost value of what they risked for it. But they cannot keep it, they cannot preserve it: they say to themselves finally, it was not worth it, he was not worth it to me, it was all as unimportant as any other emotion. She knew that she would come to say this of him, that even her feeling for him, her one faith, would fail her. He was dying so slowly: how could she keep faith until his final breath? Her fingers felt for the bruises on her arm and leg, and she said to herself, when they've faded, he'll die; and she pressed her fingers into them to make them hurt, sick with panic at the frivolity and felicity of the notion. And no, she could no longer deny them, weak, resistless, at that lonely hour; she admitted them into her, a whole host of alarms, fears, sickening misgivings, nightmare certainties. For what, after all, in God's name had they been playing at? Fast cars, card tricks, kisses, sighs, vows, the lot? And those other things which she could not bring herself to name? What on earth had they thought they were doing? It had been some ridiculous imitation of a fictitious passion, some shoddy childish mock-up of what for others might have been reality—but for what others? For no others, as nonexistent an image they had pursued as God, as Santa Claus, as mermaids, as angels, as that nonexistent image of eternity. A question of faith, it had been—but faith not justified by its object: love, human love. And for this supposed love and its dim priorities they had risked, childishly, her life and his, and those of both her children: irresponsibility glorified, a meaningless, involuntary, undirected swipe at the years of her silent childhood and her Clark's sandals and her Dutch cap.

Romantic love, that was what he had died for: how could he have allowed himself to be a martyr in so sick a cause, how could she have let herself accompany his suicidal fall? How could she ever have trusted him and the lies they had told one another? How had they found so much to say about so great a delusion? The emperor's new clothes, discussed, endlessly, stitch by stitch; and suddenly one looks in the light of undeceived day, and the man is naked, like other men, and wanting like them nothing but what all men want. What were the things that she had so admired in him, that had so moved her heart and touched her body? Nothingnesses, shadows, mockeries. What had there been so admirable in James's mother, that figure to whom she had attached such hopeful fantasies, that figure whom she had capriciously elected to redeem the maternal role? What starved and vulgar notion of glamor had so endowed her shallow attachments, her beige nightdress, her moss-green velvet ribbons? Had she not always known the reality—poor James, aged three, sitting there in her bed, nagging for his breakfast, listening to her endless amorous discussions, crying for his boiled egg.

"Just a moment, darling," she would say, turning back to the telephone. "Just a moment, James—" and then, her voice softening into the corrupt tones of adult communion, "—and, anyway, my love, he said that it was merely a question of *arrange-ment*—what? what was that? Oh, no, *no*—" and then the intimate laughter, the protests, the denials, whereupon James would start to cry about the egg once more and she would turn from the phone and say, "James, darling, why don't you play with my jewelry—" and then, later, when the jewels palled on James, but not her conversation to her man, she would tell him to play with her lipstick, and he would blue his eyes and redden his lips, a sexual object at the age of three, undefended by servants because his mother's life was too disreputable to admit them, too extravagant to afford them. This was the intimate maternal contact she had so admired. But there is no nonchalance without squalor and cruelty, no passion without its accompanying neglect.

And those cars, too: how could she have allowed herself to admire, to share his interest in such self-condemning lunacy? What waste of money, what stupidity, what marginal dishonesties. He had talked of response, as the car took off along the road, as her body flung itself from him, but what idiocy to equate a machine and a woman, neurotics though both of them were: a lump of expensive metal, a mechanical toy, and she herself not so much better, she herself responding unwilled like a machine. It disgusted her, it appalled her, and yet worse than his successes, more treacherously, she remembered his failures (for there is after all some skill in doing anything well, even an easy, subdued woman) but he had not always done it well, he had failed her, he had made mistakes that only her compliance had concealed. And she remembered, that day at the racetrack when she had first seen him driving round the track: she remembered the face of the mechanic as he gave James the car, and there had been something in it, some hint of disrespect, some suspicion of reserve that had told her what she had already known: that James could not drive well enough for the circles he had been able to move in, that his aspirations were misplaced, and known to be so. She thought, with redoubled treachery, of Malcolm, who could at least do well the thing he had set out to do: worthless though it was, pointless though it was, he could at least do it well.

For seven long years I served for you, will you not wake and turn to me? Why should he ever wake, and if he did so what name would he call? His mother's, Lucy's, any name but her own. She had heard of the effects of concussion: confusion, forgetfulness, an eternal forgetting of the moment of shock. And what more likely than that he should forget forever the whole of their intercourse, the whole of those months in which they had so wanted one another? If he woke, it would mean nothing to him: and she, if she persisted, would be left nursing a petrified, a stony memory. Better to forget, better to leave his bedside and abandon him, than to see him revive into forgetting. After such darkness, such days, such weeks of submerged darkness, how could he ever care again for the shallow waters where they had lain together? They were draining away and leaving her dry. Such a shallow, transient, selfish affair, their so-styled love had been: it had seemed necessary, but it had not been so. A question of surfaces, it had been: of skin, of touch, of admiration for hands and eyes and faces. Scars, tattoos, surface scratches merely. His skin now was dry and flaking away, wrinkling as with extreme age. The nurses could not shave him because of the damage to the skin of his face, and his hair was continuing to grow, as she had heard said that it grew in the grave. What she had so wanted in him no longer existed: the level of their communications had been taken from them,

and if ever he met other people again it would be on some
other level that she did not know—a level of kinship, of endurance, of obligation, of familiarity. Seven long years, and it was
to Lucy and his children that they had belonged. She had
hardly brought herself to think of those possibly fatherless children, deprived by her folly, as her own children had risked
death for it. Seven years, and those years of hers had belonged
not to James but to Malcolm, who had patiently endured
her afflictions, who had taken her for as long as he could, and
who still retained enough feeling for her to smash up her windows in protest against her infidelity to those years. It was Malcolm that had endured her and paid for her, in cash and sorrow, and she had felt nothing but resentment, all her gratitude
had been given to James, who had done nothing more for her
than to change an electric plug and mend the brake of the
pushchair with a bit of fuse wire and sleep in her bed. She had
been so grateful to him for these acts of kindness. She had
watched him using the screwdriver, slightly inept from the alcohol he had consumed, with such emotion: but the emotion
had been corrupt, the frivolous corrupt pleasure one takes in
watching the finally useless person performing small acts of
simulated service, of easy grace. She had magnified these trivial
cares into Herculean labors for her, heroic trials of strength and
patience; but nothing had been required of him, he had done
nothing for her, nor she for him. Oh yes, she had made him a
sandwich or two with stale bread, she had fried him an egg
and put a kettle on from time to time, she had stroked his hair,
and once, long ago, sewn a button on the sleeve of his coat.
But what of Malcolm, who had even in absence maintained
financial fidelity, continuing to pay with no returns, continuing, faithfully, to resent?

She looked back on the past and saw it crumble to dust, pre-
served dust, mummified to this point by her sick persistence.
She thought of that Christmas Day, so long ago, upon which
memory she had set such value; it had meant so much to her
that James too had remembered it, and she had been prepared
to accept their joint recollection as proof that they had wanted
each other in some gracious and inevitable way. But all that
had happened had been that they had momentarily noticed
one another's state, had felt the passing touch of such emotion
as others experience, knowing its irrelevance, each week,
each day. And she had exalted this trivial attention into significance, and forced her interpretation of it upon him because
of loneliness and poverty and need. And she had to admit,
now, that he too must have needed her: he, whom she had seen
as free and complete, had needed her. She knew, she had
known ever since Lucy's phone call the night before their departure, that there was some explanation that she would
not like to hear, but which she could not forever avoid: that he
had not wanted her through love any more than she had
wanted him in so pure a cause. Desperation had thrown them
together; past failures had held them there. They had seemed
to meet in the profound aspirations of their natures, but it had
not been so: they had met in the shallow stretches of ordinary
weakness, and what he had given her had been no miracle, no
unique revelation, but a gift so commonplace that it hardly required acknowledgment. An ordinary white rose, picked from
a hedgeful of ordinary, indistinguishable blooms, and wilting
now, crumpling and browning at the edges, subject to decay.
The seemingly endless terrain, traversed, took on once more a
look of limitation: as though it were seen suddenly from
above, from the air, from the aspect of eternity.

When they had lifted him into the ambulance, blood had been dripping from his nose and ears. Even if he lived, how could she forget such a sight?

In the morning, she would ring Lucy. There was nothing else to do. She would abandon the whole affair, take herself back to London, get in touch with Malcolm and let him do what he wanted with her. None of it mattered any more. None of it had ever mattered. It had not been worth dying for. She hoped he would recover and forget her, forget that she had once taken him so seriously, had once suffered so for him. She would take her sleeping pills and go to sleep. There was nothing else to do.

She got out of bed and went to the washstand to get the pills: she had not yet taken any, faithful to her religious dislike of cure, and she was not sure what they would do to her. She took two, as it said on the packet, and got back into bed, and waited for sleep. But it seemed as elusive as ever: she had expected it to strike her down, but nothing happened at all. Remorselessly, her mind continued to think, continued to betray. Supposing, she thought to herself, he had not even wanted her, supposing he had merely pitied her? Alone, in that large house. How could she ever have distinguished the signs in him? Why was she so afraid to question him, to speak to Lucy, to look at the contents of his wallet? Was it because she knew that his attitude to her would never have borne inspection? His wallet was in the drawer of the table by the bed: she got it out and looked at it, her hands trembling slightly at the thought of what it might contain. What did she expect to find there? Disavowals, contradictions, incriminations. She opened its soft leather. It was full of pieces of paper and she started to go through them, carefully, her heart beating with apprehension: she remembered that once, years ago, she had read Lucy's diary and found there things that she had not wanted to know. In the wallet there were petrol bills, and restaurant bills, and a library ticket. A photograph of the children. Notes of addresses. A postal order for three and sixpence. A very old letter from Lucy, saying in her familiar script: "Darling love, I'll die if you don't." She supposed it could have been worse. A letter from herself. A photograph of herself holding Laurie as a baby, at Lucy's parents' house. Lucy had taken it: she had forgotten the occasion until now. She was standing on the lawn with her baby in her arms, smiling in an unnatural and unbecoming way. Next to it, carefully folded, was an unfinished note, in James's own writing, which said, "My darling love, when I left you yesterday I . . ."

❧ I was hoping that in the end I would manage to find some kind of unity. I seem to be no nearer to it. But at the beginning I identified myself with distrust, and now I cannot articulate my suspicions, I have relegated them to that removed, third person. I identify myself with love, and I repudiate those nightmare doubts.

I knew I would find nothing in that wallet to betray me. I knew it, or I wouldn't have looked. I knew that I would find nothing there but evidence of faith. Poor James, preserving me in that dreadful photo with Laurie: all fat I was from pregnancy, and slightly out of focus too. Though I wasn't such a fool that I hadn't noticed that the baby thing attracted him as much as it repels most men: he liked having babies around, he liked the idea of taking them on clandestine holidays, and why else did he choose such a point in time to get into my bed? It can't have been merely the unprecedented vision of me in a nightdress, affecting though that doubtless was. He used to eat with avidity Bianca's disgusting tepid baby food, scraping out her abandoned plates of cereal and bone broth. It must have been something to do with his mother and all those shocking mornings in her bed. I didn't care. I loved him. And I thought how convenient it was that his inclinations should so neatly comply with my condition.

And what a coward I was to find myself unable to mention the blood that dripped so alarmingly from his head as they carried him off. He looked so dead, he looked so dreadful, I was so afraid; and in writing of it the first time I tried to pretend that that worst thing, that dripping blood, hadn't happened, I tried to protect him, to present him elegantly, even in death. I had to force myself to mention that ghastly nerveless twitch, but I hadn't the courage for the blood. But I find it. And I find, too, the courage to admit that when I thought, at first, during the crash, that he had died and the children escaped, I was relieved: I would have wished him dead, poor love, to spare them, and I knew it at the time. But he, I knew, would have forgiven me this preference: he would not have termed it a mortal offense. Nor would he have accused me for flinching from him: he would not have expected too much of me. And knowing this, how could I, even in the middle of the night, even in my thoughts, have abandoned him? How could I have thought it an unimportant affair? It had been serious enough in its consequences: we had both taken it seriously enough. The marks on my face were healing, but I rather hoped that I was scarred for life. Surface wounds they were, maybe, but then one needs a skin to live in: it is not disposable, it is not replaceable, it will mark, it will bear witness.

It may have been true, too, that need and weakness bound us, but they had bound us effectively, so what need had we to protest against the terms of our bondage? What right had I to deny the conditions of our meeting? We were starving, when we met, James and I, parched and starving, and we saw love as the miraged oasis, shivering on the dusty horizon in all the glamor of hallucination: blue water, green fronds and foliage breaking from the dry earth. Like deluded travelers we had carefully approached, hardly able to trust the image's persistence, afraid that it would fade into yet more dry acres as we drew nearer, believing ourselves blinded by our own desires: but when we got there—when I got there, for how can I speak for him, how could I speak for him, so dead and speechless—when I got there, the image remained, it sustained my possession of it, and the water that I drank, the so much longed-for water, was not sour and brackish to the taste. Nor were the leaves green merely through the glamor of distance, through the contrast with the preceding waste: they remained green to the touch, dense endless foresting boughs, an undiscovered country, no shallow quickly exhausted, quickly drained sour well, but miles of verdure, rivers, fishes, colored birds, miles with no sign of an ending, and, perhaps, beyond them all, no ending but the illimitable, circular, inexhaustible sea.

That evening, when I went to the hospital, the sister in charge of the ward led me to James with pride, and said that he was lightening. I asked what she meant, and she said that she meant that he was less deeply unconscious, he was regaining some of his reflexes. She flashed a light into his sightless eye, and I saw the iris, very faintly, contract. Life was restoring itself to that glaucous, opaque, visionary globe. I felt such relief, and I too felt pride: I felt that he was responding to my faith, as to the nurses' care. I told myself, at that point, that I would not care if he were lost to me forever, if that eye never again mirrored mine and saw in mine, as he had once said, proximity: I would be grateful if he survived, to see other things, having been removed from me by fate and not by infidelity. (I was lying to myself, of course I was lying, but how can one face such depths of selfishness?) I sat by his bed for the accustomed half-hour, staring not at him, because he did look too dreadful, despite the alleged lightening, but at the weave of my basket, which I carried everywhere in place of a handbag— I had not had a handbag for years because I never went near handbag shops, but it was quite easy to buy baskets in the local ironmongers. It was a new basket, foreign, woven of rushes, and at first glance it seemed to be merely a neutral pale-brown and yellow straw color, but as I stared I noticed in the dried colorlessness of it faint watery tender streaks of green. I can't say how much this discovery affected me. It seemed the green of the marshes where those rushes had once flourished: I saw suddenly a vision of vast acres of growing things, and it seemed so hopeful that the color of growth should persist so obstinately in such dry tender shades. Even if James had died he would have been beautifully resolved into other elements. But it was no longer possible that he should die. When I touched his hand at parting I thought that it stirred, very slightly, at my touch.

When I got back to the hotel, I had made up my mind to ring Lucy. I could not run the risk of seeing his blank lack of recognition if I were the only one to see his return. I was prepared to admit the lot—adultery, guilt, the smashed car, the vast quantities of those three hundred pounds that I had already spent. But it was not necessary: Lucy rang me. I was sitting in the lounge downstairs reading a copy of *Country Life* when the pageboy came and said to me that Mrs. Jane Gray was asking for me on the telephone. I had such a shock at the sound of my own name that I could hardly stand up: it all seemed too absurd, like some dreadful Elizabethan comedy of impersonation and substitution and mistaken identity. I don't know who I thought would be on the other end of the phone: fate itself, perhaps, or my schizoid double. But I recognized Lucy's voice instantly.

"Mrs. Otford, eh?" she said, when I said hello into the receiver. "Mrs. Otford, is it? Well," she said, in a tone of such venom, force, and feeling that I could hardly believe my ears, "I've only got one thing to say to you, and that is that I wish to God he'd been killed and that you'd been killed with him."

And then she rang off.

I was so amazed that I kept on saying hello for some time into the mouthpiece, and then I went back into the lounge again and opened the *Country Life* and stared at a picture of a horse jumping over a fence. The astonishing thing is that, hav-

ing got what I'd asked for, I didn't much care. I hadn't foreseen it, I'm not saying I'd foreseen it, any more than I'd foreseen Malcolm's onslaught when he dragged me out of bed and
beat my head against the wall; but at the same time I accepted
it, as I had not accepted Malcolm and his violence. And I was
not surprised when, five minutes later, I was called to the
phone again. It was Lucy once more, of course, but this time
speaking in her accustomed manner.

"I'm sorry," she said. "I'm sorry. I didn't mean it."

"That's all right," I said.

Then there was a long silence, and I said, "How did you
know where we were?" and she explained that Malcolm had
visited her the night before, very drunk, and told her that he
had seen me with James. So she had rung the Norwegian
cousin (a character whose very existence had entirely slipped
my memory), who said that he'd not heard from James, and
anyway, if she was James's wife, why wasn't she with him as he
was expecting both of them.

"Then I got in a panic and rang the R.A.C. and the police,"
she said, "and they told me what had happened to the car. So
I rang the hospital and they told me where you were."

"What did they say about James?" I said, thinking that they
might have been prepared to tell her more of the truth than
they would have told me, being his wife, and Lucy being
merely, as she had claimed, his sister-in-law.

"They said he was recovering, that they thought he'd recover," said Lucy.

"It seems that he will," I said.

Then there was another long silence, and finally she said,
in a tone so like her, so like her old exchanges that I wondered
if the other thing that I had heard had been a mistake, a hal-

lucination, "Would you mind very much if I came and joined you?"

"Mind? How could I mind?" I said.

"I'm nearer than you think," she said, and it seemed that she was at the station, having taken her children during the day to her mother's and come up on the evening train.

"Shall I book you a room?" I asked her, and she said that I should, and that she would get a taxi to the hotel at once; and before I had finished speaking to the girl at reception I heard the taxi draw up and saw her pushing feebly at the heavy glass door.

We stared at one another across two yards of carpet, and then she crossed toward me, and put her case down, and said, "Whatever happened to your face?"

I touched the plaster, defensively. "It's nothing," I said.

And then she turned to the girl at reception, who was smiling politely, glad, I think, to see that I had company at last, but disappointed by the lack of visible emotion, by the chill that marked our demeanor: she would have liked embraces and tears. I had booked the room for Lucy in my own name. She signed, and then looked at me, and said, "Whose address shall I put?"

"I had to put yours," I said, so she bent her head and wrote mine and then she looked up at me and said, "I can't understand it. Do you think it has any kind of meaning, all this?"

"I think it must have," I said.

❋ In bed that night we talked, Lucy and I; we slept in the same bed, divided by Laurie. Lucy said she could not face her own room. She had bought a bottle of Scotch in the bar below, and we lay there drinking it, lying on our backs, staring at the ceiling. She told me some of the things that I had known I would have to hear: about the dreadful, endless, exhausting conflict between herself and James, and I could see that the harmony of silence that had so touched me between them had been in part the silence of rejection and fatigue. "He's so insanely jealous," she kept saying, "he wanted all of me, all of me, and he knew it wasn't there even when I met him, he knew it was gone already—" and I thought of how unqualified, how unpreceded his possession of me had been, and I could see why he had so wanted it. "He wants babies," she said, "he kept going on about babies, until I started to hate him for it—I hated having children, they drive me to despair, how could one have more than three children? It wouldn't be possible." She started to cry. "I couldn't bear him to touch me," she said.

Then she told me that she was having an affair—the most recent of several, I gathered—with one of the directors of the company where she worked: the same director, she claimed, who had been having an affair with James's mother when she had first met James. "I can't understand it," she said. "I simply can't understand it. Why am I doing it, why has it turned out like this? It seems so obvious that it's because of James's mother, some kind of revenge I suppose, but it doesn't feel like that when I'm with him. I think—" and she started to laugh, hysterically, smothering her laughter for the children's sake, "I really think that it's nothing to do with all that at all, it's just because we work in the same building. Proximity, that's all it is. The basis of all incest. Take what's nearest."

"It can't be so," I said, though I had thought the same thoughts myself.

"No, of course it can't," she agreed, "but I can't understand all the other reasons."

"There's not much point in trying to make sense of it," I said.

"Perhaps it's something to do with you and me," she said.

"I've thought of that, too."

"You've thought of everything."

"No. Not everything. I didn't think Malcolm would go and see you."

"He wants you back," she said.

"I'd have rung you anyway," I said, defending myself from accusations that she would never have voiced. "But I couldn't bring myself to do it, at first."

"Malcolm seemed in rather a bad way," said Lucy.

"Oh, forget about Malcolm," I said, thinking that the next thing I'd have to hear would be that Lucy had slept with him to cheer him up.

"I told him where you were, when I'd found out," said Lucy. "He said he'd come and collect the children and take them home to your mother's. Then you could say you were here to keep me company. And anyway it would give our mothers something to do. Looking after their grandchildren."

"I'm not letting him have them," I said, without thinking.

"They're his children," said Lucy. "And, anyway, they can't like it much here. However long were you prepared to stay here?"

"Until James's money ran out, I suppose," I said, to revenge myself upon her for sympathizing with Malcolm: I had had enough explanations, I was longing already for the dim obscurity of misunderstanding in which we had hitherto lived.

"You realize what this'll have cost us?" said Lucy. "You realize there was some fiddle with the insurance of that car?"

"What do I care about that?" I said.

"It's all right for you," she said, "your husband must be earning a bloody fortune."

"I'll take you to see the car tomorrow," I said. "I'll take you to see all the sights of the town. The car looks horrific. I go and have a look at it from time to time and think what a good time we could have been having in Norway."

"What a bastard he is," said Lucy. "He really is unspeakable. You're not the first, you know. Whatever he says."

"I didn't think I was," I said, untruthfully.

"Anyway," she said, "I suppose we shouldn't speak ill of the unconscious."

"I haven't spoken ill of him," I said. "I haven't even thought much ill of him."

The next day we went to visit those two wrecks, James and the car. It was a cold, bright, clear morning: there was ice on the puddles in the gutter, and frost on the rooftops. Charming, we must have looked, Lucy and I, walking along in our head scarfs and our thick coats, with me pushing the pushchair, and Lucy holding Laurie's hand. Two sisters, spending an idle morning. I took her to the garage first; the car was in a shed at the back. She stared at the crumpled metal, and shivered, perhaps from the cold. She had told me over breakfast, sitting up in bed—we had breakfast in the room, always, the children and I, to spare the other guests—sitting up in bed building a small tower with the little oblong paper parcels of sugar lumps, she had told me of how frightened she always had been of just such an accident, of her disgust at the race tracks, of her withdrawal from James's infantile enthusiasms. "It was all the worse," she had said, her face frowning slightly from her efforts at justice, efforts I too well recognized, "it was all the worse because I'd once liked it, I'd once found it exciting. There's nothing more dreadful than having to live with an outworn affectation." She sighed, and drank some tea. "Sometimes," she said, "I thought he was getting tired of it too. And I couldn't think which would be worse, his caring or his not caring any more." They had had one accident together, years ago, Lucy and James, but so mild a one compared with our sensational disaster: they had driven into the back of a station-ary car and broken the radiator. "The crunch was so soft, we were going so slowly," she said, "that I couldn't believe it had done any damage, and when James started to moan about it, and said the car was finished and we'd have to have it hauled away by a garage, I had no sympathy with him, I told him he must be mad, that there couldn't be anything wrong with it at all. I told him to get in and drive away." And all the time the rust-colored water had been seeping before her eyes onto the road. "I've come to dislike myself so much," Lucy said. And that statement, too, I recognized and took to my heart.

When we had inspected the corpse of the Aston Martin, we went back to the hotel and had a cup of coffee. We sat around as though we were on some kind of holiday.

In the evening, Lucy went with me to see James. By now he was almost alive: he was moving slightly, restlessly in his sleep. It was lovely to me to see him move. The nurse said he had spoken a word in the morning: I asked what word it had been, but she said she could not catch it, it had not been clear. The sight of him was a shock to Lucy, but I had expected no less, for she had not been through my initiation; and even so I don't think she appreciated quite how grave the situation had been. She didn't question me about the accident, and I volunteered no information. As we stood there together by the bedside I wondered if we would both return into our private discretion. I hoped so, I could not take too much intimacy. We returned to the hotel, and as we sat in the bar drinking a final drink, she said, "It makes no difference, to him, what we think. Does it?"

And I said no, how could it. But we knew better, both of us. Why else had those stories been created, those tales of entranced lovers kept alive through the years by faith, those fables of sleep-

262 | THE WATERFALL

ers and dreamers awoken finally by the intensity and endurance of desire? Will you not wake and turn to me? I must have been mad to think these thoughts. And yet madder still to abandon them. Lucy lit match after match and dropped them into the heavy glass ash tray and let them burn out. As children, we had played a game with matches: we would light one and let it burn, then reverse it and hold its other end. We would make each match represent the life of a person we knew: and if we dropped the match because it burned our fingers, or if it extinguished itself of its own accord, then the natural life span of that person would be curtailed by the amount of soft white wood that was left. We did not believe in it, but we suffered a pang when we idly lopped twenty years from the life of an admired friend or school mistress, and we triumphed when the match dwindled and withered and blackened to its very end. For certain people I would have endured any burn, any scar, but sometimes there was something in the quality of the wood or the currents of the air that prevented my efforts. Superstition. Childish nonsense. I wondered if Lucy, as she dropped those idle matches into their small pyre, was recollecting, in the dim reaches of her mind, that childhood game. I did not recall it to her. I have a respect for the rational, for what others call reality, but I gazed at the withering splinters with more attention than I listened to the prophecies of the nurses at the hospital.

263 | THE WATERFALL

Malcolm did not come for the children: I had not thought he would. What could he have done with two small children, one of which he had never even seen? He could not even have got them south on the train. I wondered how long Lucy and I would stick it out together. On the second night, we had dinner in the hotel dining room, an event which I had until that point avoided, making do with fish and chips, purchased on the way home from the hospital, or sandwiches and hamburgers from the local snack bar. We sat opposite one another, across a small table covered in white linen and heavy cutlery, and read the menu, and ate paté and steak and rolls and butter and sherry trifle. It seemed years since I had eaten a meal in such a place. We did not talk much: we had reverted, both of us, to silence. The time for any confidence had passed. I could see that neither of us would find an opportunity, now, to say, will you relinquish him to me? how long do you intend to stay? I had come to think I would live in that town forever: there was no point in going away, it was as good a place as anywhere.

As we drank our coffee I remembered, absurdly, something that a friend of Malcolm's had once said to me at a party: a grand friend he was, a well-known concert pianist, whose kindness in speaking to me, young and unmusical as I was, I conceived humbly as condescension. He was speaking of himself, as performers do: a handsome fellow, dark and flashy; and r@@@@@@@@@@@@@@@@ff@@@@@@@@@@@@@@@@ fff@@@@@@@@@@@@@@@@@@f.f.f.f.f.f.f.f.f.f.f.f.f.f.f.f.

he said that a megalomaniac was a man who, when run over by a car, thought at the point of death that fate had done it to him from a sense of personal spite, to prevent him from achieving better things. I thought of this irrelevant remark, and I remembered the poems that I intended still to write, and I thought of the rushes, green in death, dry but still green and immortal, like Keats and his cold pastoral. And I thought that those rushes were the color of poetry, and that I would write, because writing is the thing that one can do anywhere, in a hotel bedroom, in solitary confinement, in a prison cell, a defense more final, less destructible, than the company of love. I could feel it stirring in me. Descending. I could see the changes in the color of the air, the faintly approaching presences of words. Forgive me. It is no less than the truth that I try to express.

The next day James's eyes were open: he could see out of them, though what he could see it was impossible to tell. The day after that he started to speak, but his words were slurred and indistinguishable. Lucy and I took turns with my children so that one of us could be with him all the time, in case he should know us, but he recognized nobody. The nurses said it might take days, even weeks, for him to regain full consciousness, and that it would in any case be hard for us to recognize the true moment of his recognition: there would be no amount of revelation, no sudden light. And they were right: his speech grew gradually clearer, phrases became distinct, he would ask for a drink or a cigarette and seem to see me, and then, before he took the proffered glass, he would sink away again into sleep or lassitude or obscure mumbling. It was so slow, the process, that I could see it wouldn't matter which of us he knew first: and indeed, on the third day after he had first spoken, he suddenly said to me as I stood up to go:

"Jane. Where did they put my book?" as though he had known me all the time, had known all the time that I was there, but of course there was no book, there never had been a book, and by the time I had taken out of my basket the only book that I had with me to offer to him—a picture book of Laurie's, it was—he had relapsed once more, and would not even lift his hand to take it. I recounted this to Lucy, and she said it was the same with her: at times he seemed to know her, at other times he was confused or indifferent.

Finally, just over a fortnight after the accident, he took the decisive step into this world. I arrived for my evening visit to be met at the entrance of the ward by an agitated nurse, who expressed relief to see me, and said that he was weeping and screaming for me. I followed her to him and heard her say to him, "Look, Mr. Otford, here she is, here's your wife," and I heard his dreadful sobbing. I would, I suppose, had things been simpler, have gone then to look for Lucy, but how could I? Being there, I did what I could. He clutched at me and would not let me go, and in the end he became quiet, and spoke for the first time reasonably.

"It's a hospital, isn't it?" he said, and then he said, bewildered, "I suppose I must be ill."

"It was an accident," I said, wondering if he would ask any more, but he didn't. He shut his eyes and said, "Oh God, I'm so tired, I'm so exhausted." He was still holding on to my hand. Then he said, "I'm so glad you were here, I'm so glad you didn't leave me."

"I wouldn't leave you," I said, but he was already asleep. I asked the nurse what all his agitation had meant, and she said it was a usual thing, it would have done him good. And indeed, when he woke again the next morning, he found it quite easy to identify both me and Lucy, and even the nurses, and even asked the occasional question about how he had got there, and what had happened, though he never attended to the answers. He did not seem at all surprised by our presence: I wondered, guiltily, if he remembered what he had known of me, or if he remembered me merely as Lucy's cousin. It was impossible to tell from his manner.

At lunch that day Lucy looked at me suddenly and sharply across the table, and said that she was going home. I said nothing, and she buttered a piece of roll and said, "I've got to get back. I've got to get back to work, I've got to get back to the children. I've been away long enough."

I continued to say nothing because I did not know what to say. I did not even know whether I wanted her to stay or to go.

"I'll leave him to you," she said. "One of us is quite enough for this job. I've had enough. I'll leave it to you, I'll get off out of it."

"If that's how you see it," I said, inconclusively, for I did not know how she saw it, nor what she meant by her departure. I have often wondered, since then. Perhaps she meant what she said, that she had to get back to the children. Perhaps I was helping her, by staying to keep him company? Perhaps she was acknowledging my claims by leaving him with me? I would have kept him forever, but I think I knew already, from the ways in which she had spoken of him that night when she told me of their unhappiness, that I would never be allowed to keep him. It was a loan that I was offered. I accepted it, being more interested in possession than in the terms of possession.

And so she left. I had to lend her ten pounds of James's money, as she'd run out, and parting with such a sum made me take stock of my own finances and realize I couldn't afford to live at the Saracen's Head forever. So I moved out into a boarding house, having paid my already staggering bill. I thought I might as well stay on there until James was ready to move. What else had I to do? It would be another month before he could leave, they said, but I was prepared to stay for a month. It was so strange, to see him recover, so slowly, with such fatigue. He always seemed glad to see me, he addressed me as darling and held my hand, but the whole journey, the Aston Martin, the notion of Norway, the lot, had been wiped from his memory entirely. He began to talk more and more easily, but all he talked about was the hospital itself: what he'd had for breakfast, what a bore it was having to get up to sit in a chair for five minutes, what the old man in the next bed had said, the nurses' stockings. I didn't know whether to be annoyed or encouraged by his interest in the nurses' stockings; certainly he showed no interest in mine, and I told myself that I could not expect him to. I regulated my reactions to his words so carefully: as carefully as I had, in earlier days, my jealousy. I was glad, really, of his preoccupation with hospital life, because what else would we have talked about? Many a regretted confession must have been made, through desperate boredom, at a hospital bedside. I remember my mother, lying in bed in a nursing home after some gynecological operation, was driven most unadvisedly, through lack of other topics, to tell me about one of my less respectable great uncles. She could think of nothing else to say to me, a distant captive visitor.

Lucy came back on the weekends, and James's mother came once, in the fourth week. I kept out of her way, not knowing what she had been told of the situation, not knowing when Lucy had informed her, thinking that she might well resent the silence and delay for which I had been so largely responsible. I did not think she would resent my connection with James: she would be as indifferent to it, I assumed, as my own mother would have been appalled. But nevertheless, I was myself so acutely conscious of my grotesquely false position that I avoided her. She stayed at the Saracen's Head, whence I had removed myself, and doubtless had to endure much embarrassing and confusing chat about her daughter-in-law and grandchildren. She stayed for one night only and then got quickly off back to London. I was apprehensive, visiting James for the first time after her departure, afraid of the ways in which she might have affected him, and indeed when I got there he seemed in a very curious state. He was lying back on his bed, staring at the ceiling, and muttering silently to himself, moving his lips anxiously, as though trying to find some difficult, elusive word. When he saw me he paid me no attention, so I sat down on the chair by him and prepared to wait. And after a while he turned to me and what I saw in his face was so beautiful, so amazing, so unhoped for, that I felt my breath stop and the blood leave my head. What I saw was recognition.

"Jane," he said. "Jane." As though he had not known who I was until that moment, as though he had just worked out who I was.

"Yes," I said.

"Darling," he said, and I began to get frightened, because I could see his face working, I could see some awful fear in his eyes, something he could hardly bring himself to speak. "Darling," he said, bending toward me, "darling. Tell me. Whatever happened to Laurie and the baby. They were on the back seat. Whatever happened to them." And as I said to him that they

were all right, as I reassured him, he started to cry, hiding his
face against me, crying and shivering like a child. He'd remembered nearly all of it, he said, and he'd suddenly thought
of the children, and thought they must be dead, because he
hadn't seen them, because I hadn't brought them.

"You're so kind, so kind," he said to me, "you'd never have
let me know that I'd killed them, you'd never have let me
know . . ." and so I tried to explain to him about the accident, to tell him that it hadn't been his fault, that it had been
an act of God lying in the road, that nobody had suffered any
injury but he himself. But my explanation tired him: he
couldn't follow it, he couldn't concentrate. He held my hand
and repeated, "Thank God I didn't kill you all, thank God I
didn't kill you." And I could tell from the way that he was
holding on to me that he remembered me, that he'd remembered what he'd known of me. I was filled with such admiration and tenderness by the nature of his first conscious thought:
it vindicated all that I had ever hoped of him. Later, when he
was well enough to discuss these things, he told me of his bewilderment at finding me in the hospital, and his inability, at
first, to account for my presence there: he had accepted my
presence, he said, it had seemed natural to him, but he had
been unable to work out why it should seem natural, nor why
I let him hold my hand. "I used to say to myself when you'd
gone," he said, "that perhaps she'd let any dying man hold on
to her, perhaps any woman would hold the hand of any man,
and I didn't like to ask you why you did it in case I frightened
you away, I didn't like to ask you why you knew so well what
I wanted." And then he said, "I didn't dare to touch you, I
hardly dared to touch you until that day when I remembered
that car and the journey and remembered that you had been

mine. It was so lovely," he said, "when I remembered that, it was like finding you all over again, like opening my eyes and finding you and knowing you had been there by my bed the whole time." He always told elegant lies. But it may have been true, what he said. All I can say for myself is that it was only when he awoke and remembered me that I admitted to myself how bitterly painful I had found his forgetfulness: how selfishly, how painfully I had longed for his attention.

The next day I took the children to see him for a few minutes, as he no longer looked too disgusting to witness: I thought he should see that they were still alive. The nurses were reluctant to admit them, but since they thought they were James's own children they relented. It was so touching to see his feeble smile, his efforts to connect.

The matron told me that she had known few patients make so complete a recovery. All the fractures mended, and before we left he was able to walk a little on crutches though his leg was still in plaster. But more remarkable was the degree of recollection that he finally achieved. It is normal, it appears, in such cases, to forget the whole of the preceding sequence of events: certainly the crash itself, and usually the whole journey. But James, by the time he left the hospital, had remembered our departure, the broken window of our house, the Scotch in the front pocket, the car registration number, and our destination. He claimed, later, that this reflected well on the quality of his emotions, and I'm sure he was right.

Our last week there was really quite enjoyable. We sat there discussing what we would have done in Norway had we got there, and whether it would be bad luck ever to plan to go there again: it seemed quite like our old life together, a fantasy life, a fake marriage with borrowed children and substitute names. Perhaps, I thought, we were better with this kind of thing than we would have been at reality: Norway would have been too much for us. I fed him with recollections, with anecdotes, with carefully edited little pieces of the past. One significant change was that we now spoke of Lucy, in this new context—not much, but a little, as though our relationship could now bear the forbidden syllables of her name, as though her deliberate leaving of him had given us the right to acknowledge her existence. I saw him revive, slowly, as he must have felt me revive for him at the beginning of the year: I felt so strong, watching him, I could measure my own change. One evening, toward the end of those weeks, as I was sitting there, he suddenly said to me: "They were playing "Chimborazo" when it happened," and we laughed and wept because it had been so, because he had remembered it all, right up to the moment of impact, he had suppressed nothing, he had let it all come back to him. He claimed that he had remembered it through love for me, because nothing undergone with me could be forgotten: two holes in my skull couldn't let you out of me, he said, holding my hand, threatening, smiling, and I, drunk on his protestations, did not protest too much.

We were happy, in that hospital. Such imprisonment suited our natures. Dialogues in a sick room, in claustrophobic proximity. Dependence, confinement, solicitude.

It could not last, of course. The price of his restoration was his loss. When he was well enough to move, his mother came for him and took him away, home to Lucy and a resident nurse. Jane watched him go, waving goodbye to him and his mother with a calm that surprised her. She did not try to claim him: she had known he would go, and he had known that she knew it. There was no question of keeping him: he had been lent to her, and the loan was over. So she packed up her things and caught the train back to London. Returning home after so long away was like returning from a foreign country: she gazed from the taxi on the way home at the passing unfamiliar city architecture, at the hoardings, at the grime, at the posters advertising films she had never heard of, and she felt that she had been away for years. The house was in a dreadful state: the front room, which had clearly been inhabited by vagrants of some kind, was full of old egg boxes, newspapers, old cardigans, sardine tins, and fag packets. The cardboard had come away from the broken window, and cats ran in and out. The front passage was silted up with weeks of filthy old mail, mostly free samples and circulars. A pipe had burst and half the kitchen ceiling had fallen in, exposing the rafters. Moss and fungus were growing from the walls. Malcolm had been back during her absence, because the piano room at the top of the house showed signs of his occupation. He or one of the tramps had mended the burst pipe with elastoplast. She stared at the wreckage, and decided that there was nothing for it but to try to clear it up. How could she leave it, how could she live any longer in such decay? It had rotted so quickly, it had become so quickly derelict. She had thought it bad enough before, but now she could see that her residence, however inattentive, had at least kept out the elements.

In the ash tray of the room upstairs she found a little clipping from *The Times*, screwed up in a ball: it said that Malcolm

Gray was the most accomplished guitarist of his generation, and that he had played on November 8 with unparalleled brilliance and plangency. She did not think that such a man as he would be kept warm in bed by such cuttings, nor that they would be enough to make him forgive himself for having abandoned a wife and two children in the leaking pipes and the moss. He would pay forever: he would never be able to buy them off. She knew that she would hang around his neck, the slaughtered albatross, forever, and she resolved to lighten that guilt by setting her own house in order. She owed it to him, she thought. She would clean the place up, and thus prove to him, if he should pass or hear of her, that she was not entirely dead, that he need not bear the weight for life. And yet, she thought, perhaps it might cause more offense than death, to fly off on snowy unbroken wings? Which would do him more good, to know that he had killed her, or to suspect that she had escaped him? There was no way to spare him.

It took her some days to get around to sorting out the accumulation of second-class mail that lay around the hallway: she could not throw it out without looking at it, though little of it repaid inspection. The first interesting missive that she found was a letter from the secretary of the play group that Laurie had attended: it was presented as the minutes of the last committee meeting, and she read it with growing amazement because it was mad, quite mad, madder than she had ever herself been in her worst moments. The secretary woman had been unpopular, or had managed in some way to offend the other mothers and committee members involved: the minutes, which started off on a note of amateur intimacy of a peculiarly feminine nature—"The meeting was held in Mrs. Hibbert's drawing room, where the newly sanded floor was much ad-

mired, and on which young Master Andrews was requested
not to drive his new tractor"—ended up in a flood of irrelevant,
masochistic, self-denigrating abuse—"Mrs. Starkey, the present secretary, was informed that unless she resigned the Treasurer and the Chairman would no longer continue to serve on
the Committee, and that her services were no longer required:
whereupon Mrs. Starkey burst into tears, which were wiped up
on a nice clean pink Kleenex offered by the hostile Treasurer.
Mrs. Starkey then said that since her help was not appreciated
she had no option but to . . ." and so on, and so on, in a nightmare of tangled emotions and official language that made
Jane, reading it, sigh and shake her head. She had always suspected that all such women were mad, that such lives could
lead only to madness. She did not know why the typed and
duplicated pages looked so significant. Perhaps she saw them as
a warning.

The next letter that she opened, a dull-looking official brown
envelope, was a letter from Malcolm's solicitor, telling her he
was seeking a divorce. She could not make out what it was at
first, and nearly threw it out, it looked so irrelevant.

> *Jane Gray.*
> *Head on the block.*
> *And all the whirring birds flew upwards.*

James Otford, the solicitor's letter said. It named him. Poor
James, who was in a rehabilitation place, learning to walk
again.

Why was I always so interested in being innocent? Is it a
common preoccupation? The most grotesque falsehood I have
told is when I said that I didn't much care when Lucy wished

me dead, over the telephone, in that hotel. I cared more than I could express, I cared so much that I could not bear to relive it. I was paralyzed, I was numb with guilt. I did not think I could ever endure it. Why was I let off? What charity, what certainty in her allowed it?

At the beginning of this book, I deliberately exaggerated my helplessness, my dislocation, as a plea for clemency. So that I should not be judged. Poor helpless Jane, abandoned, afraid, timid, frigid, bereft. What right had anyone to point an accusing finger? Poor Jane, lying in that bed with her newborn child, alone. Poor Jane, child of such monstrous parents. How could she not be mad? And as for that note of consecutive calm on which I opened these pages—that surely I have managed to deny?

I don't like guilt. I don't like being human. I don't like my own actions. But they are, after all, mine. And I don't think that any indictment could touch me now.

There's nothing wrong with my parents, anyway. Quite often I like them. Much of what they say is perfectly true, and even quite amusing.

One might as well face it. Particularly when one sees it in black and white. Adultery with James Otford. Ah well. Worse crimes have been committed, no doubt. Though it did not seem so at the time. It seemed to be the worst thing, that I was so willingly undertaking. Perhaps I did not make this clear. Perhaps I should have nerved myself, and said more about guilt. Guilt, the gilded crown of the martyrs.

But instead, I wrote about love. The more I emphasized my sorrow, I must have thought, the more claims I made for my love. The better I would emerge. Damaged before birth, I think I described myself. A curious plea for acquittal. In fact there probably wasn't much wrong with me at all. Looking back, with the wisdom of my present knowledge, I could well claim to have been perfectly well adjusted all the time: merely waiting, I might have said, for an opportunity to prove it. What, after all, was I complaining about? Nothing very significant, surely? An unhappy childhood, an unsatisfactory marriage, my own laziness. I had been perfectly all right all the time, and in trying to claim that there had ever been anything wrong with me I was merely trying to defend myself against an accusation of selfishness. Judge me leniently, I said, I am not as others are, I am sad, I am mad, so I have to have what I want. I cannot be blamed, I said. Let me off lightly.

But I judge my past now, in the light of the present. It had seemed so clear to me, always, that people could not change, that they were predetermined, unalterable, helpless in the hands of destiny; and if, therefore, I had ended up sleeping with James and liking it (and God, how I liked it), if I had ended like this, conniving with Lucy, rejecting Malcolm, if I had ended up thus human and thus corruptly happy, then surely I had always been capable of such an ending, and the other symptoms had been merely false warnings, misleading evidence, portents misunderstood? In seeking to avoid my fate, like Oedipus, I had met it. In seeking to avoid the sin of treachery, I had embraced it, I had forced its inevitability upon me, and those sick withdrawals had been nothing more than the sighs by which I summoned James to my side. In presenting myself, in this narrative, as a woman on the verge of collapse, on the verge of schizophrenia or agoraphobia, I had been lying: I had been pleading nonexistent desperation, unfulfilled hypochondriac spiritual fears. I knew, as I lay in the bed with newborn Bianca, that I would be saved, that there was no possibility that I might lie there alone forever. I would have James: there was no possibility of refusing him. I have to rethink it all, in terms of what I now know myself to be, in terms of the things I have done since then. Had I been destined for collapse, I would have collapsed. But I was not. So to plead its past imminence, as I did in this first chapter of this book, is illegitimate: a false plea, falsely based.

And yet, that can't be the whole truth. There are certain facts that remain, and I turn back to them, not seeking extenuation, but seeking, perhaps—and ah, what lost nobility I could thereby claim—seeking perhaps the truth. It is a fact that I lived alone and lay there alone, that I spoke to no one, that I was unable to confront the sight of a human face. It is a fact that I regarded James as a miracle, and that when he touched me it was as though I had another body, a body different from the one I had known. Perhaps I had always possessed it: but without him, where would it have lived? What shadowy realms would it have inhabited? A body must take on flesh for us to know it. And without James, where would it have been, where would I have been, where would have lived the woman that writes these words? He changed me, he saved me, he changed me. I say it again, there is nothing else to say. It is too much to lay at his charge, but it was he that did it: but for him, where would I now have been? Alone and mad, perhaps, or reunited with Malcolm, more likely, dragging out his days in endless faint reproach and sick resentment.

James changed me beyond recognition. I bow to circumstance, I acknowledge it, I acknowledge the things that brought him to me. Foolish to deny them, foolish to deny the accidental, foolish to deny the personal. I lay myself at its feet.

In a sense, perhaps, I have always believed that a passion adequately strong could wrench a whole nature from its course, and that all the romantic accouterments of torn skies, uprooted trees, gaping earth, and white torrential waters would follow meekly such a natural disaster: Lucy's father had an old oil painting of just such a scene, a storm of dismal varnished rage, the effect of which was somehow immensely heightened by a rip in the canvas itself, which as a small child I took to be part of the painting, and which only in later years revealed itself as the work of time, not of the artist. This belief itself, this obstinate faith, so at odds with my sense of predestination, may have been a part of me, presaging James and all those violent convulsions. Had I not expected such events, they would not have occurred: the force of the current admits them, and a shifting of the landscape effects them. They could not occur, surely, in a flat and empty plain. And so it is all foreordained, after all: I was merely a disaster area, a landscape given to such upheavals. I saw, once, in reality, the effects of such a storm. In Scotland it was, and I heard there stories of roofs blown off high buildings, and whole tenements crashing in the gale, and I saw with my own eyes the country roads littered with pine trees, the branches in the drooping fronds of telephone wires, the hairy roots reaching for the sky, the red bleeding earth. But then, in so wild a country, even the unnatural seemed expected, the violence inevitable. And I must conclude that I did not summon James (that revolution in the elements) from nothing, I did not draw him like a ghost from the outer sky. He pre-existed. It was our meeting that was not foreseen: though what lovers have not believed that the whole of time has been watching over their convergence? As those pine trees had grown to crash in that January gale?

There is one thing that I can find no way to explain, and

that I must recount in amazement, in gratitude. Who would have thought he would ever take such pains to make good in me the new courses, the new ways, the new landscapes? I spoke of violence and convulsions, but he made the new earth grow, he made it blossom. It cannot have been an easy task: it cannot have been easy for him, to find the words and the persistence, but for some reason—for obstinacy, for kindness, for love—he found them both. He changed me forever and I am now what he made. I doubt, at times, I panic, I lose faith; but doubt, as they say, is not accessible to unbelievers.

Malcolm didn't divorce me. After that first letter from the solicitor, stating his intentions, I heard no more about it. I didn't give the matter much thought, myself, at first; it seemed irrelevant.

James wrote to me, from the rehabilitation place, where I did not dare to visit him, having silently accepted the fact that he had been returned to Lucy, that I had lost him. He had never much cared for writing letters, as he could hardly ever find in the written word the occasional felicities of his speech, but he had taken the trouble to write to me. His handwriting strayed helplessly and straggled on the page, for he had lost a certain amount of physical control, only gradually to be regained; and his words strayed equally, searching for a phrase that would unite and condone us, as I searched for an image to express my assent to my fate, as I search now for a con-

clusion, for an elegant vague figure that would wipe out all the
conflict, all the bitterness, all the compromise that is yet to be
endured. He said that he knew I would start to think badly of
him, now that I was so far away, and to think that it hadn't
been worth doing: you'll think, he said, that the accident was a
judgment on us both. He said that I would start to doubt him
for the very things that I had once so liked (and I thought of
that night in bed when I had judged him for the cars and
the card tricks) and then he started to apologize for those
things, to say that he hadn't been able to avoid being what he
was, that he couldn't have been anything else, with such a
mother and such a home. He offered me, in fact, as dispiriting
an account of himself as even I, in my worse moments of disaffection, could have thought up. And as I read his words I
could feel in myself such strength of attachment that I knew
we would never be able to part, that I would never be able to
leave him; whether the attachment existed because of or despite those defects was no longer relevant. It had been: it was
no longer so. I would flow in the course that he had made
for me: there was no way of returning to the old confines, the
old high banks through which I used to run.

There isn't any conclusion. A death would have been the
answer, but nobody died. Perhaps I should have killed James
in the car, and that would have made a neat, a possible ending.

A feminine ending?

Or I could have maimed James so badly, in this narrative, that
I would have been allowed to have him, as Jane Eyre had her
blinded Rochester. But I hadn't the heart to do it, I loved him
too much, and anyway it wouldn't have been the truth because
the truth is that he recovered. When he came back from the
rehabilitation place he was cured of nearly all his afflictions

except for a boring tendency to recount the details of the accident; he likes to flash about a disgusting document, drawn up for the insurance, which catalogues the quantity and location of his fractures, but this is a tendency that does not take much heroism to endure. Nothing like what Jane Eyre had to put up with. In fact I have grown quite fond of that document, as he has, and no longer wince from phrases like "a fracture across the base of the skull through the pituitary fossa and into the sphenoid sinus—." I read them calmly, with affection, and don't blame him at all for trying to horrify the susceptible with tales of what he went through. The document also has its amusing moments: for instance, James and I were highly entertained by the following sequence of statements:

11 OCTOBER *Answered questions about his name and age.*
12 OCTOBER *Recognized his wife and spoke to her. Mostly semiconscious.*
13 OCTOBER *Awake most of the day.*
14 OCTOBER *Appeared to relapse: failed to recognize his wife, appeared in some confusion over his sister-in-law's identity.*
15 OCTOBER *Talking well but still confused.*
16 OCTOBER *Awake all day. Less confused.*

Even Lucy, apparently, could not resist the charm of this report, but I couldn't fully enjoy the thought of her conditional forgiveness, because I was too jealous at the thought of their laughing together over it and excluding me. But such, I see, is my lot: alternate jealousy and possession. It could have been worse. But it's hardly a tragic ending, to so potentially tragic a tale. In fact, I am rather ashamed of the amount of amusement that my present life affords me, and of how much I seem to have gained by it. One shouldn't get away with such things. In a way it makes the whole business seem, in retrospect, less serious: when we laugh together over my foolish expectation, at the moment of impact on the A1, of a personal message from God, I look anxiously over my shoulder and cross my fingers lest I should be struck down.

When James got back he came to see me instantly, and started to complain about the way I'd cleaned my house up. He said that all the shining paintwork and well-swept floors made him feel uncomfortable, so I let it lapse a little. He didn't much approve of my plans to acquire a girl to look after the children for me, either, and was really highly critical of my new-found desires to see my poems in print. He doesn't like my literary friends, and nags me about them in a pleasantly dull way. I think, too, that he is afraid that I will start to discuss him with Lucy, and I allow him to suspect that if provoked I might: though in fact never, never would I risk such a thing. Lucy and I, we remain locked in passionate exclusive discretion. I do not understand it. I do not understand it at all.

We should have died, I suppose, James and I. It isn't artistic to linger on like this. It isn't moral either. One can't have art without morality, anyway, as I've always maintained. It's odd that there should be no ending, when the whole affair otherwise was so heavily structured and orchestrated that I felt, at times, that I could see the machinery work, that I was simply living out some textbook pattern of relationship. Perhaps the pattern is not completed: the machine, which throws up every month some new juxtaposition and some new reflection, is striving for an effect too huge to conceive, or for some finale too grand and too full of poetic justice to be approached without forty years of hard and intricate labor.

I took up publication, and James took up driving again, so we both have our interests. As our adventures resolved into comedy, not tragedy, what I worry about most now is their financial aspect: people were too kind to tell me what the outcome of the Aston Martin insurance disaster was, and what the whole escapade cost, but it can't have been cheap. I shall probably know, in the end: James already makes veiled allusions to the business, which in retrospect he finds entertaining, and these allusions will doubtless resolve themselves finally into pounds, shillings, and pence; he won't be able to resist letting me know what he paid for me. Why should he? It was an impressive gesture. He and Lucy seem, in any case, to have recovered their own old standards of living—indeed, they never noticeably abandoned them. They are a resilient couple. I envy them.

I wrote a very good sequence of poems while James was in hospital, while I thought he was dying. I shall become like a man I know who wrote his only great poem on the death of his small child, and who has lived on its reputation ever since. But James, of course, didn't die, so I am mercifully quit of such dubious prestige. I had the experience without the loss: for free. And the poems are none the worse for the fact that they were founded on an unfulfilled terror. I have been writing better ever since that episode. Soon, no doubt, I shall begin to worry about writing too well. James was annoyed when I published the poems about him: he claimed that it was sacrilege to speak of such matters. But by a little casuistry I managed to persuade him that I would have destroyed them had he died, and that since he had not it was only right to bear witness to our escape, for the sake of luck, for the sake of the future. I said that it was an act of affirmation, at once a defiance and a distant grateful bow to providence, like his reunion with his car, and he accepted the analogy, though I daresay it would not bear inspection.

I was glad that he did not abandon driving. It would have been sad for him, and for me, I must confess, a deprivation and an inconvenience. I had become very keen on fast driving: I liked ripping along fast roads with him, wearing a head scarf and dark glasses, and pretending I was some other kind of person entirely. I liked to pretend that he was mine. I liked the sensations of speed, and the devouring of space and time. By his side, when his physical presence was no longer enough in itself to subdue me, I could sit very peacefully and quietly, re- leased from my own disgusting nervous restlessness by the noise and the vibrations. The first time he took me out, after the acci- dent, was so moving. I remember that we went out together from the house, and there it was, at the curbside, the familiar car. I must have hesitated, very slightly, as he opened the door for me to get in, because he looked at me with something in his face—apology, bravado, defiance, inquiry, I don't know—that compelled my knees and heart to their accustomed fluttering, and I got in quietly and sat down, consigning myself to him yet once more, with more unfounded and yet unquestionably more profound trust. I love his face. I love the expressions of it. "I won't kill you, I don't suppose," he said, as we moved off, and I said, "No, I don't suppose you will." I liked it, in his car. It was worth a few risks, to be there.

I heard no more from Malcolm after that first official letter. Perhaps he will turn up again one day and claim me, I don't know. I don't believe much in the sacrament of marriage, but it is to him that I am married, for all that. I follow his career in the papers, and I take the children to Croydon to see his parents: I don't know why I do this faithfully and punctiliously. As a kind of expiation, maybe, as a way of acknowledging the past. I sit there in their drawing room and accept their hostile affability, their suspect forgiveness. Had I constructed a form of social torture for myself, a year ago, two years ago, it would have consisted of just such a scene—myself exiled, guilty, stranded, among my enemies, among those with a supreme right to judge me—but now I take it with apparent calm. I am even entertained by some of the conversations that I hear there.

It is all so different from what I had expected. It is all so much more cheerful.

When Galsworthy had an affair with his cousin's wife, they carried on for years in alleged secrecy, taking long holidays abroad together, and Ada Galsworthy is said to have remarked that it was most convenient (from the point of view of passports and hotel bedrooms) that she and John already shared the same surname. What mixture of wit and common sense must have informed her: can they have laughed together over it, or were they above a sense of the ridiculous? One wonders why, in the circumstances, they bothered to marry at all. Similarly James and I, in not dissimilar circumstances, have found my family likeness to Lucy quite useful on occasion. I wonder from time to time whether the fact that I now find this not painful but amusing is a sign of maturity, or a sign of the total depravation of my character. It would be hard, I think, to decide. Anyway, I envy Ada Galsworthy those long trips to the Continent. Her first husband must have been very undemanding or very unobservant; the most James and I have ever managed, since that abortive Norwegian attempt, is a weekend in Yorkshire, though why I should speak of it with disparagement I don't know, because it was lovely. It was so lovely, in fact, that I can't resist attempting to evoke it, gratuitously, as a finale, however irrelevant—and it must be irrelevant because the only moral of it could be that one can get away with anything, that one can survive anything, a moral that I in no way believe (and if I did believe it I wouldn't tempt providence by asserting it). I write about it simply, as I say, because it was so lovely.

We went in the early summer, the summer after the accident; we went to Bradford, to see a man about a car, and I left the children at home with the *au pair* girl. (It's not possible, it's not possible that I acquired an *au pair* girl, but I did, I really did: like everyone else, I learned to swallow neurosis for the sake of convenience. What have I come to, I am incredulous.) We went up the motorway this time, and we got there without mishap, in a disgracefully short time. We went to see the man about the car, and when that was finished I made James take me to see a piece of scenery that I had always wanted to behold—a man at a party once gave me such an impassioned description of it that I had wanted to go for years, knowing that parties are for just such exchanges of information, and that such intimations, such stirrings, must not be denied. It is called Goredale Scar, the piece of scenery, it is part of the Pennines: it is real, unlike James and me, it exists. It is an example of the sublime.

We drove up to it, through the summer evening; it was late by now, for we had wasted time in Bradford, having tea and chips, but the evenings were long and it was still light. As we approached I grew slightly nervous, as it was clear that we could not drive the car right into the scenery, and that we would have to get out and walk and I was not at all confident about James's walking capacity. But we drove the car as near as we could, and parked it by a piece of dry stone wall, and then we got out and walked along a footpath through the short grass, along a kind of rift between two high hillsides that led toward the as yet unrevealed scar. At the bottom of the rift by the footpath flowed the small brook, source of the River Air, I believe, that would produce higher up, when we reached it, the celebrated waterfall. I looked at James anxiously from time to time, as we walked, as I was worried about his health, about his bad leg, about his unsuitable shoes, about whether he was bored or not by this purposeless expedition. I was worried about my own shoes, too, and my stockings; it was years since I had walked in the countryside. And I was worried by the fear that the view, when we reached it, would lack the significance with which I had, for anticipatory years, endowed it. We had to walk for ten minutes or so, perhaps a quarter of an hour, before we reached the curve in the rift which revealed the view—a view which suddenly disclosed itself, after murmuring watery premonitions: we turned the final bend and suddenly found ourselves within the roofless cave of the scar itself, where huge curved echoing rock sides stretched up above us, and water leaped down through the side of the cleft, pouring itself noisily downward across brown rocks that are twisted and worn like wood, like the roots of trees. It is impressive not through size, as I had perhaps expected, but through form: a lovely organic balance of shapes and curves, a wildness contained within a bodily limit. The water flung itself out from the rock. A rabbit ran on the grass. Plants and trees grew from the cliff face, and birds nested there. We were alone. There was nobody else there.

We climbed up the scar. We started the ascent almost by accident, climbing up the first rocks to see if we could see where the water came from higher up, but before we knew what we were doing we had climbed so high that we found it less frightening to continue than to return. Neither of us liked looking downward. It was not difficult, it was a route familiar to human feet, as several cigarette butts and candy wrappings bore comforting witness. The last stretch, right up toward the top, was the worst: the grass had been worn away, by sheep and men, into crumbling slippery earth, but we made it quite easily. We walked across the top to look down the other side of the valley and sat there together, high up, out of breath, pleased with ourselves and our exertions. We could see the sheep in the valley below: indeed, there were some up around us, including some very overgrown lambs, harassed by over-protective mothers. We looked down at the shapes of the clouds moving on the hillside, and we saw a brown crying bird that I said was a curlew, though without any evidence. I identified it from poetry I had read, and not from any ornithological knowl-edge. There were some of those very tiny pale-yellow wild pansies growing up there: Heart's Ease, I think they are called. James looked quite gray and ill from the climb: he looked his age, as he had done ever since that accident, but he looked so lovely with it that I could not but feel that age was a necessary handicap to him, and that the accident had merely been an attempt to attach him more firmly to the human earth. It was beautiful, up there. We could see the car on the road, very small, miles away beneath us. On the opposite hillside there was a man with a sheep dog. I suppose he must have been a shepherd.

Later, in the hotel in Manchester where we spent the night, we looked at one another in the bedroom mirror, as the porter put down our suitcase and left us: we were both muddy and faintly disheveled, my stockings were in shreds, and James had bits of grass stuck all over his jacket. We could have got away with it, perhaps, had we been different people wearing different clothes: tweeds, cashmere, brogues. We smiled at one another through the glass: united by a vanity so tentative, so mutually dependent, what separation could we contemplate, could we ever have contemplated? I speak for myself. How could I speak for him?

We had a bottle of whisky with us, which we had bought, by unusual impulse, in Bradford: we must have bought it, I think, to exorcise the recollection of that other smashed and reeking bottle that we had left in splinters on our last journey on the A1 the autumn before. I poured myself a glassful, in the tooth mug, and went to have a bath, to wash off the mud. When I came back and got into bed I must have left my glass at James's side of the bed because much later in the night he took a mouthful of the unfinished drink, and spat it out again violently, saying that it tasted unbelievably foul. I protested, and tasted it myself, but he was right: it tasted dreadful, ancient, musty, of dust and death, and when we put the light on to examine it we saw that I had spilled talcum powder into it, that the Scotch was covered with a thin white chalky film. Scotch and dust. A fitting conclusion to the sublimities of nature.

No, I can't leave it without a postscript, without formulating that final, indelicate irony. I had at one point thought of the idea of ending the narrative not so much with James's death as with his impotence: the little, twentieth-century death. (I feel ashamed, now, to have had so vicious a notion.) But in fact the truth is quite otherwise, for if we hadn't had that accident, I would quite possibly have died myself of thrombosis: since Bianca's birth I had been taking the relevant pills and would probably have gone on taking them until they killed me, which they might have well done, preferring the present to the future, however dangerously. I think I mentioned that on the eve of our departure to Norway I lay awake imagining a pain in my leg: well, it was a real pain, it was a swelling, a thrombic clot. The price that modern woman must pay for love. In the past, in old novels, the price of love was death, a price which virtuous women paid in childbirth, and the wicked, like Nana, with the pox. Nowadays it is paid in thrombosis or neurosis: one can take one's pick. I stopped taking those pills, as James lay there unconscious and motionless, but one does not escape decision so easily. I am glad of this. I am glad I cannot swallow pills with immunity. I prefer to suffer, I think.

Plume

LOOKING BACK—AT PEOPLE AND PLACES

27 million Americans can't read a bedtime story to a child.

It's because 27 million adults in this country simply can't read.

Functional illiteracy has reached one out of five Americans. It robs them of even the simplest of human pleasures, like reading a fairy tale to a child.

You can change all this by joining the fight against illiteracy.

Call the Coalition for Literacy at toll-free **1-800-228-8813** and volunteer.

Volunteer Against Illiteracy. The only degree you need is a degree of caring.